DANGEROUS DREAMS

"I'll sleep on the floor. I'll be fine. I've slept rougher plenty of times."

She blew out the lamp, and he thought the matter was settled. He lay down on the blanket and pulled it up around him.

Bedsprings creaked, and the lavender scent of Ellen surrounded him as she lay down beside him.

"What are you doing?" he asked.

Her eyes were huge in the dim light. "I can't sleep in that bed, knowing you're down here on the floor."

"Get back in the bed."

"No." She lay down with her back to him.

"Please."

"Only if you come with me."

He shook his head. "It wouldn't be proper."

"Why not?" She sat up, hugging her knees to her chest. "Everyone thinks we're married. Won't they think it strange if they found out we're not sleeping together?" She hesitated. "I mean, that's all we would be doing—sleeping."

She put out her hand and found his. A groan escaped him at her touch, but he let her pull him to his feet and lead him to the bed. He lay down on the edge of the mattress and turned his back to her. He had every intention of getting up and returning to the floor as soon as she was asleep. He lay rigid, every fiber aware of her body inches from his own. He could feel the warmth of her, sense every movement she made. He listened to her breathing, unconsciously matching the rhythm. In . . . out . . . in . . . out . . .

A Husband By Law

Cynthia Sterling

JOVE BOOKS, NEW YORK

If you purchased this book without a cover, you should be aware that this book is stolen property. It was reported as "unsold and destroyed" to the publisher and neither the author nor the publisher has received any payment for this "stripped book."

This is a work of fiction. Names, characters, places, and incidents are either the product of the author's imagination or are used fictitiously, and any resemblance to actual persons, living or dead, business establishments, events, or locales is entirely coincidental.

A HUSBAND BY LAW

A Jove Book / published by arrangement with
the author

PRINTING HISTORY
Jove edition / March 2001

All rights reserved.
Copyright © 2001 by Cynthia Myers.
This book, or parts thereof, may not be reproduced
in any form without permission.
For information address: The Berkley Publishing Group,
a division of Penguin Putnam Inc.,
375 Hudson Street, New York, New York 10014.

The Penguin Putnam Inc. World Wide Web site address is
http://www.penguinputnam.com

ISBN: 0-515-13028-1

A JOVE BOOK®
Jove Books are published by The Berkley Publishing Group,
a division of Penguin Putnam Inc.,
375 Hudson Street, New York, New York 10014.
JOVE and the "J" design
are trademarks belonging to Penguin Putnam Inc.

PRINTED IN THE UNITED STATES OF AMERICA

10 9 8 7 6 5 4 3 2 1

For Denise
A sister-in-law who's better than a sister

Chapter One

San Antonio, March 1846

Lieutenant Michael Trent had enjoyed better accommodations in his twenty-six years than this guardhouse cell, but then again, he'd endured worse. One thing about the Army: the brass would see that you were fed regularly, with a roof over your head, right up to the moment they hanged you.

"None of this would have happened if you'd learn to stay away from the ladies." Dr. Marvin Sullivan scowled at the jagged cut in Michael's left forearm and opened his leather bag.

Michael leaned against the iron bars of the cell and grinned at the doctor. The bright morning sun streaming through the ventilation slit near the ceiling shone like a spotlight on the doctor's face, forcing him to squint, thus ruining the effect of his frown. A thick-muscled man who was rumored to have trained in the finest hospitals in Europe and New York, Solly played at being the hard-drinking, rough-talking "character" who generally filled the post of Army physician. But the act did not extend to the care he gave his men, even those, like Michael, whose wounds couldn't be said to have been received in the line of duty.

"Now, why would I want to stay away from women?" Michael drawled. "A man might as well cash it in for good if he's forced to forsake the fairer sex."

Solly gave a less-than-gentle jerk on the bandages he was wrapping around Michael's arm. "I'm not saying you need to become a monk. Just think before you go rushing in where it's none of your business."

"Act rationally, you mean?"

"Exactly."

"Michael."

Michael laughed. "And ruin my reputation as a fearless devil?"

"All your tomcatting around has landed you in more hot water than you'll admit. Now you've gone too far." He tugged the sleeve of Michael's blue uniform tunic down over the bulky bandage. "I'll want another look at that dressing tomorrow."

Michael frowned at the jagged tear in the left sleeve of the uniform. That made the second tunic this month he'd ruined. Chivalry was definitely hard on a man's wardrobe. "How was I supposed to know the brute manhandling that girl was her husband?" His frown deepened, the memory of the way the dark-eyed beauty had cowered beneath the man's blows still rankling. "Any right-thinking man would have stepped in to stop it."

"Any man with an ounce of sense would have known better than to pull a knife on a civilian!"

"I never claimed to have sense." When this remark did not draw so much as the hint of a smile from his friend, he shrugged and looked away. "I'm not sorry I did it."

"Even if it ended you up in Company Q—again?"

Michael struck a nonchalant pose against the bars—or as nonchalant as one could appear when shackled hand and foot. "I'll welcome a few days rest. When you get a chance, smuggle me the novel I was reading."

Solly stepped back and shook his head. "You're not taking this seriously enough. Peabody's had his fill of your run-ins with the locals. He might decide to make an example of you and send you to the gallows for good."

"They don't hang men for knife fights." Michael's smile wavered only a little.

"The Army can hang you for anything they damn well please, and don't you forget it."

Michael absently rubbed his wrists above the manacles, where the flesh was already chafed raw. So Colonel Peabody was angry. He'd been angry before. He'd get over it. Next time Michael got into an argument with a civilian, he'd be more careful not to get caught.

He was about to say as much to Solly when a freckle-faced private hurried down the narrow hallway toward them. "What is it?" Solly barked.

"Colonel Peabody wants to see the prisoner, sir." The private snapped to attention in front of them.

Solly glanced back at Michael. His eyes telegraphed *I told you so*, though his mouth never moved. He stepped aside and watched the private unlock the cell door and swing it open. "Come with me . . . sir," the private said.

Michael bent and picked up the twelve-pound iron ball attached to his leg irons and, with as much dignity as he could muster, followed the private out of the cell, down the hall, and into the harsh light of San Antonio at midmorning.

The First Dragoons had set up camp next to abandoned Mission Concepcion along the San Antonio River. The triple domes of the mission, gleaming white in the harsh Texas sun, provided an elegant backdrop for the comings and goings of the troops. As a child, Michael had sometimes sought refuge from the rain and cold within those hallowed walls; they offered no sanctuary for him now.

He followed the private past the mission toward the colonel's tent. The leg irons chafed with every step, and his chains clanked like a junk-man's cart, so that every man they passed turned to gape at his disgrace. He fixed a haughty look on his face and met every gaze head-on, as if this were all just another lark, a minor inconvenience in his adventurous life. Never let them see your fear.

He'd learned that lesson before he'd learned to read. A boy didn't survive long on the streets unless he mastered that one.

"So, what kind of mood is Peabody in this morning?" he asked the private.

The private slid his pale eyes over in a sideways glance at Michael. "Didn't seem too happy with you. Said he was going to straighten you out for good this time."

Michael's gut clenched. What did that mean—straighten him out for good?

He didn't have time to ponder the thought. They were already in sight of the headquarters tent, with its tied-back flaps and billowing company flag. He looked for Colonel Peabody, hoping to read his intentions on his craggy face. Instead, his gaze locked on the vision beside the colonel, a tall beauty with hair the color of a Texas sunset. He blinked, wondering if he'd lost enough blood in the fight to make him hallucinate.

He closed his eyes for a moment to clear his head, but when he opened them again, she was still there. Her blue velveteen riding habit clung to every generous curve, and a black campaign hat with a jaunty white ostrich feather sat like a crown atop her glorious hair.

She looked up as Michael approached, fixing him with eyes the same royal blue as her habit. In a city of diminutive, dark beauties, this woman stood out like a diamond among rubies. She had skin as translucent as fine china, with a faint blush of pink at cheeks and lips. And her hair—he could not remember seeing hair this particular shade of red gold, cascading in rich curls from beneath the rakish hat. He clenched his hands around the iron ball, imagining the feel of those shimmering locks sliding through his fingers.

Rather than blush, or look away when their eyes met, the beauty continued to study him as he came to a stop in front of the colonel. Michael involuntarily expanded his chest and drew himself up to his full height, cursing the chains that bound him. He wasn't a stranger to the admiration of women, but usually they surveyed him from the concealment of fans or veils. Never had he found himself the object of such an open, considering look.

Unable to doff his cap, he still managed to bow before the woman. "Lieutenant Michael Trent, at your service."

She nodded, the slightest inclination of her head. Up close, he could see the firm line of her jaw, as if she were clenching her teeth. Her fingers, encased in kid gloves, were laced tightly together. He had the impression that she was trying very hard to keep from shaking.

"This is Miss Ellen Winthrop," Colonel Peabody said. "She's only recently arrived in this country from her home in England. She wishes to travel to California, where she has family."

Michael flashed a smile at the enchanting Miss Winthrop. She was only a couple of inches shorter than his own six-two. Rather than seeming awkward, the added height made her appear regal. "I wish you a safe trip, Miss Winthrop."

Colonel Peabody frowned. "With the threat of war with Mexico, travel to California has been seriously curtailed. Learning we were soon to set out for that territory, Miss Winthrop has asked to travel with the troops. I've explained to her the Army's policy that only soldiers' wives may travel with us. Miss Winthrop is willing to marry one of the men in order to get to California."

Michael's smile faded. It was no secret that laundresses and other camp followers sometimes married enlisted men in order to travel with the troops. But Miss Winthrop looked much too high-born for that sort of arrangement.

"I've suggested you, Lieutenant, as a suitable groom."

He stared at the colonel, unsure he had heard him correctly. When he opened his mouth to protest, no words came out.

He looked at the woman, who gave another jerky nod, then had the decency to blush. "Colonel, may I speak with you a moment?" he said in a strained voice that did not sound like his own. "In private?"

Peabody nodded. "Miss Winthrop, why don't you wait inside the tent for us? I'll have my aide bring you something to drink."

Michael waited until she had gone inside before he followed the colonel to stand beneath a smooth-barked cottonwood. He struggled to regain his composure. What the colonel was proposing was absolutely impossible. "With all due respect, sir, why would you suggest *I* marry this young woman?"

The colonel studied him, saying nothing. As the minutes passed, Michael became aware of the wrinkles in his uniform, the dusty toes of his boots, and the wild tangle of his hair. "I chose you, Lieutenant Trent," Peabody said at last, "because you are an officer, and despite your appalling lack of judgment at times, for the most part you are a gentleman. All of the other officers are already married, and I couldn't very well turn Miss Winthrop over to one of the enlisted men. She's obviously a young woman of breeding."

"But why not—"

The colonel held up a hand to interrupt him. "And I chose you, Trent, because I think you would do well with the good influence of a woman. God knows I've tried everything else to keep you in line." He cast a pointed look at Michael's chains.

Michael clamped his mouth shut. When he finally spoke he could barely contain his irritation. "What happens if I refuse to marry Miss Winthrop?"

Peabody's steely expression never wavered. "I'll begin court-martial proceedings tomorrow."

He clenched his jaw so tightly his teeth ached, then decided to try a different tack. "What if Miss Winthrop refuses to marry me?" He hefted the iron ball, setting his chains to swaying and rattling together. "She can't think I'm much of a catch trussed up like this."

"I certainly can't force her to wed. Why don't you ask

her yourself?" He summoned the private. "Remove the shackles."

The private produced a key and began unlocking the bonds. Gathering up the ball and chains, he started to leave, but the colonel put out a restraining hand. "Don't go too far," he said. "I might need those again." He gave Michael a meaningful look and motioned toward the tent. "Go on. I'll wait out here until you're ready."

Michael paused outside the tent flaps to straighten his coat and adjust the angle of his cap. His mouth felt as dry as cotton lint, and he noticed his hands were shaking as he brushed a bit of dust from his shoulders. What he wouldn't give for a shot of brandy just now.

Miss Winthrop sat at one end of a wooden table, holding a china teacup. He removed his cap as he entered the tent and nodded to her. Clearing his throat, he searched for some thread with which to weave a conversation.

"You are not wanting to marry me," she said, her fingertips stroking the side of the cup. Her voice was low and clear as the contralto notes of a pipe organ, with the lilt of her homeland softening each word.

His shoulders sank when he heard the sadness in her voice. Any moment now, she'd no doubt dissolve in tears, and if there was anything he didn't want to deal with, it was a woman in tears. Especially not one so beautiful.

"It's not you in particular, Miss Winthrop." He closed the distance between them in two strides. "I just hadn't planned on marrying anyone at this point in my life." He looked down at her bent head, at the white ostrich feather stirred by his movement. "And I can't imagine why you'd want to marry me. You don't even know me."

She raised her head, mesmerizing him with those sapphire eyes. He'd expected to see tears, but her gaze was clear, though troubled. "I know no one here. And I must reach California."

She sounded so desolate. He fought the sudden urge to pull her into his arms, to comfort her, as if he would indeed be capable of relieving her suffering. "But surely marriage to a stranger isn't the answer," he said softly.

"We would learn to know each other." She straightened her shoulders. "If marrying you is the only way of getting to California, then it is what I must do."

"Why is it so important for you to get to California?"

"I have relatives there . . . an uncle." She took a deep breath, as if gathering strength. "The colonel assured me you are a gentleman. I'm sure I could do worse."

And I could do worse than a beauty like you, was the surprising thought that flashed across his mind. He pushed the errant idea away. "I'm flattered, I'm sure," he said. "But you don't know what you're getting into. How many gentlemen do you meet trussed up in chains?"

She took a deep breath, her cheeks two spots of red against her pale face. "Lieutenant, I have traveled hundreds of miles across the ocean. I have no family, no friends . . . and very little money. What choice do I have but to be going along with this scheme?" She glanced at him. "The colonel seems to think we would be suitable."

He shifted his eyes to focus somewhere besides the rounded curves encased in blue velveteen. He'd already stared at her more than a gentleman ought. "The colonel thinks I need a good influence," he said. "I have a reputation for getting into scrapes more often than he'd like. I'm not one to run away from a fight, even when a more prudent man might do so. I like to gamble when I get the chance, and I've had affairs with several of the women in town." He meant to shock her, to make her see how unsuitable he was to be anyone's husband, much less one to a lady such as herself. "I'm too much of a rounder to ever make a proper husband for anyone, much less a woman of your obvious, uh, breeding."

To his consternation, she began to chuckle. "My breeding, is it?" she murmured, as if to herself. "It is my breeding that has me in this fix in the first place." She raised her head and looked at him again. "If it's being saddled with a wife you have no use for that worries you, could not we just pretend to be married, until we reach California? I'll cook and clean for you in exchange for my board, and you can continue fighting and gambling and . . . and seeing your women friends. I promise not to interfere. When we reach California, we can break it off, and no hurt feelings all 'round."

She raised her chin, full lips set in a stubborn line. Everything about her, from the straight shoulders to the jaunty angle of her hat, spoke of a woman with pride. He wondered what it had cost her to come here and make her request. What would it do to her to have him turn her away?

Michael understood pride. Hadn't his own been trampled more times than he cared to remember? Would it really be so bad, to help this woman out, for just a little while? Maybe the colonel was right. It might do him good to have a feminine influence around, even if it was clear that it would be a purely platonic arrangement.

"You'd agree to that?" he asked. "Pretend to be my wife until we reach California?"

She took a deep breath and nodded. "And when we reach California, we can go our separate ways."

He hesitated only a moment, the determined look in her eyes softening his last reserve. "All right. As long as you understand this isn't a permanent situation."

She stood and offered her hand, and he took it. But rather than a brief clasp, she held him fast and brought her other hand up to cradle his fingers between her gloved palms. She looked up, capturing him with her steady gaze as much as her touch. That look made him believe he could do anything, be anything, as long as he had that kind of faith to support him.

She made a move as if to release her hold on him, but he reached out with his free hand and drew her to him. An occasion like this called for a kiss, and lips as ripe as hers should not go ignored so long.

He felt her stiffen as he drew her near and heard the gasp that escaped from her lips, her breath warm against his skin. He encircled her with his arms, smoothing his hands down her back in a gentling motion. His senses filled with an awareness of her—the sough of her breathing, rapid and shallow, the feather touch of her gloved fingers against his neck. She smelled of lavender, and the mint tea she'd been drinking. Tall and handsome as she was, she felt fragile in his arms, and he took pains to be gentle with her. He inclined his head slightly, anticipating the feel of her pliant, parted lips against his own.

"Hrrrmph!"

They snapped apart, and Michael looked up to see Colonel Peabody standing in the doorway of the tent. "I see you two have come to some agreement," he said.

Michael glanced at Ellen. She stared at the floor, her delicate complexion the deep pink of an evening primrose. He cleared his throat and turned to the colonel. "Miss Winthrop has agreed to . . . to be my wife." The words sounded strange on his tongue, even though he knew they were not true, merely necessary for this deception they were carrying out.

The colonel looked at Ellen. "You're sure this is what you want, Miss Winthrop?"

She nodded.

Peabody walked over and stood behind the table. "All right, then. Find a priest or a preacher, or whatever you like, and make it official as soon as possible. Lieutenant, you may show your intended to your quarters, then report to me for orders."

As soon as Lieutenant Trent left her alone in his tent, Ellen sank down on the end of the cot, the last bit of strength deserting her. Feeling a nudge at her ankles, she absently lifted her skirts, and her Scots terrier, Bobby, emerged from beneath the petticoats, nose raised to catch the scent of this new environment.

She followed the little dog's progress around the perimeter of the tent, taking in the pile of dirty laundry in the corner, the unwashed dishes on the table, and the open trunk from which spilled more laundry and a fearsome assortment of weaponry—a saber, pistols, rifles, and what appeared to be a machete in a heavily ornamented scabbard.

Her own luggage stood just inside the doorway of the tent. For the hundredth time she felt a twinge of guilt, looking at the bag. No doubt the others at her father's castle had branded her a thief by now. She'd never meant to take anything with her when she ran away, other than her own clothes and a few mementos. How could she have known that the bag she'd mistaken for her own was actually an extra one the Lady Gennette had packed for a trip to the earl's hunting lodge?

She fingered the fine material of the royal blue velveteen riding habit. Everything in the bag was much fancier than anything she'd ever worn. The red cambric day dress with its white lace fichu was far nicer than Ellen's best clothes. And the underwear seemed too fine to ever wear: French lace drawers and a ribbon-trimmed lawn shift with its rows of tiny pin tucks. There was even an embroidered silk nightdress and matching robe, fine enough for a princess's trousseau. She'd have gladly traded all Gennette's fine clothes for her own humble dresses and her mother's prayer book.

At least she still had Bobby. She smiled as the dog pounced on a bread crust he had discovered on the floor under the table. She could never have made the long trip from England without this one true friend.

She drew a deep breath and mustered her failing courage. Everything would be all right. Her mother's brother in California would surely take her in. It had been a long while since she'd seen Uncle David, but he'd always been fond of her. Everyone back at her father's castle would forget all about her, and she'd live the rest of her life in peace, as simple Ellen Winthrop, settler.

She shook herself and went to bring the portmanteau farther into the tent. Lieutenant Trent had dropped it just inside the door, declining to follow her inside. Indeed, he'd seemed reluctant to even look at her since they'd left the colonel's tent.

The memory of his embrace brought a flush to her face not entirely from embarrassment. She still could not believe she had let a stranger touch her that way. And yet, when Michael Trent had put his arms around her, she'd felt safe and protected in a way she hadn't felt since her father died. Despite his height and the strength evident in the muscles of his arms and chest, which the dragoon's uniform did little to conceal, Lieutenant Trent had held her with tenderness, as if she were a fragile treasure.

When he had looked at her with those ice-blue eyes, it had seemed the most natural thing in the world to respond to his gentle urging. All the worry and fear she'd been wearing like a cloak slipped away in his arms, and a warmth spread through her that had nothing to do with the Texas sun, but came from deep within, radiating outward.

She'd almost panicked when he'd shown up wearing those chains. The colonel hadn't mentioned anything about that. But by the time he came into her tent, he was unshackled, and though a little rumpled looking, he'd had nice manners and the decency to try to talk her out of this wild scheme. She was sure all his talk of fighting and gambling and . . . affairs had merely been designed to frighten her away.

Though it was easy to believe that Lieutenant Trent could have all manner of women begging for his attention. He was one of the tallest men in the camp, and the dark blue dragoon's uniform emphasized his broad shoulders and muscular legs. With blond hair, brilliant blue eyes, straight nose, and firm chin, Lieutenant Trent might have been some ancient Greek warrior, rather than a modern American soldier.

Would a true gentleman really have tried to kiss her like that? She was sure he *would* have kissed her if the colonel had not interrupted them. Would Lieutenant Trent try to kiss her again—and perhaps want more? She pushed away the thought and stood, brushing dust from her gown as if to brush off bad memories. What was done was done. She'd have to make the best of it. And she'd start earning her keep right now, by cleaning this pigsty Lieutenant Trent mistook for decent living quarters.

Chapter Two

Michael's mood had improved considerably by the time he returned to the tent. He'd spent a painful half hour with Colonel Peabody, being chewed up one side and down the other for fighting with a civilian. He'd been threatened with flogging, and worse, if he let it happen again.

Then all his aggravation had dissolved when the colonel announced that the company should be prepared to head out within the week. After months of cooling their heels on the prairie, they were finally off to California and action!

Feeling more lighthearted than he had in days, he shoved back his tent flap and stared at the transformation that had taken place in his quarters.

Gone were the dirty dishes of last night's supper, replaced by a silk shawl draped over the tabletop. The cot was neatly made, blankets tight enough to please a drill sergeant, and the mounds of soiled clothing had vanished, perhaps within the trunk, which now sat closed, its brass gleaming. Where his forage cap had hung, now reposed a black campaign hat, white ostrich feather waving.

The woman responsible for such industry had transformed herself as well. Ellen Winthrop had changed out of the velveteen riding habit and now wore a simple red dress with a white scarf at the throat. Her head was bare, a red-gold braid trailing down her back, though her energetic cleaning had loosed a few tendrils, which framed her lovely face.

She sat at the table, a pair of his trousers in her lap, needle and thread in hand. "Good afternoon, Lieutenant," she said.

"Good afternoon, Miss Winthrop." He jerked off his cap and advanced toward her, but froze at the sound of a low growl from beneath the table.

"Bobby! Hush at once! Lieutenant Trent is our friend."

A small black dog regarded him with a less-than-friendly look and backed up to sit at his mistress's feet. Michael frowned at the animal. "I didn't realize you had a dog."

"Bobby's come all the way from England with me." She reached down and stroked the dog's back.

The sadness of her expression made him vow not to utter another word against the dog. He moved carefully around the animal and sat at the table across from Ellen.

She turned her attention back to the trousers she was mending. "I've been thinking," she said after a moment.

Thinking you're sorry you got into this mess, I'll bet. "Yes?" he prompted.

She glanced up, then hurriedly averted her eyes. "I've been thinking that if we're to be married, then we should address each other by our Christian names."

He could not remember seeing anyone with such translucent skin. Even now, as she spoke, he could see a flush of pink making its way up the open neck of her dress, over her cheeks, to the tips of her ears. The movement fascinated him, so that at first he was unaware of her words.

"What?"

"I was saying we should call each other by our Christian names. Unless you would prefer me to call you Lieutenant Trent?"

"No. No . . . Ellen. Please. Call me Michael."

She nodded. "All right . . . Michael."

He watched as she took tiny stitches in the leg of the

trousers. "You don't have to do that," he said. "I can take those to one of the laundresses."

"Nonsense. I can cook, too, if you'll tell me where I can buy food."

"You mustn't trouble yourself. I can eat at the mess. . . ."

"And where will I eat?" She looked up, a challenge in her eyes. "I *want* to cook for the both of us. And to do your mending. And the washing, too. That was the bargain we struck." She knotted the thread and bit off the end, revealing even, white teeth. He found himself recalling how close he had come to feeling those lips against his own, and quickly looked away.

"Tell me something about yourself," he said. "How old are you?"

"Eighteen. How old are you?"

"Twenty-six." He couldn't remember what it had been like to be eighteen, except that now it seemed a terribly young and naive age. "Where did you live in England?" he asked.

"In Lanesmore, near Penrith."

"Is Lanesmore a very big town?"

"It's not a town really, just a village around Lanesmore Castle."

"This castle, did you live there?"

She hesitated a moment, then nodded.

"Oh. Was your father some sort of nobleman, then?"

"My father was the Earl of Lanesmore."

He was quiet, digesting this information. He hadn't been wrong about her being high-born, then. She must have been desperate to agree to an arranged marriage with the likes of him. He looked up and found her watching him, though she quickly ducked her head. Were those tears he'd seen?

"I'm sorry. Does it make you sad to talk about your home and family?"

She nodded, and began stitching once more. "I would

rather talk about something else," she said after a moment. "Tell me about yourself. Where did you grow up?"

He considered what to tell her. She was obviously under the impression he was some upper-class gent. Would the truth send her running away, or was she so committed to her decision she'd stay, but be miserable knowing she'd been deceived? "My mother and three younger sisters live in Hockley, a little town not far from Houston, but I grew up here in San Antonio."

"And Mr. Trent, your father, is he dead, then?"

"I don't know."

Ellen Winthrop would make a lousy card player. All her emotions showed so clearly. Right now, she was obviously shocked at his answer. "You don't know?"

"My father ran off when I was six."

"Do . . . do you remember him much?"

How could he forget? Dan Trent had cut a wide swath wherever he went. He was a cheerful, hearty man, always eager to be on to the next scheme, the next adventure, the next bit of excitement. His wife and family followed him from one mishap to the next, until one day he simply stopped coming home at all. Michael always thought his mother had been relieved, though her relief transformed to grief as she watched her son grow up as restless and eager for excitement as his father.

"What's wrong?"

He looked up, realizing he'd been lost in thought for some time. "I'm sorry?"

"You were frowning. Does your arm hurt?"

Until that moment he hadn't paid much attention to his wounded arm, though now he noticed it was throbbing. He gingerly folded back the torn sleeve and studied the bandages, wondering what the cut beneath looked like now. No telling what that wife-beater had on his knife.

She laid aside her mending and went to fetch something from her bag, which she'd placed beside his trunk. "I believe I have something in here." She withdrew a flask and read the label. "Yes. Here it is." She grabbed up a cup of water and dumped in half the bottle. "Here. Take this."

"What is it?" He frowned at the muddy drink she shoved at him.

"Hartshorn. It's good for fevers and aches." She brought the cup, to his lips and braced one hand behind his head. "Drink it all up at once."

She tilted the cup, and he closed his eyes and drank, grimacing at the taste but managing to swallow it all. She moved the cup away from his lips, though he could still feel her hand at the back of his neck, a silken touch, kneading at the tense muscles, sending shivers of pleasure down his spine.

When he opened his eyes, she was looking down on him with an expression of concern. He'd seen many emotions when he'd looked into women's eyes—greed, lust, passion, even disgust. But when had a woman ever looked on him with such care? He half raised his arm to pull Ellen close, wanting to capture this moment, to hold it as he held her.

But he remembered who he was, and who she was. He let his arm fall back, and looked away, breaking the spell. He may not have been the true gentleman Ellen believed him to be, but he knew better than to treat her like some Spanish doxy. She'd promised to mend his clothes and cook his meals. She'd said nothing about warming his bed, and he fully intended to respect their bargain.

"Hello in there!" The shouted greeting made Michael jump to his feet, one hand on the Bowie knife strapped to his thigh. An out-of-tune trumpet sounded a blast just outside the door, followed by furious strumming on a guitar and the loud rattling of castanets. Ellen's little dog spun in circles, barking at a deafening pitch.

Solly ripped back the tent flap. "Make yourselves decent! Company's come!"

Words of protest strangled in Michael's throat as Solly marched into the tent, followed by a three-piece mariachi band, half a dozen laundresses, a waitress from his favorite cantina, three privates, and a brown-robed friar. The holy man clutched a black-bound prayer book in one hand and an earthenware jug in the other. The women carried armfuls of wildflowers, giggling and whispering in Spanish as they filled the tent. The privates saluted, then stood at parade rest behind the women, rolling their eyes at one another and grinning.

By the time everyone was inside, there was scarcely room to turn around. As one of the women stepped forward and began to tuck flowers into Ellen's braid, Michael found his voice once more and shouted above the din, "Solly, what the h—!" He glanced at Ellen and amended his speech. "What in blue blazes do you think you're doing?"

The band squeaked to a halt, and the women's voices subsided to a hushed murmur. The dog retreated beneath Ellen's skirts, and everyone turned to face Michael. Solly held his arms wide. "Everyone knows a wedding requires a wedding party."

The women began chattering once more, and the soldiers relaxed and joined in. The waitress relieved the friar of the jug, uncorked it, and began passing it around. As it neared Michael, he inhaled the sharp odor of *pulque*, the fermented cactus juice favored by the locals.

He didn't know whether to grab the jug and take a swig or unsheathe his saber and order them all out. He was leaning toward the latter when he felt a timid tug at his sleeve. "Perhaps you should be introducing me to your friends."

He looked down into Ellen's wide eyes. He'd expected she might be shocked or even afraid. Instead, she had the eager look of a child at the circus. "I never dreamed we'd have so many guests at our wedding," she whispered.

He resisted the urge to draw her to him and kiss her soundly for being such a good sport. Instead, he took her arm and turned to Solly. "Miss Ellen Winthrop, may I present Dr. Marvin Sullivan, Solly for short. If you ever need advice on anything, Solly is very free with his. At least, he delights in telling *me* what to do."

Solly took Ellen's hand and bent low over it. "My pleasure, I'm sure." Keeping hold of her hand, he straightened. "My first advice is to keep a close eye on this one." He nodded to Michael. "I've saved his bacon more times than I can count."

She wrinkled her brow. "Bacon? What are you saving it for?"

Solly chuckled. "I meant I've gotten him out of trouble too many times to count. Always charging into the fray, he is."

Ellen was going to think she'd pledged herself to a fool. He pulled her along toward the women, his spirits sinking with every step. This bunch wasn't going to do anything to improve Ellen's opinion of him. "These are the camp laundresses," he explained.

The women wore what he had come to think of as the camp-follower uniform—full skirts and loose white blouses, colorful shawls about their shoulders, feet bare. They smiled and nodded and exchanged "how-dos" with Ellen, all the while openly staring at her.

She had the grace not to acknowledge this lack of manners. Instead, she nodded to each in turn and thanked them for coming to her wedding.

The cantina waitress, Trini, stood at the end of the row of women. She had dressed up for the occasion in a green dress trimmed in lace, a dozen silver bracelets jangling about each arm. Her pretty mouth, outlined in red, shaped into a pout when they stopped in front of her. "I see you have found for yourself a real lady, Lieutenant," she said.

Ellen coughed, covering her mouth with her hand. "Excuse me. Must be the dust."

"Come, we will help you get ready for your wedding." Trini took Ellen's arm.

"Oh, yes," one of the laundresses agreed.

"We will help you, even though half of us are sick with envy that you would take him away from us," another woman added.

"And the other half are glad for a rest!" a fourth woman exclaimed.

With an explosion of giggles, they herded Ellen to the far corner of the tent, while Solly pushed Michael toward the opposite corner. The priest stood in the middle of the room, arms folded in his sleeves, eyeing everything in silence.

"Here, you'd better change." Solly shoved a clean tunic toward him.

He unbuckled his saber and peeled off the torn tunic and tossed it onto his cot. Already his arm felt better. He guessed he had Ellen's medicine to thank for that.

"Don't you have any polished boots?" Solly frowned at the scuffed toes of Michael's footwear.

"No. It doesn't matter, anyway." He shrugged into the clean tunic and began buttoning the row of brass buttons that ran the length of the right side.

Solly spat on a handkerchief and knelt to attack the worst spots on Michael's boots. "Maybe not to you, but I guarantee to her it will."

Would it? He glanced over at Ellen. She was smiling at the women as they brushed out her hair and decorated her with flowers. What must she think of him? Did she see the truth in the women's crude jokes and Solly's sharp comments? He was a man made for a life of temporary attachments, always looking forward to the next adventure. Just like his father, he didn't have in him the stability to settle down in one place, with one woman. He'd never deliberately hurt Ellen, but he knew he wouldn't be able to help doing so.

"I have to hand it to you, friend. When you decide to do something, you don't do it by halves." Solly had straightened and was standing beside him, looking toward Ellen. "She's a beauty, all right."

"I had little enough to do with it." He turned and picked up the scarlet sash draped over the end of his cot. "She's only marrying me in order to get to her relatives in California. All this—" He nodded to indicate the laughing wedding guests. "All this isn't necessary."

"Peabody sent me to make sure you go through with the wedding."

Michael jerked a knot into the sash. "He did, did he?"

"Seems he's determined to replace one ball and chain with another."

Michael shook his head. He wouldn't have described gentle Ellen as a ball and chain. More a brake to slow him down, for a little while at least. Suddenly he felt the need of a drink. "Where's that *pulque*?" he asked as he refastened the saber around his waist.

"None of that poison for you." Solly clapped him on the back. "You want to remember this day for the rest of your life."

As if he was likely to forget it. He stood at attention as the women brought Ellen to him. "Are you all right?" he asked, taking her hand. Her fingers felt as fragile as a bird's wing in his palm.

She nodded, her eyebrows lifting in question. "Are you?"

As all right as a man could be when he was on the verge of taking the biggest gamble of his life. "Yes." He squeezed her hand and leaned over to whisper in her ear. "Just remember. When we reach California, you have no further obligation to me. We'll arrange a quiet divorce. Or better yet, an anullment."

She ducked her head in a nod, and they turned to face the friar.

The minute the priest began reading from his prayer book, Michael understood the reason for the man's earlier silence. Every word he uttered was in Spanish; it must be the only language he spoke.

"I don't understand," Ellen said.

Michael shook his head. "Neither do I."

"How will we know when to answer?"

"Whenever he pauses, say 'I do,'" Solly advised. "That should do it."

Solly had to elbow Michael in the ribs a few times to remind him it was his turn to speak, but at last the padre closed his book and beamed at them. The deed was done. For better or worse, he was a married man, at least for a while.

He looked at Ellen. Though she smiled brightly, the expression seemed forced. He wanted to apologize for such a dismal day. Surely young women dreamed of something better for their weddings.

"Kiss the bride!" Solly nudged him from behind.

A fresh chorus of laughter arose from the laundresses at these words. "Kiss her! Kiss her!" they called.

Ellen blushed but didn't drop her gaze. Michael bent and planted a chaste kiss on lips soft as satin. Eyes closed, he inhaled deeply of her lavender scent, and felt the flutter of her lashes against his cheek.

The band struck up again, and reluctantly he straightened and prepared to play the part of eager bridegroom. The women began passing the *pulque* jug. "Go on now, leave us alone," he urged, shooing them toward the door.

"Thank you all for coming," Ellen called, and seemed to mean the words.

Solly was the last to leave. Without warning, he pulled Ellen close and kissed her soundly on the cheek. "I guess I'm the closest thing to best man," he said. "I'm at least owed a kiss from the bride."

Ellen smiled at the doctor and continued to hold his hand too long to suit Michael. He pointedly reached out and broke the contact, enveloping Ellen's fingers in his own. "I'm sure Solly has duties to see to," he said. "So we won't keep him."

Solly laughed. "Just like a newlywed, wanting to have her all to yourself." He replaced his cap on his head. "Stop by in the morning and let me take a look at that arm." He nodded to Ellen. "I'm sure I'll see you again. I can tell you all Michael's bad habits."

He left, closing the tent flap behind him. Silence folded around them like a shroud. Everyone and everything else seemed very far away. "Well, it's done, then," he said, not looking at her, fearful of the disappointment he might find in her eyes.

"Yes. It is done."

The awkward moment stretched. He didn't have any idea what to do. "I . . . I guess that's not what you always thought your wedding would be like."

She smiled and shook her head. "No. Still, I'll not be forgetting it. And you? Did you think your wedding would be like this?"

He plucked a drooping lily from a jar on the table and twirled it in his fingers. "I never thought I'd have a wedding."

"Whyever not?"

He shrugged. "Some men aren't cut out for that. I'm one of them."

"I don't understand."

Unable to keep his eyes from her any longer, he found her gaze fixed on him, filled with the same concern that had shaken him earlier. "No need to fret about me," he rushed to reassure her. "It's like a job, I guess. Some men are good carpenters. Some are soldiers. Some men make good husbands. Others don't."

"How do you know you wouldn't make a good husband if you've never tried?"

"Let's just say I'm too restless."

She began pulling flowers from her hair, dropping them onto the table. "Restless people are looking for something. Maybe you're really looking for the right person to settle down with."

He didn't like the turn this conversation was taking. Had she already set her sights on making him into the perfect husband? He wanted to argue, to protest that she was setting herself up for disappointment, but words fled as she picked up a brush and began to smooth her hair.

Freed of their braid, the red-gold locks flowed to her waist, shimmering like rippled water, the color of heat and the setting sun. He wondered if they would be warm to his touch or cool as silk. His fingers twitched to touch her, while other parts of him ached for closer contact still. "I . . . I have duties to see to." He grabbed his forage cap from atop his trunk and clapped it onto his head. "I'll be back later."

If anyone thought it strange that the new bridegroom was rushing from his tent at such a pace, they had the sense not to ask him about it. For that, at least, he was grateful. He'd survived barroom brawls and armed combat, forced marches and Army rations, but nothing had prepared him to survive a hundred nights of looking at, but not touching, the woman who was suddenly his wife.

Chapter Three

Ellen opened her eyes to darkness, pulled to instant wakefulness by the strangeness of her surroundings. She scanned the unfamiliar shadows illuminated by the first hint of dawn showing through the white tent top and slowly let out the breath she'd been holding, remembering the events of the previous day.

Bobby rose from his curled position at her feet and crept forward across the blankets to nudge her with his cold black nose. She raised her arm to make a place for him next to her, then rolled onto her side and let her eyes come to rest on the blanketed form on the floor beneath the table.

Lieutenant Trent . . . Michael . . . had insisted on giving her the cot, saying he was used to sleeping rough. He was curled with his back to her now, only his tangled locks showing above the fold of the blanket.

She recalled the feel of those curls against the back of her hand when she'd given him the hartshorn for his sore arm. She had thought then that he might kiss her. She'd stood there, with her fingers kneading his neck, unable to stop herself, wanting to prolong the contact between them.

When he had finally kissed her, after they'd said their vows, the contact had been too brief. She put one hand to her mouth, trying to recall the feel of his lips there. She remembered warmth and the scrape of his beard, and then he was gone.

He had left the tent, after all his talk of not being the sort of man for marriage, muttering some excuse about attending to his duties. When he returned, much later, he said little, merely rolled into his blankets and fell asleep.

Was the truth so obvious to him, then? Despite her fine clothes and the half-lies about her life in England, did he see that she was nothing more than a peasant—the bastard daughter of the earl and his paramour? A timid woman who knew little about life in general and men in particular?

She closed her eyes and thought again of the things she knew about him. The colonel had called him an officer and a gentleman. Others said he was daring, an adventurer. The very word sent a shiver of pleasure through her. Oh, to be brave enough to charge into life that way! Back in England, she had always been "shy Ellen," looking on while others took chances. Even her running away had been the result of desperation, not bravery. Maybe Michael could see that she was a coward at heart, no match for a man like him.

The first notes of reveille interrupted her thoughts. Michael stirred, and she sank lower in the covers. He struggled out of the blankets and shoved up onto his knees, groaning. Then he rose to his feet, white woolen undergarments illuminated in the pale light.

She caught her breath at the sight of his body so clearly outlined. He stood with his back to her and stretched, and she luxuriated in the chance to study him so thoroughly. Her eyes traveled over the broad expanse of his shoulders, tracing a line down his backbone, the pace of her breathing increasing as her eyes settled on the outline of his firm backside. She dropped her gaze to his muscular thighs and calves, a delicious warmth spreading through her that she was at a loss to explain.

Bobby chose this moment to bark, and Michael jumped as if shot. He dived for the blankets and came up again, facing her in a low crouch and brandishing a wicked-looking knife.

She gasped and shrank back at the sight of the weapon.

He dropped the knife and snatched up a blanket and wrapped it around his waist. "You're awake," he said, his face flushed.

"Good morning," she said, the greeting somewhat muffled by the covers she had pulled up to her nose. She sat up on the side of the bed, still clutching the bedclothes around her, and leaned over and lit the little lamp she'd placed on a crate by the cot. "I imagine it will take a few days to get used to our situation," she said, avoiding looking at him. "I'll prepare breakfast, if you'll show me where to get food."

He nodded, seemingly unable to pull his eyes away from her. "All right. Get dressed, and I'll show you where to draw our rations."

She waited a moment, but he did not move. She looked around, already knowing there were no partitions in the tent and nothing she could hide behind in order to dress with modesty. She looked back at Michael. "Would you turn around, please?" she asked, a blush warming her cheeks.

"Oh. Oh, yes. Of course." He whirled to place his back to her, and she eased out of the blankets and reached for her clothes.

Michael stared at the floor and listened to Ellen moving behind him, heart still hammering in his chest from the shock of finding her in his tent. Embarrassment had in turn replaced amazement as he realized he was standing before her, practically naked. And the sight of her generous curves outlined by the thin blankets had done little to lessen the swelling that strained the fly of his small clothes.

This was never going to work. He'd have to find some way to convince her to give it up, before the troops moved out. Maybe he could find a freight company for her to travel with, or convince one of the other officers to take her in.

His jaw tightened at the thought of another man waking each morning to gaze on that lovely face. No, best to get her out of the company altogether. He raised his head to stare at the canvas wall of the tent, as if to find a solution written there.

But the image he saw on the wall ended all attempt at logical thought. Before him, like a picture in a magic lantern slide show, Ellen dressed in the wavering light of the lamp, every feature carefully silhouetted against the canvas. His breathing grew shallow as he watched her pulling the laces of her corset, drawing in her waist and thrusting her breasts up. His mouth went dry, and he stifled a groan when she propped one foot on the edge of the cot and began rolling stockings up her long, well-shaped legs.

A gentleman would have left the tent or turned his eyes away. But Michael was no gentleman, and he could not bring himself to ignore the intimate play before his eyes. Stockings and garters in place, Ellen pulled on petticoats and slipped a dress over her head, fingers working the buttons up the front. Then she undid the long braid and began brushing out her hair.

He stood transfixed, miserable with desire, guilt and fascination warring in his fevered brain. She bent forward at the waist and stroked the brush through her thick tresses, and he swallowed hard, imagining the feel of that spun gold against his skin.

Hair neatly braided and coiled atop her head, she pinned a cameo at her throat. "I'll wait outside while you dress." She walked past him, the dog trotting at her heels.

By the time he walked out to meet her, Michael had managed to regain his composure. He'd wiped the worst of the dust from his boots and dressed in the newly mended trousers and his last clean tunic. With Ellen on his arm, he set out across the compound.

News of the marriage had quickly circulated, and their progress was frequently interrupted by men stopping to give their congratulations and be introduced to the new Mrs. Trent. Ellen smiled and blushed prettily, and Michael stood tall by her side. "I believe I'm the envy of every man here," he said as they started out once again.

He enjoyed walking with someone who did not require him to bend over at an uncomfortable angle in order to hold her near, and Ellen had no trouble matching her stride to his own. But this led to thoughts of other ways in which they might be physically well matched, and his earlier discomfort returned.

By the time they reached the quartermaster's headquarters, in the rear of the mission, he was glad to leave her to pick out whatever she needed, to be added to his account. "I'll be back for breakfast," he told her, and hurried away in search of Solly.

He found the doctor in the hospital tent, unpacking supplies. "Well, good morning, Trent!" he boomed, looking up from a case of sharp-toothed saws. "Wedding night send you in need of a physic? I'll bet that British Amazon you married put your usual choice of feminine company to shame."

Michael bristled, one hand riding the hilt of the Bowie. "I'm not sure I like what you're insinuating," he growled.

"Oh, beg pardon." Solly threw up his hands. "No offense intended. I'm sure your wife is every bit the lady she appears to be."

"She's not my wife, and you know it." Michael sank onto a stool beside the doctor's worktable. "Don't tell me I have to pretend with you, too."

Solly put aside the blade he'd been polishing. "Then maybe it's a quantity of saltpeter you'll be needing, if you intend sharing your tent with a beauty like that and leaving her untouched." He chuckled, stroking his thick gray beard. " 'Course, they do things different in those foreign countries."

"What do you mean?" Michael frowned at him.

"Oh, those lords and ladies don't look at sex as quite the taboo we do. They change partners over there like a regular square dance." He looked down his nose at Michael. "Your 'lady' just might surprise you. Might make this a very interesting campaign indeed."

Michael stared at him, then rose slowly and left the tent, trying to absorb the doctor's observation. Was he saying Ellen might actually *expect* him to take her to bed?

The notion shook him up so much he forgot all about having his arm seen to.

The enticing aroma of bacon and eggs greeted him when he reached the tent. Ellen sat on a stool beside a cook fire and turned bacon in a skillet. "I hope you don't mind, I bought some pans and things as well as food," she said, reaching out to lift a coffeepot from the coals.

He stepped forward and took the pot from her. "It all smells wonderful." He couldn't remember when he'd eaten more than cold bread and beans, or tortillas and chili, washed down with whiskey.

"I've made scones, too." She pointed to a pan of biscuit-shaped breads. "Go on inside, and I'll serve it up."

She brought him a platter heaped with food, then sat across from him with her own plate. "What will you be doing today?" she asked.

"Drilling mostly. Trying to get the men ready to move out."

"How long will it take us to reach California?" she asked.

He shrugged. "Weeks. Several months. It all depends on what we encounter along the way."

She nodded and fell silent. Was she already regretting her decision to come with him, now that she knew it could be many weeks or months before they reached their destination? Yesterday he had laughed at the idea of being saddled with a woman to take care of. Now he found part of himself dreading the thought of seeing her go.

"I thought I'd do the laundry today," she said before he could think of anything to say.

"There are laundresses to take care of that. Enlisted men's wives and local women."

She shook her head and stabbed at a piece of bacon with her fork.

Bobby's barking interrupted their conversation.

"Lieutenant, we've come with a present from Colonel Peabody," a man called.

He rose and held back the tent flap, and three privates entered, carrying several large pieces of wood between them.

"Why, it's a bed," Ellen said as they moved past her and began assembling the wood into a double bedstead.

"What?" Michael stared at the bed taking shape before his eyes.

While two of the men worked, the third stripped the linen from the cot and folded it up, then went out and returned with a feather mattress rolled up under his arms. "A wedding gift from Colonel Peabody," the private said as he unrolled the mattress, revealing sheets and blankets and two pillows stacked in the middle. He looked up. "Would you like me to put on the linens, ma'am?"

"No, that's all right," Ellen said, smiling. She looked back at Michael. "Isn't it beautiful?"

He stared at the bed, and words stuck in his throat.

"Tell Colonel Peabody thank you very much." Ellen reached out to feel the mattress. "I'll send a proper note to him later."

The privates saluted and filed out, taking the old linens and cot with them. Ellen sat on the bed, running her hands along the smooth ticking. "Now you won't have to sleep on the floor," she said.

He swallowed hard, staring at her. Maybe Solly was right. Maybe Ellen did see things differently. The air inside the tent felt too close. He was having difficulty getting his breath. "I'd better go," he said. He turned and hurried away, leaving her sitting on the edge of the bed.

After she'd made up the bed, washed the breakfast dishes, and packed them away, Ellen gathered up her own and Michael's dirty clothes and walked toward the river.

The day was already warm, and her wool dress felt heavy and close. She passed a group of soldiers drilling in the sun, the steady tramp of their feet raising clouds of dust, the officer's shouted commands echoing over the parade ground. She wondered how the men bore the heat, burdened as they were with weighty haversacks and weapons.

She was aware of more than one pair of eyes turned her way as she walked by, and she held her head up and quickened her pace. She didn't like the hungry, animal look she saw in some of those eyes—the same look her cousin Randolph had given her before she'd found the courage to run away. Had she come halfway around the world to find things were not that much different where she was concerned?

Only Michael did not look at her in that way—as if she were a delicacy to be devoured. Instead, his gaze held an unexpected tenderness.

Out of sight of the men, she slowed and unbuttoned a button at the neck of her dress. Raising her head, she felt a slight breeze brush her bare skin. A line of trees marked the riverbank, their shade beckoning.

But before she reached the river, she came upon a group of women gathered under the trees. A thin, dark-haired woman almost as tall as Ellen herself was holding court in their midst.

"Can one of you ladies tell me the best place to find a husband?" she asked as Ellen joined the group.

Ellen stared at the woman. Other than her half-sister, Gennette, this was the first female she'd met who was as tall as she was. But there the similarities ended. Where Ellen was well-endowed, this woman was small-breasted, with long thin arms and bony hips. Even her dark hair was thin, fine tendrils escaping from the knot at the back of her neck and waving in the breeze. Her dark brows and lashes stood out from her white, white skin, and a single brown mole drew attention to her well-shaped mouth.

She smiled, revealing large teeth. "They tell me gettin'

hitched is the only way to travel with this army, so that's what I intend to do."

Ellen returned the smile. So she wasn't the only one willing to wed for convenience. "I can help you," she said. "We'll go talk to Colonel Peabody."

If the colonel was surprised to see yet another woman wishing to marry one of his men, he had the grace not to show it. "A friend of yours?" he asked Ellen, surveying the newcomer's coarse dress and coarser manner.

"No. I . . . I don't even know her name." Ellen looked at the woman.

"It's Katherine. Katherine Shea." She stuck out her hand, and Ellen took it.

"All right, Miss Shea. If you can find a man willing to marry you, you can travel with us," the colonel said, waving them away.

Katherine grabbed Ellen by the arm and pulled her away from the colonel's tent. "What are you doing?" Ellen asked, hanging back.

"Goin' to find a husband!"

Ellen's eyes widened as Katherine dragged her toward the parade ground. The soldiers she had seen on her way to do laundry had been replaced by a group of dragoons. She recognized Michael's tall frame astride an ink-black horse.

Katherine walked right up to that horse, taking Ellen with her. Michael stared down at the two of them, choking off the order he'd been about to give. Ellen stared at the ground, feeling her face grow red. What must he be thinking of her now?

"Yes?" he asked after a long moment.

"This won't take a minute, Lieutenant," Katherine said, and stepped out in front of the men.

Ellen shrugged and shook her head, indicating she had nothing to do with this interruption. Katherine strode the length of the mounted troops, studying each one, the men staring back. Then she stopped, hands on her hips. "My name's Katherine Shea, and I'm lookin' for a husband!

Who wants to marry a woman with five hundred dollars in gold and the longest legs in Texas?"

All semblance of order dissolved as the men began to talk among themselves. Michael glared at Katherine and then at Ellen. "What is the meaning of this?" he demanded.

She shrugged again and looked away, too proud to let him see how his anger hurt her feelings.

Katherine walked up to a sorrel gelding and grabbed hold of the bridle, staring up at the skinny private in the saddle. "What's your name, soldier?" she asked.

"W-W-Watson," he stammered, turning red up to his earlobes. "St-Sticks W-Watson."

"I kinda like you, Sticks." Katherine grinned up at him. "What do you say you and me get hitched?"

Before Private Watson could stutter out an answer, a burly, bearded fellow rode up and slid out of his saddle beside Katherine. He wrapped his arm around her and glared out at the crowd. "Any man who thinks he wants Katherine the Great here will have to fight me for her."

Katherine looked at him, one eyebrow raised. "Katherine the Great, is it? What's your name?"

"Bear Roberts," he said, pinching her soundly on the bottom.

She reached over and calmly pinched him back. "As long as you remember I can give as good as I get, we'll get along fine, Bear."

A shout went up from the men at that, and Ellen thought the ranks would dissolve into a melee until a blast shook the air. She looked around and saw Michael glaring down from his horse, a pistol raised over his head and gunsmoke settling around him. "The next man who steps out of formation can expect to get a ball in his a—er, backside," he said, glancing at Ellen.

The men quietly resumed their places. Bear Roberts climbed back onto his horse as well. Michael directed his attention to Katherine. "Miss Shea, you may wait for Private Roberts in his quarters. Mrs. Trent"—he glared at Ellen—"will take you there."

Red-faced, Ellen turned away. "Who was that?" Katherine asked, hurrying to catch up with her. "That officer."

"That was . . . my husband!" Ellen spat out the word. Michael acted as if he blamed her for his troops breaking rank. If he couldn't control his men any better than that—

"I'm sorry." Katherine plucked at her sleeve. "I didn't mean to make him mad." She looked sorrowful. "Sometimes I do things without thinking."

Ellen nodded. When the gun went off, Bobby had taken refuge under her petticoats, and he was still there now, making it difficult to walk without tripping. She stopped and lifted her skirts. "Get out of there," she ordered.

Katherine laughed when the little dog emerged from beneath her skirts. "Ain't he cute?" she said. She reached down and petted him, then smiled up at Ellen. "Friends?"

Ellen nodded and returned the smile. "Friends."

"So, how long have you and the lieutenant been married?"

"One day." Ellen saw Katherine's obvious surprise and began to laugh. "I did the same thing you did," she said. "Well, almost. Colonel Peabody told me I'd have to marry if I wanted to travel to California with the troops, so I did."

Katherine shook her head, chuckling. She nudged Ellen with her elbow. "All I want to know is, how did you end up with a lieutenant—and a good-lookin' one, too? All I got was a private—and he's a real 'Bear'!"

Both women began laughing then. By the time they reached the row of enlisted men's tents, Ellen was in a better mood. She'd made a new friend. So what if Michael Trent was mad at her? She'd fix steak and kidney pie for dinner and stewed apples with cinnamon sugar. She'd dare him to eat that meal and remain angry!

Michael thought about going into San Antonio for a few drinks and a game of cards to take his mind off things. But a night on the town didn't have the same attraction now that he knew Ellen was waiting for him.

Not that he could expect any excitement with her. More

frustration was all she offered. At least he would stop by the tent and check on her before he headed into town. Maybe he'd find a willing woman there to take his mind off his troubles.

The canvas of his tent glowed golden in the lamplight, a welcome beacon. When he pushed aside the flap, Ellen looked up from the table and rose to meet him. She was wearing the red dress again, a white lace shawl around her shoulders. At her smile, Michael felt his spirits soar, then plummet. What would it have been like to come home each evening to find her waiting like this, with a smile just for him?

"I'm glad you're home," she said, dishing food onto his plate. Simple words. But when had he ever heard them before? Even Bobby seemed glad to see him, wagging his tail when Michael bent to stroke the wiry fur.

He couldn't remember eating such good food before, either. "This is delicious." He forked up a portion of the meat and pastry. "You'll make me fat, feeding me like this."

She smiled at the compliment. "I did all the wash today, mended two of your shirts, and sewed the buttons back on one of your uniforms."

"Thanks to you, I'll be the best-dressed soldier in the dragoons."

"I don't want you to be sorry you agreed to let me stay."

"Why would I do that?"

She shifted in her chair. "You looked none too happy with me this morning."

He looked down at his plate and stabbed at a bit of steak. "Do you blame me? One of the points of drilling the men is to instill discipline. Your appearance with that woman put an end to any attempt at order."

He glanced up and immediately regretted ever speaking. She looked so wounded.

"I was only trying to help her. She wanted to find a husband, the way I found you."

He swallowed hard, all irritation evaporating. How could a woman like Ellen, raised in the sheltered confines of a family castle, have any concept of the harsh realities of Army life? "I'm sure you meant well." He reached across the table and took her hand. "But Texas isn't like your English village. There are a lot of different kinds of people here, and not all of them can be trusted."

She looked troubled. "Are you saying I shouldn't have trusted Katherine?"

He shrugged. "She's obviously no lady, but that doesn't mean she's up to no good. I was thinking more of the men."

"What about the men?"

"Some of them, seeing you walking around camp unescorted—they might get the wrong idea. They might try to bother you."

"Then they would have you to answer to."

He could not hold back a surge of pride when he heard the certainty in her voice. "Yes, they would have me to deal with." Heaven help the man who would touch one hair of her pretty head. "Still, I want you to promise me you'll be careful."

She bowed her head. "I promise." Without waiting for an answer, she stood and carried the dishes outside to wash them.

He removed his boots and stretched his stiff limbs. He was sore from sleeping on the floor last night. His eyes strayed to the bed set up against one side of the tent. The mattress looked soft, almost as soft as the woman who proposed to share it with him.

Ellen returned with the clean dishes, and he guiltily looked away from the bed. "What will I need to do in the morning?" she asked.

"Pack everything in the trunk," he said. "A detail will come around to load it and the furniture into the baggage wagons, and to take down the tent. Can you ride?"

She nodded.

"Then I'll find you a horse. You'll have to ride with the other women and the baggage wagons. We'll probably travel most of the day and we'll camp rough for the next few nights."

She compressed her lips into a thin line, her fair skin growing paler. "It's late," she said, turning away. "We'd better get ready for bed."

"You take the bed," he said. "I'll sleep on the floor."

"No!" She shook her head. "There's plenty of room for two people, and I wouldn't feel right having it all to myself."

He watched her eyes, hoping for some clue as to what she wanted, but they were as innocent as a child's. Apparently she truly saw no problem with two adults of the opposite sex sharing a bed.

"I'll sleep on the floor," he said again. He picked up a folded blanket from the foot of the bed and spread it on the floor underneath the table. "I'll be fine. I've slept rougher plenty of times."

She blew out the lamp, and he thought the matter was settled. He lay down on the blanket and pulled it up around him. Not that he was likely to get much sleep anyway, but he had to keep up appearances.

Bedsprings creaked, then he felt a draft, and a weight settling beside him. The lavender scent of Ellen surrounded him as she lay down beside him and pulled a second blanket over them.

He rolled to face her. "What are you doing?"

Her eyes looked huge in the dim light, bright with anger. "I can't sleep in that bed, knowing you're down here on the floor."

"Get back in bed."

"No." She lay down, her back to him.

He leaned over her. "I order you to get back in that bed."

She crossed her arms over her chest. "I'm not one of your soldiers. Is that the way American men talk to their wives?"

"Please." The word emerged as a whisper, the closest he had come to begging in years.

Her expression softened. "Only if you come with me."

He shook his head. "It wouldn't be proper."

"Why not?" She sat up, hugging her knees to her chest beneath the blanket. "Everyone thinks we're married. Won't they think it strange if they find out we're not sleeping together?" She hesitated. "I mean, that's all we would be doing—sleeping."

She put out her hand and found his. A groan escaped him at her touch, but he let her pull him to his feet and lead him to the bed. He lay down on the edge of the mattress and turned his back to her. He had every intention of getting up and returning to the floor as soon as she was asleep. He lay rigid, every fiber aware of her body inches from his own. He could feel the warmth of her, sense every movement she made. He listened to her breathing, unconsciously matching the rhythm. In . . . out . . . in . . . out . . . until they were both sound asleep.

Michael burrowed deeper under the covers, clinging to that blissful state between sleep and wakefulness. The bed was so warm, his companion so soft. Smiling to himself, he moved closer to the woman beside him, pressing against the rounded backside. Was this perhaps a new lover or one of his former paramours?

Eyes still closed against dawn, he buried his nose in the sweetly perfumed skin of the woman's neck. She smelled of lavender and a subtle, spicy aroma he could identify only as female. He let his tongue trail along one shoulder, the skin soft as satin, tasting sweet and clean. Awake and fully aroused, but reluctant to break the spell by opening his eyes, he slid one hand around to cup a delightfully full breast. Not someone he'd bedded before. He would never have forgotten a shape as pleasing as this.

He dropped his hand to the curve of his companion's waist and felt her tremble at his touch. So his bedmate was awake and already shaking with desire for him. He brought his hand to her breast once more, feeling the tip, firm and erect between his hand and the thin fabric of her shift. He

A Husband by Law 41

stroked the delicate nub with his palm and heard the woman gasp.

Eager to know the identity of this delightful paramour, he opened his eyes and stared into the astonished face of Ellen Winthrop.

Chapter Four

Michael swore and pulled away as if scorched by the touch of Ellen's flesh. He leaped out of bed and began pulling on his trousers, his back to her. He silently berated himself as he struggled to fasten the buttons of his fly. What had he been thinking? Those hadn't been trembles of desire and cries of pleasure he'd heard! She'd obviously been shaking with fear. He'd terrified the girl, his hands all over her as if she were some Houston Street whore.

He shrugged into his tunic and did up the buttons. Balancing on one leg at a time, he pulled on his boots. From the trunk at the end of the bed he dug out his spurs and buckled them on, then drew out his saber and belted it around his waist, along with the Bowie knife in its scabbard. Cartridge box, canteen, sash, and a brace of pistols finished off the outfit.

He splashed water on his face from a bowl on the table, then raked a comb through his curls and settled a tall blue shako on his head. He was ready for battle. And right now he'd rather face a hundred enemy soldiers than the woman in his bed.

When he finally mustered the courage to turn around, Ellen was sitting up. She stared at him, wide-eyed and flushed, blanket pulled around her shoulders as if to shield her from his sight. "I'm sorry," he said, holding out his hands in apology. He could not meet her eyes, afraid of the hurt or fear he would see there. He shook his head. "I'm sorry." Then he turned and started out of the tent.

"Wait, I'll prepare your breakfast." She rose from the bed, though she still did not raise her eyes to meet his.

"I'll have coffee at the mess. There's no time for more." He allowed himself a brief look at her, realizing his mistake as a jolt of renewed desire rushed through him. Tendrils of red-gold hair had escaped from her braid and framed a face still soft with sleep. The blanket she held about her did little to hide the generous curves he'd so recently embraced. When he dropped his eyes, he saw that her shift fell only halfway past her calves, revealing shapely legs and ankles and bare feet. He turned away from her once more, his voice gruff. "You'd better pack. We'll be heading out soon."

He lifted the tent flap and ducked out into the humid morning air. He waited until he was out of sight of the tent before he raised his canteen and took a long drink, though the water did little to damp the fire that raged within him. Maybe it was best that this had happened, he thought as he headed toward the stables. Now that Ellen had seen his true nature, she'd no doubt leave before the troops headed out. That would be best.

Best for her. As for Michael, he knew Ellen's departure would leave a void in his life he'd never before known existed.

Ellen's hands trembled as she fastened the buttons on the blue velveteen riding habit. In fact, she hadn't been able to stop trembling since Michael had left the tent. It was as if he'd taken all the warmth she had with him.

How stupid she'd been! How wanton he must think her, insisting that he share the bed with her. She'd only meant to save him the discomfort of sleeping on the floor. She'd never realized what lying beside him would feel like, how being so close to him would make her yearn to be even closer.

And this morning, when she'd awakened to find his hands on her, his body pressed against her, she'd been horrified at the reaction of her own flesh, alternately trembling and burning at his touch. Her breasts and her loins ached for him, while her mind told her that this was not the way a lady would behave. What a gentleman he was to take the blame upon himself, to apologize for what she'd driven him to do.

Yet even while she berated herself for her behavior, a part of her thrilled at the memory of Michael's touch. Her very nature fought against all her pretense at being a lady.

With a heavy heart, she stripped the linens from the bed and packed them into the trunk, along with the dishes and pots and pans and leftover food. By the time two privates arrived to load the baggage and take down the tent, she and Bobby were waiting outside.

As the men worked, the camp physician, Dr. Sullivan, approached, leading a large-boned mare, its coat almost the same coppery shade as Ellen's own hair. He pulled off his cap and waved to her. "Good morning, Madam Trent."

She reached up to stroke the neck of the mare as the doctor brought the horse to a halt beside her. "She's beautiful," she whispered.

"Her name's Fly. Well, Dragonfly really, but the Army shortens everything." He patted the mare's rump. "The lieutenant ordered a sidesaddle for her, said you'd be more comfortable riding than in one of the baggage wagons."

Her smile faded at the mention of Michael. "Thank you, Doctor. I'm sure I'll enjoy riding her."

"Call me Solly." He looped the reins around a spindly post oak but made no move to leave. He stood by the horse, his gaze fixed on Ellen until she began to feel uncomfortable. "I reckon if anyone can tame our headstrong lieutenant, you might be the one to do it."

She stiffened. What did he mean, calling Michael headstrong? Was it so wrong for a man to decide on a course and stick firmly to it? Or did he mean something else entirely? "Have you and Michael been friends very long?"

He shrugged. "Long enough to know he's a good man. He leads with his heart instead of his head sometimes, but I don't know as how that's such a bad thing."

She wove the mare's reins through her fingers and thought about keeping silent, but in the end she couldn't hold back the question. "Do you think marrying me was a decision of his heart or his head?"

He looked at her so long without answering that she wondered if he was trying to concoct an apt lie. Then a throaty chuckle escaped him, making her look at him sharply. "I'd say a little of both, my dear. A little of both." Still chuckling, he looked over her shoulder, then the laughter abruptly vanished from his eyes. "What the devil?"

She looked around to see Katherine Shea, now Katherine Roberts, riding toward them astride a raw-boned Army mule. Her long skirts were hiked to reveal several inches of black-stockinged leg on each side of the high-pommeled saddle. "Ellen, let's ride together!" she called, kicking the mule in an effort to speed her progress across the compound.

"I'd better be going." Solly turned away, but too late. Katherine had already spotted him. "Well, don't this beat all!" she exclaimed, kicking the mule into a rough trot. "Solly, you old scalawag! What are you doin' here?"

"Hello, Katherine." Solly tipped his hat, eyes fixed on the new laundress with all the wariness of a fox faced with a well-remembered trap. "One usually expects to find an Army doctor with an Army," he said. "The better question might be—what are *you* doing here?"

She grinned and looked over the long line of troops. "Looks like I'm goin' to California."

Solly replaced his hat on his head. "Is Private Edwards with you, then?"

She shook her head. "No. Me and him had a partin' of

the ways, you might say." She shrugged. "I got me a new man now. Private Bear Roberts."

Solly pursed his lips. "Roberts. A brawny, bearded fellow as I recall." He nodded. "He's taller than you, at least, something that can't be said for most of the men I've known you to favor."

She laughed. "And he thinks he's big enough to fight off the competition—for a while."

Ellen thought Solly was trying hard not to smile. "I see you haven't changed much in ten years."

"Well, you sure have! Gone gray as a grizzly bear!" She leaned over and stroked his neatly trimmed beard. "But, say, I like it! Makes you look all distinguished."

"You two are old friends, then?" Ellen said.

Katherine straightened and looked contrite. "Solly, you made me plumb forget my manners. Ellen, this here's an old friend of mine, Doc Solly. Solly and I knew each other in Florida, during the Seminole campaign. Solly, this is Ellen Trent, Lieutenant Trent's wife."

"I've already had the pleasure of meeting Mrs. Trent."

"Doc—I mean Solly—brought me a horse to ride," Ellen explained.

"May I help you mount, ma'am?"

All around them, people were lining up in formation, ready to move out. "I suppose you'd better." At her nod, he made a step with his hands and assisted her into the saddle. She took the reins and arranged her skirts. "Would you hand Bobby up to me?" she asked. "I'm afraid if I don't hold him, he might be trampled."

He obliged, and the dog stood before her, balancing against the horse's broad neck, ears erect, black nose twitching with excitement, short tail wagging.

"Now ain't that the cutest sight!" Katherine turned to Solly. "You'll ride with us, won't you?"

He shook his head. "Not today."

"Oh, come on now. Just once, for old times' sake."

He relented, as Ellen had known he would. He hadn't stopped looking at Katherine for more than two seconds since she'd arrived. "Meet me by the baggage carts," he said, and hurried away.

A few moments later they fell in line with the baggage carts, Solly riding between them on a clean-lined strawberry roan. "That's a good-lookin' mount," Katherine observed. "How long you had her?"

"Five years." He patted the mare's neck. "Pepper is the finest horse I've ever owned. She's got a gait like a rocking chair. I won't ride anything else."

"What have you been up to since I saw you last?" Katherine asked.

"The usual. 'Poking, pilling, and purging.'" His eyes wandered back to her once more, his gaze sliding over the shapely stocking-clad legs showing between the hem of her skirt and the tops of her boots. "What have you been up to?"

"I stayed in Florida a while, then traveled some. Spent a year or two in New Orleans." She grinned. "Had a fine time. But I missed the Army, so when I heard there was another war coming on, I decided to join up."

"I see. Just another volunteer?"

"In a manner of speaking."

"How patriotic of you." He turned to Ellen. "I should warn you, Mrs. Trent, that our friend Katherine here is to be taken seriously only half the time."

Ellen smiled. "And which half might that be?"

"Ahhh. There's the rub."

"I'm always on the level with other women," Katherine protested. "It's just the men I have to keep guessing."

She winked, and to Ellen's surprise the crusty old doctor flushed red as his horse. "I . . . I'd better go make sure everything is in order with the ambulance," he muttered. Not waiting for a reply, he spurred the mare and trotted away.

Katherine stared after him, a tender smile on her face. "Solly always was a funny one," she said. "And he could kiss better than anybody I ever met."

It occurred to Ellen that Katherine probably knew a lot

about kisses . . . and about all the other intimacies between a man and a woman. Perhaps she'd know better why Michael had fled their tent this morning like a man possessed. But then, she could never bring herself to tell such things. She looked away.

"It's a beautiful day for travelin', ain't it?" Katherine said.

Ellen nodded, looking around the encampment. The sun had risen, cutting through the dawn mist and bathing the compound in a clear golden light. All around them, tents had been struck and wagons loaded. As she watched, the company band began to play, and soldiers fell into formation, a mass of dark blue uniforms, glinting weaponry, and sable and chestnut horses.

"Ain't it a thrillin' sight?" Katherine asked, gazing out over the troops. "There's nothing like a man in uniform to get the blood stirring. And when you've got *three hundred* of 'em, well, my heart gets to goin' to beat sixty."

Ellen smiled at her friend. "They do look handsome," she said. Without meaning to, she found herself searching for Michael. She found him at the head of his men, arm raised as he gave the order to march. A thrill shot through her at the sight of his tall, muscular figure in the saddle, and she caught her breath at the sudden memory of that body pressed against her this morning.

"He's a huckleberry above a persimmon, for sure," Katherine said, following her gaze. "I hear tell he broke a lot of hearts in San Antone when he married you." She waved and pointed. "And there's my man. Hey, Bear!"

Her voice carried clearly, and Private Roberts turned in the saddle and grinned at his enthusiastic bride.

"You two seem to be getting along well," Ellen said as they waited to fall in line behind the troops.

"Oh, passable fine." She winked at Ellen. "He's lusty enough all right, and aimin' to please, but he just don't give me the shivers."

"The shivers?"

Katherine leaned over and slapped her on the shoulder.

"You know! That shakin' all over like you're gonna bust, and then it's like you do explode and you're on fire from head to toe. I'll bet that handsome fella you're married to can sure 'nuff do it to you."

Ellen swallowed hard, remembering the way Michael's touch had set her to trembling. Still, exploding and being on fire didn't sound very enjoyable.

"Yessiree, it's a fine day for a parade." Katherine turned her face up to the sun. "I always feel grand at the start of a march." She turned to Ellen once more. "We're setting out on a great adventure, you know. No telling what marvelous things we'll see and do between here and California."

California. The very thought of that paradise had sustained her through the long ocean voyage. In California she'd have family again. In California she'd find a home at last. For weeks she'd thought of nothing but her destination. She'd never dreamed the journey itself would hold so much attraction. During the next weeks she'd see things and meet people she'd never known before. And she'd come to know the man who had agreed to be her husband, if only for a while. That in itself might be the greatest adventure of all.

As the stirring strains of "Boot and Saddle" rang out across the compound, Michael concentrated on forming up his men and moving out. His gelding, Brimstone, danced beneath him, as if excited by the prospect of travel. The mood was infectious, leading the men to sit taller in the saddle, their mounts to move with a livelier step.

The band switched to "The Girl I Left Behind Me" as the troops passed through San Antonio. A crowd gathered in Military Plaza to cheer them on. Bearded Texans in rough buckskin and Mexicans draped in blankets lined the street. Anglo women in flowered bonnets waved handkerchiefs and cheered, while the Mexican señoritas hailed the soldiers with more lusty cries. Michael spotted Trini looking his way, and he quickly turned his attention to the opposite side of the square. There, in the shadow of the Bexar

Exchange Saloon, a group of Lipan Indians in paint and feathers surveyed the scene, their gaze fixed on a spot behind Michael's company.

Something about the Indians' stern, almost resentful expressions sent a prickle of apprehension up his spine. Slowly he turned his head just enough to look in the direction of their scrutiny. His hands tightened on the reins as he recognized the half-dozen irregulars who had brought their shaggy mounts alongside the orderly column of soldiers. Though they called themselves Texas Rangers, Michael thought of them as barbarians. Loud-mouthed and greasy-haired, dressed in outlandish costumes of buckskin and wild-animal pelts, and bristling with knives, pistols, sabers, and every other kind of weapon, the six had laid siege to the city two weeks before. They drank constantly, gambled often, and brawled with anyone who did not jump to do their bidding. Only the week before, Michael had seen one of them gun down a bartender in cold blood when he had the audacity to demand payment of their bill. Only Solly's iron grip on his wrist had stopped Michael from retaliating. Even now he had half a mind to ride back and order them away—

"What are you staring at with such a murderous look?"

Michael snapped his head around to discover Colonel Peabody by his side. He brought his hand up in a crisp salute. "I was noticing that band of rangers who have fallen in with us, sir. If you like, I'll ride back and order them to disburse."

"You'll do no such thing, Lieutenant." Peabody folded his hands atop the high pommel of his McClelland saddle in a relaxed pose that belied the steely alertness in his eyes. "The rangers are to accompany us as scouts and trackers."

"Accompany us!" He could scarce believe his ears. "Those men are the lowest sort of thieves and troublemakers."

"I don't recall asking your opinion, Lieutenant."

"Yes, sir, but surely our own men could do a better job, with half the trouble."

"That's quite enough, Lieutenant!"

Michael choked back further protest, but inside he seethed. The idea of having to work alongside the undisciplined rangers rankled. He'd have to be sure to warn Ellen to steer clear of them.

"Captain Dunleavy and his men know the territory between here and Santa Fe far better than any of our troops," Peabody said. "And it appeases the local politicos to have their own forces involved. Damned independent lot, these Texans."

Michael sat even taller in the saddle. "I'm a native myself, sir."

Peabody gave him a measured look. "So you are."

And just what is that supposed to mean?

"How is your wife, Lieutenant? Settling in all right?"

"She seems to be, sir." He watched the colonel out of the corner of his eye, wary.

"Glad to hear it. I'll daresay a woman like that will keep you home nights and out of trouble."

"Yes, sir."

"Carry on, then."

Michael watched the colonel ride toward the head of the column. Was Peabody lumping him into the same bunch as those rangers—just another independent, trouble-making Texan? It wasn't as if he went looking for trouble, after all; not like the rangers, who boasted of the hell they raised.

But neither was he one to live passively, to ignore an insult or turn a blind eye to injustice. It was true he had a taste for recklessness; he supposed he could say he'd been bred to it, considering his father's love of adventure.

His mother always said Dan Trent's penchant for excitement had led him to desert the family, and she'd long predicted the same fate for her only son. *So be it*, Michael had always thought. He could think of worse ways for a man to spend his life.

Now that Ellen was in the picture, he wasn't so sure. He'd thought the burden of responsibility for another would weigh too heavily on him. Instead, he found himself longing to be the hero in her eyes, to prove himself worthy of her kind regard.

He smiled as he thought of how she'd looked this morning, mounted on the mare he'd chosen for her because its shimmery red-gold coat nearly matched her own sun-washed tresses. She'd sat very erect in the saddle, the ostrich plume of her campaign hat waving in the breeze. She looked every bit as noble as she was, as fine and rare as strawberries in February.

And every man Jack thought she belonged to him. They'd no doubt laugh him out of the Army if they knew the truth. He'd have laughed himself if anyone had ever told him he'd end up in such a predicament. Ellen wasn't the sort of woman a man bedded then left behind. She deserved better, but he didn't have it to give. He groaned and took a firmer grip on the reins. By the time this campaign was over, he had a feeling he'd be wishing he'd taken his chances with an Army tribunal, rather than endure this torture of wedding vows unfulfilled.

Chapter Five

When they halted at noon to water the horses and eat a cold meal, Michael walked back to the baggage wagons. He told himself he was only doing so because Ellen was his responsibility, and it was his duty to check on her. But he knew the lie of that the moment he saw her, and her smile pierced his reserve like a sword.

"Hello, Michael," she said in her soft, throaty voice, and the sound of his name on her lips made his heart pound.

"How are you doing?" he asked.

She looked around at the men unloading food from some of the carts, and others drawing water for their mounts from the barrels strapped to the sides of the wagons. "It's very exciting, isn't it?"

He smiled at her enthusiasm. "Would you like to get down, stretch your legs a bit?"

"Oh, yes, please." She handed Bobby to him. He took the little dog, who thanked him by licking his face and dancing about his feet once he set him on the ground.

"He likes you," Ellen said.

He reached up to help her dismount, and for a heart-stopping moment she was in his arms once more, the warmth of her skin burning into his hands, her face even with his own, lips so close . . .

He looked away, breaking the spell, and stepped back, searching for some safe topic of conversation. His eyes fell on the dog. "I've never seen a dog ride a horse before," he said.

She laughed, a bright sound that only added to the heaviness of his heart. "Oh, Bobby's a good traveler." She knelt and ruffled the black fur.

"He means a lot to you, doesn't he?"

She looked up, sun lighting her face and illuminating those brilliant blue eyes. "My father gave him to me."

"Your father, the earl?" He offered her his arm, and they set out walking, away from the wagons and the press of other people. "So what was it like, growing up royalty and all?" Could there be anything further from his own hardscrabble childhood?

"Oh, but we weren't royalty!" She looked shocked at the idea.

He loved the way her cheeks flushed such a soft pink. He had to fight the urge to reach out and stroke her skin. "Oh, come now, not even a little?" he teased.

"Well, *I* certainly wasn't!" She smiled. "Though when I was very little, I did think my father was at least as important as the queen. But I suppose all little children feel that way about their parents."

He nodded. "When I was a boy, I thought there was nothing my dad couldn't do." He still liked that memory of his father best—Dapper Dan, always togged out in a pressed suit, full of enthusiasm for his latest scheme. Young Michael would have followed him anywhere.

"And you wanted to be just like him."

He looked at her, startled. "What makes you say that?"

"Because that's the impression you give—that there's nothing *you* can't do." She smiled, and her blue eyes shone with mirth. "I've been listening to people talk about you, did you know? Whenever I meet someone new and they find out I'm your bride, everyone has a story to tell."

The thought alarmed him. Depending on which stories people chose to tell, he might come off looking like a reckless idiot or a dangerous fool. "Don't believe everything you hear," he cautioned.

"Then it isn't true that you once harnessed a man to his own cart when you caught him beating his mule?"

"The cart was overloaded. That was the best way to demonstrate the point to the oaf."

"And did you really fight four card players who tried to cheat you at a game in a San Antonio saloon—and win?"

"Yes, but they were all half drunk at the time."

"And did you really break the nose of a man you caught beating his wife?"

He shrugged, uncomfortable under her bright-eyed scrutiny. "I suppose so. You must think I spend all my time thinking of scrapes to get into. You mustn't get the idea that life with me is one troublesome time after another."

She looked at him thoughtfully for a long moment, then nodded approvingly. "I think life with you will never be boring."

Boring. No, that's not how he'd have described life wed to Ellen Winthrop either. Different, arousing, even physically torturous, but never boring. He glanced at her again and saw that she was watching the goings-on around them with keen interest. Maybe he needed to rethink his opinion of his demure English bride. She might have lived a sheltered life until now, but she wasn't the shrinking violet he'd first expected. Who knew what other surprises she held in store for him?

"Ellen! Halloo!"

A female voice of uncommon strength hailed them, and Michael turned to see the woman known around camp as Katherine the Great hurrying toward them.

"There you are!" She arrived in front of them, scarcely winded from her charge across the campground. She nodded to Michael, then put a hand on Ellen's arm. "Let me borrow your lady a minute, Lieutenant. I've got to visit the bushes."

Ellen looked around, a puzzled look on her face.

Michael could almost read her thoughts at Katherine's strange pronouncement. The flat prairie stretched around them on all sides, dry grass undulating in the hot wind, the occasional cactus breaking the monotony of the view with a spiny silhouette. "I don't see any bushes," Ellen said.

"Exactly," Katherine said, dragging her along. "I need you as a stand-in."

Ellen looked back at Michael, puzzled. "I don't think . . ."

"Go on." He shooed her away, trying to maintain an appropriately serious expression on his face. Katherine was about to teach Ellen a lesson she'd need to know for traveling on the prairie. After all, there were some things a husband couldn't be expected to take care of!

They hadn't gone far before Katherine burst out laughing. "Guess you never had to pee on the prairie, huh?" she said as her chuckles subsided.

Ellen flushed, still not sure what this bodily function had to do with bushes, or the lack thereof. "Where are you taking me?" she asked.

Katherine shook her head and didn't say anything until they were some distance away from the wagons. Then she stopped and spread her full skirts. "See, you stand like this, and I go behind you. Then I do the same for you."

Understanding brought a fresh rush of heat to Ellen's face. She glanced back toward the line of men and horses. "But they can see us. I mean, they'll know. . . ."

"Well, of course they'll know. But they won't really see anything, not if we hide behind each other's skirts." She patted Ellen's arm. "Honey, it's not like we'd be doin' somethin' every one of them ain't done. Except we're lucky if most of these yahoos have the decency to turn their backs before they unbutton their pants and whip it out."

Katherine's manner was so frank and her language so descriptive, Ellen began to laugh. It was true that more than once today she'd found herself looking the other way as a soldier stopped to relieve himself. "All right," she said, holding out her skirts. "You go first."

When Katherine finished, she moved over a few feet and arranged herself to shield Ellen from view. "Don't sit on a cactus," she said, grinning.

Ellen was just preparing to raise her skirts when a shot rang out, scattering pebbles at her feet. She screamed and stumbled back, clutching at Katherine.

"Sorry to frighten ya', lass, but you'll do well to pay more heed to where you're runnin' off to." At the sound of the clipped Scottish accent, Ellen whirled, heart in her throat.

A stocky, bearded man with long black hair and flashing black eyes strode toward them through the tall grass. He was dressed in a fringed buckskin shirt, tight fringed pants, and tall boots. The wide-brimmed hat on his head looked as if it had been trampled by a herd of horses, then punched into shape again. An assortment of knives, daggers, and pistols hung from belts and scabbards about his body. When he reached them, he bent and scooped something from the grass. Ellen screamed as a headless serpent swung into her view.

The man grinned at the snake in his hand. It stretched almost six feet, its body as big around as Ellen's wrist. Though the snake was clearly dead, she couldn't contain the shiver that swept over her as she stared at it.

"Rattler," he said, showing large white teeth. "As common out here as rats in a granary. And a sight more deadly." Still holding the snake in one hand and a long-barreled pistol in the other, he gave a slight bow. "Captain Gregory Dunleavy, Texas Rangers, at your service."

"I don't care if you're a Texas Ranger or the goldurned King of England!" Katherine stepped forward, glaring at Dunleavy. "What do you think you're doin', spyin' on a couple of ladies tryin' to find a moment of privacy, and then scarin' the livin' daylights out of us with that horse pistol!"

Dunleavy looked at the weapon in his hand, then shoved the gun under his belt. "Samuel Colt's revolver is a far cry from a horse pistol, madam." He hefted the snake in his hand. "I suppose next time I should just let the rattler have you, and save your precious modesty."

"No. No, thank you, Captain Dunleavy." Ellen put a restraining hand on her friend's arm and somehow managed to find her voice. "I had no idea the snake was there. Your quick thinking saved our lives."

Dunleavy smiled again, eyes sweeping over her with open admiration. "Anything for a lass as bonny as yourself," he said. "And would I be right in thinkin' you're from across the pond, too, then?"

Before she could answer, she heard a familiar voice shouting, "Ellen, are you all right?" She turned and saw Michael galloping toward them on Brimstone. He'd barely reined the horse to a stop before he vaulted out of the saddle and came to stand between the women. "What's going on here?" he demanded of Dunleavy.

"I was just warning the ladies not to venture away from the wagons without beatin' the grass to flush out the snakes." Dunleavy frowned. "Not that it's any concern of yours, Lieutenant."

Michael put a hand on Ellen's shoulder. She wanted to turn and huddle against him, letting him calm the tremors of fear that still ran through her. But this was not the time or place to make a scene. She contented herself with that brief contact on her shoulder, drawing strength from the warmth of his hand and the firmness of his grip as he caressed her. "It's my business when one of the women in question is my wife," he said, anger edging his voice.

Dunleavy raised one eyebrow in a mocking look. "I'd think a man lucky enough to have a bride so lovely would do a better job of looking after her."

Ellen felt Michael's hand tighten on her shoulder. "I'll certainly be more careful in the future," she said quickly.

She might as well have not spoken, as much as the two

men paid any attention to her. They continued to glare at each other like two stallions facing off over a mare. She exchanged a knowing look with Katherine.

"So, Captain, are you going to eat that thing or wear it?" Katherine asked.

Dunleavy looked at Katherine, as if seeing her for the first time. "You're the one they call Katherine the Great, aren't you?" he asked.

She nodded. "That's me." She took his arm and turned him back toward camp. "Why don't you show me how to skin that monster? If there are so many of them around here, I might decide to make me a new pair of boots."

When Katherine had led Dunleavy away, Ellen collapsed against Michael. "I've never been so terrified in my life," she said with a gasp.

"I should have warned you," he said, his arm around her shoulders. "Dunleavy's right. I should do a better job of looking after you—"

"Michael Trent! I do believe I ought to be able to relieve myself without instructions from you!" She straightened and looked him in the eye. "What happened was my own fault for not paying attention to where I was going."

"I promised to protect you," he said, his gaze never wavering from hers. "That's one of the reasons the Army requires women who travel with the troops to be married. A single woman isn't safe out here."

"And I promised to be a pleasing companion—not a burden." She squeezed his hand. "I really will be more careful from now on. Don't worry."

He looked away. "We'd better get back. We'll be moving out soon."

He turned toward the wagons, but she hesitated. "What's wrong?" he asked.

She blushed and looked away. "I haven't had a chance . . . I mean, Captain Dunleavy came along before I . . ."

His face reddened as well, but he straightened and drew

his saber. "Allow me, madam." With that he began beating the grass in a wide circle around them. Then he sheathed the weapon and turned his back. "You'll be safe now. I'll wait for you."

Michael frowned at the playing cards laid out on the blanket before him. The Queen of Spades looked up at him with baleful eyes, the Jack of Hearts beside her. With the eight of hearts face down beside them, he'd clearly lost this hand.

"I'm thinking *vingt y un* is not your game, Lieutenant."

To Michael's great annoyance, Dunleavy had assumed a position behind him and was now shaking his head and making tutting sounds under his breath.

"I don't remember asking for your opinion, Captain," Michael said, the coolness of his voice belying the anger simmering within. "Deal." He shoved his cards away.

The card game had begun pleasantly enough, a way to pass the time between the evening meal and sleep. Michael, Solly, Bear Roberts, and a corporal named Martin played on a blanket spread out not far from Michael's campsite. He'd planned to be close enough to Ellen to hear if she needed help, and far enough away to afford her a little privacy.

They'd arrived at this spot about sunset and pitched camp. Though from time to time he chafed against the Army's interminable and sometimes insensible rules, Michael had to admit they had it all over anyone else for efficiency. In no time at all campfires were laid, bedrolls distributed, and suppers cooked.

Ellen had weathered her first day's travel in good spirits, despite her terrifying encounter with Dunleavy and the rattlesnake. He glanced back at the Scotsman again. No one had invited him to join them, but he had insinuated himself into their circle as if no one would dare to object.

"And how is your lady wife, Lieutenant?" Dunleavy asked as Martin dealt another hand.

Michael bristled. Why was the captain so concerned about Ellen? "She's fine."

Dunleavy grinned. "I must say, if I had a woman as bonny as that one, I'd not be wastin' my time playin' cards."

Michael glared at the captain, hands itching to punch that smug grin off his face. But he'd nothing to gain from striking a superior officer—even if Dunleavy was an irregular. "You seem to have plenty of time to waste tonight, Captain," he said with exaggerated lightness. "I suppose it's because no woman would have you."

The others burst out laughing at the exchange, and Dunleavy's face darkened. Michael let one hand drape casually over the hilt of the Bowie, just in case the captain was foolish enough to demonstrate his offense.

"Care to share the joke, fellas?"

Michael looked up and saw Katherine Roberts sauntering toward them. He frowned at the interruption, until he noticed Ellen following her friend. He smiled at her, and the look she gave him in return warmed him through.

Katherine swaggered over to Bear Roberts, who reached out and pulled her to him. "Maybe we were talkin' about you," Bear said.

"I've a few tales I could tell on you, too." She thumped him on the head. "So watch your tongue if you want your secrets kept." She settled down beside him, studying the cards with interest.

"Do you mind if I watch?" Ellen came to stand next to Michael.

"Not at all." He moved over to make room for her beside him on the blanket. She sat and arranged her skirts around her. Bobby came and lay at her feet. The scent of lavender, which she pressed between the folds of her clothes, drifted to him, and he inhaled deeply of the perfume he'd come to think of as Ellen's special fragrance. Sitting next to her like this was an indulgence, rendered safe by the presence of so many others about. The cards before him went unnoticed now that he had a more pleasing diversion.

"I trust you've seen no more snakes about?" Dunleavy sat on Ellen's other side and smiled at her.

"What? Oh, no, thank goodness."

Michael glanced at her, surprised to see her blushing under Dunleavy's open stare. The man had the manners of a goat. "How thoughtful of you to remind her of that unfortunate incident," he said, frowning and shoving his bet forward.

"Ah, but I cannot think of it as unfortunate, when it allowed me to make the acquaintance of such a lovely lady."

A lovely lady who happens to be my wife, Michael almost said. But then, Ellen wasn't his wife—not really. And she might not appreciate him making such claims on her. He looked to her again for a clue as to how he should behave, but her attention was on Dunleavy.

"What part of Scotland are you from, Captain?" she asked.

"A little village just below Ben Nevis. Clan Dunleavy has lived there nigh on three hundred years."

"I've never been there but I've heard it's beautiful." She turned to Michael. "Ben Nevis is the highest mountain in Scotland. The country there is still very wild and unsettled."

"A rugged land for rugged men, we say." Dunleavy looked at Michael when he spoke, a challenge in his eyes.

He's itching for a fight, Michael thought, glaring at him. *He keeps this up, he'll have it.*

"Do you miss your home?" Ellen asked. Did Michael imagine a wistful note in her voice?

"Sometimes." Dunleavy stroked his beard. "But I wanted to get out in the world, have a few adventures. And my father's healthy as an ox—he'll not be ready to turn over the reins as laird of the clan for a few years yet."

Michael groaned to himself. Was Dunleavy saying he

was the son of a lord as well? Had all the British nobility decided to foist their offspring onto Texas?

"And where did you say you're from, lass?" Dunleavy asked.

She shifted on the blanket and twisted her fingers in Bobby's thick fur. "A little village. I'm sure you wouldn't have heard of it."

"She's being modest," Michael said. "Ellen's family . . ." He felt her fingers digging into his wrist and he stopped speaking, understanding washing over him when he saw the pleading in her eyes. For some reason, Ellen didn't want Dunleavy to know who her family was or where they were from.

"What were you saying, Trent?" Dunleavy asked.

He shook his head. "Are we going to finish this game or not?"

"Aw, hell, I've got picket duty!" Bear Roberts threw his cards onto the blanket in disgust.

"I'll take your place." Katherine plopped down on the edge of the blanket and pulled her skirts over her crossed legs. "I'll show you fellas some real card games, not this Frenchy playparty stuff."

"Will you teach me to play?"

Michael felt a soft touch on his shoulder, and the warm brush of her breath as Ellen spoke.

"Sure, we'll show you how." Katherine gathered the cards and began to shuffle. "But first you have to show us something in return."

Michael felt Ellen stiffen. He reached for her hand and glared at Katherine. What was this wild woman suggesting?

"I . . . I don't know what you mean," Ellen stammered.

Katherine grinned. "If we're gonna teach you how to play cards, you have to teach us something first."

Ellen looked perplexed. "But I don't know how to do anything."

"Sure you do." Katherine leaned toward her. "Everybody has *some* talent. Something they can do the average fellow can't. For instance, I once knew a gal who could tie cherry stems into a knot with her tongue. And I knew a fellow who could imitate all kinds of bird whistles. I even met a man once who was double-jointed all over his body, so he could knot himself up in all sorts of interesting positions."

Ellen's look had transformed from puzzlement to amusement. "I can't do any of those things," she murmured.

"I don't imagine any of those talents are much called for among the kind of company Ellen is used to keeping," Michael said.

"Ahh, but a lady such as yourself has many other talents." Dunleavy wore a smug grin as he spoke. "No doubt a lass such as yourself has been educated in all the maidenly arts. Perhaps you would favor us with a recitation of a poem."

Ellen stared at her hands, knotted in her lap, and shook her head.

"Can you sing?" Katherine asked. "You could teach us a little ditty."

A red stain crept up the slender column of Ellen's neck as she shook her head more insistently.

"Surely you must be able to do *something*," Katherine said.

Michael glared at the other woman. He had a mind to put a stop to this at once. Couldn't they see how Ellen, a genteel lady, was suffering from their coarse taunts?

"I . . . I can dance."

She spoke so softly, he scarcely heard her at first. Then she raised her head and said again, "I can dance . . . a little."

"Yee-haw, that's the ticket!" Katherine clapped her hands together, then scooted back on the blanket. "I could use a little help in that department myself." She gestured toward the cleared space in the center of the blanket. "Show us what you can do."

Face still flushed a becoming pink, Ellen rose and gathered her skirts in hand. "Well, this is called the Sir Roger de Coverley." Humming softly, she curtsied, then lifted her right arm and stepped forward, as if to touch hands with an imaginary partner. Step back, step forward, twirl around, all with infinite grace and in perfect time to the lilting notes of the song.

"Allow me, madam." Dunleavy stepped in front of her and bowed. "No one so beautiful should dance alone." She hesitated a moment, then took the Scotsman's proffered hand.

Michael's mood darkened as he watched them. Hand in hand, they advanced and retreated, turned and twirled, promenaded and do-si-doed. He clutched at the blanket, fingers digging into the dirt beneath, as if he might physically restrain himself from leaping up and tearing Dunleavy's hand from Ellen's. But that would only mark him for the lout he was, wouldn't it? He hadn't been raised a gentleman in a lord's castle. He was Dapper Dan's son, a boy educated on the street. He knew how to fight and how to gamble, not how to cut a courtly figure on the dance floor.

Ellen and Dunleavy finished their demonstration with an elaborate bow and curtsy. Even in his rough clothes, Dunleavy had a certain grace about him, an unexpected courtliness. Blood will tell. Michael had heard that saying often enough. For all his rough looks and vulgar ways, Dunleavy was at the core a noble's son, who not only knew how to dance with a lady like Ellen—he knew the very songs to which they danced.

Bile rose in Michael's throat as he watched Dunleavy bow low over Ellen's hand, the ranger's lips caressing her fingers while his eyes raked over her. Were these the gentleman's manners Ellen was accustomed to? Her blush deepened, and she pulled her hand away and dropped down once more at Michael's side.

"You dance beautifully," he managed to say, avoiding her gaze. There was nothing she did that was not beautiful, he could have added.

"That sure was some fancy footwork," Katherine said. "A little tame for my tastes, but downright pretty when you do it." She gathered up the cards and began to shuffle them. "All right now, who wants to play some poker?"

Ellen leaned closer to Michael, her voice soft in his ear. "Will you teach me now?"

There were a lot of things he'd like to teach her. . . . He forced his mind to the matter at hand, to instructing Ellen in the art of playing poker. "All right. Come here so you can see." She obligingly scooted in close beside him, and he moved his arm so that they sat shoulder to shoulder, her breast against his side, her cheek almost touching his as they studied the cards.

"The picture cards—the jack, queen, and king—are worth more than the number cards," he said. "And all the cards are in suits—like families."

"How pretty they are," she murmured, reaching out a finger to trace the elaborate drawing of the Jack of Hearts. "Like little paintings."

He smiled, looking not at the cards, but at her face. "Yes, beautiful." They might have been alone, for all he heard, or saw, or felt anything but her. He breathed her presence like air and warmed himself in the sensation of her body against his own. When she raised her eyes to meet his, he could have fallen into the deep blue of her gaze.

"Are you two lovebirds going to make calf eyes at each other or play cards?"

Katherine's taunt pulled Michael out of his trance, back to the moment at hand. He stared at the cards in his hand, but they made as much of an impression on his fogged senses as a collection of paintings. "Fold," he said, laying them facedown on the blanket. "That's enough for me. I think I'll call it a night."

Ellen rose also and followed him out of the circle of firelight. "Where are you going?" she asked.

He took a deep breath, his mind clearing some. *What*

I'd like to do is take you back to my bedroll and make love to you properly, he thought, grateful for the darkness that hid his expression from her. "I thought I'd take a walk."

"May I come with you?"

Walking off into the darkness with Ellen was the last thing he knew he ought to do. But he couldn't bring himself to say no. He nodded and offered his arm to steady her on the rough terrain, and they set off together.

Chapter Six

Ellen leaned on Michael's arm, enjoying the solid feel of him against her. She'd come to treasure the moments when they were together like this, close not only in body, but it seemed in spirit as well. She marveled that, having known this man only a few days, she could find herself caring so much for him. Was this what it was like to fall in love?

Sometimes, when she looked in his eyes, she believed she could tell what he was thinking. And sometimes what she saw there mirrored her own whirling emotions, a kind of fear and a nameless longing that came over her unexpectedly. She feared what would happen, what she might become, if she abandoned herself to her feelings, yet she thrilled at the thought of answering that longing, of allowing sensation to overwhelm reason for the first time in her life.

They walked in silence, finding their way around the compound by the light of glowing bivouac fires. She studied his profile in the dim light. As usual, his hair was a tangle of curls, tucked behind his ears and trailing past his collar. She had a sudden urge to run her hand through those locks, teasing them to smoothness. He glanced at her, eyes veiled behind golden lashes, then quickly looked away.

She heard music, the gentle strains of a violin floating on the night air, and thought at first her mind was playing tricks on her. But after a moment they came upon a group of soldiers gathered around a fire. One man cradled a violin to his cheek and coaxed from it lilting music. Impulsively she took Michael's hand and faced him. "Dance with me," she said.

He shook his head and tried to pull away, but she held him fast.

"I'm afraid I don't know the type of dancing you're used to," he said.

She tilted her head, listening to the music a moment, taking note of the rhythm. "This is a waltz," she said. "Surely you can waltz. If you can't, I can teach you."

"I can waltz." He didn't sound pleased, but she could change all that.

"Dance with me," she said again, pulling him toward her. "Please."

He held her lightly, as if she were made of spun sugar, and tentatively guided her into the first steps of the dance. She smiled and gave herself up to the lilting music and the soaring feeling of being in his arms. Michael's steps became surer. He held her more firmly and pulled her closer.

She closed her eyes and reveled in the feelings that flooded her senses. This was dancing! Those measured steps with Captain Dunleavy had been mere formal exercise. But waltzing—waltzing was something she was rarely allowed to do at home. After all, she was a mere poor relation, little better than a servant. Waltzing was for ladies, ladies being courted by fine gentlemen, not for the likes of her.

They danced on in the darkness, the music weaving around them in the cool night air, the moon like a lantern lighting their way. She dared to open her eyes, to gaze into the face of the man she feared she was fast losing her heart to. Michael's eyes were dark pools, fixed on her with an intensity that stole her breath. What did he see when he looked at her this way? Did he read the confused emotions she sought to hide? Did he look beneath the fancy dress and see her true humble nature? Did he, an officer and a gentleman, disdain to be yoked to the likes of her?

But she saw no disdain in his eyes, only a fierce longing that mirrored her own muddled feelings. She stumbled in the dance, caught off guard by the naked emotion he quickly masked. He caught her and stepped back. "I think we'd better get back to camp," he said gruffly. Without waiting for an answer, he turned and started back the way they'd come earlier.

She stared after him, a hard knot in her throat. Had she been wrong to encourage his affections this way? Did he think she meant to trap him in a relationship he did not want? He had told her in the beginning that he was not a man for marriage. Did that mean he did feel *something* for her? Enough to worry she might weaken his resolve?

In silence she followed him back to where they'd made their camp, near where Katherine and Bear had spread their blankets. Trying to cover ground quickly, the troops didn't bother to set up tents for each night's brief stay. Instead they slept in the open, their bedrolls spread wherever they could find a place.

Ellen removed her hat, shoes, and jacket and loosened her corset before lying down and wrapping herself in the blankets. Bobby curled at her feet. For a long time she lay awake, restless, looking at the stars overhead.

Muffled noise to her left distracted her. Bobby raised his head and looked toward the place where Katherine and Bear had spread their bedrolls. Ellen turned her head and saw the mound of blankets shift and change shape, then heard a woman's muffled, frantic cry and a man's low groan.

She drew in her breath, imagining that Bear was hurting her friend. But the cries were followed by laughter and more vigorous movement from the blanket-covered mound.

Blushing even in the darkness, she realized the true nature of the cries. Katherine and Bear must be making love, their passion unrestrained even out here on the prairie.

She had never understood, until now, why her mother had always sent her to spend the night with Mrs. Spence in the next cottage over whenever the earl came to visit. Her mother had explained to her once how babies were made and indicated that what a man and woman shared under the covers was a wonderful experience. But it had never seemed real to Ellen until now.

She rolled over, her back to the scene, and found herself face-to-face with Michael. His eyes met hers and held her, like a hand pinning her down. His face was solemn, almost fierce in the intensity of its expression. She lay there, scarcely daring to breathe, the cries of Katherine and Bear's mating loud in her ears. Michael shifted his gaze from her face to her body, raking his eyes over her in a slow, devouring sweep. She felt naked beneath that look, and a longing grew within her, a tension in her breasts and a heat in her loins that made her clamp her thighs together and draw her legs up to her stomach in an effort to ease the ache. The things she thought frightened her as much as the things she felt. "Michael."

She spoke his name as a plea, and he blinked, as though coming out of a trance. "Michael," she whispered.

"Go to sleep, Ellen," he said, and rolled over, pulling the blanket across his back.

"Michael, I . . ."

"Shhh. Go to sleep."

Michael wondered sometimes if he had been drawn to the military by the dash and polish of its uniforms as much as anything else. He could remember standing on a street corner as a child, watching a regiment pass through town. Dressed in little more than rags himself, the spotless blue coats and gleaming boots swelled his heart with the kind of desire others might have for gold or jewels.

Given a choice of positions upon his graduation from West Point, he had opted for, to his mind, the most swashbuckling of regiments, the Dragoons. Not only did the dark blue, gold-faced coats with their red sashes appeal to his idea of sartorial elegance, but a Dragoon posting was one of the few positions that guaranteed the chance to cut a sharp figure on horseback.

Except for occasional lapses due to various adventures, he prided himself on upholding the proud image of the United States Army. He shined his boots and the brass of his uniform, oiled his carbine, and sharpened the Bowie. His saber gleamed in the scabbard on his hip, and his shako sat tall atop his golden curls. Mounted on his black gelding, Brimstone, he was a sight to instill fear in the enemy, pride in his fellow soldiers, and, not the least of importance, adoration in the eyes of any female he passed.

But it wasn't adoration he saw when he looked in the eyes of Ellen Winthrop. Too often she regarded him with a veiled, studied expression, one he might have labeled concern—or was that just another word for pity?

He pondered this as he knelt along the bank of the Pecos River, using the water as a makeshift mirror as he scraped at his face with a straight razor. He and Ellen had been traveling together almost a week, and he was no closer to figuring her out than he'd been that first day in Colonel Peabody's tent.

He didn't seem to be able to put his thoughts in order around Ellen. Part of him knew how he should behave toward her, but another part of him ignored all propriety and responded altogether inappropriately.

And then there was the whole matter of their marriage. How would a real gentleman act? Where did he leave off being a gentleman and take up being just a man? A gentleman might say it was all right to live with a woman and not sleep with her, to treat her like a lady and not offend her honor, especially when he'd made it pretty clear up front he had no intention of marrying her in truth.

But the real man he was wanted her, and honor be damned!

He heard a light step behind him, then saw the object of his thoughts reflected in the water, her lovely face smiling down at him. "Good morning," he said, half turning and starting to rise.

"No, please finish." She waved him down and sat on a log a little ways away. Bobby scampered in the leaves around her feet. "I didn't mean to disturb you. I brought you breakfast." She held out a tin mug of coffee and a plate of fried pork and biscuits.

"You didn't have to do that." He turned to study his reflection once more. "It's one thing when we're encamped, but out here—"

"I promised to see that you're well fed, and I always keep my promises," she said, a hint of exasperation in her voice.

He was conscious of her eyes on him as he scraped the razor over the flesh of his cheeks and neck. He remembered his sisters watching him when he'd first begun to shave. They'd teased him about the hair that had sprouted on his face and chest, and tried to imitate his changing voice. Though he'd complained loudly, he'd been secretly delighted at this feminine acknowledgment that he was, indeed, becoming a man.

That had been a long time ago, and Ellen was not his sister. The feelings he had for her were not the feelings of a brother toward a sister, but the emotions a man felt for a woman. A woman he admired, desired . . . loved?

"Damn!" He swore as the razor nicked his throat, and dabbed at the cut with his neckerchief.

"Here, let me." She dampened her handkerchief in the river and knelt beside him, applying firm pressure to the cut. "If you hold it like this, you'll stop the bleeding."

Her face was inches from his own as she faced him,

one hand to his throat, the other braced on his shoulder. He put a hand to her waist, as if to steady himself, wanting to pull her to him, as he had that first day in the colonel's tent.

As if seeing his intentions in his eyes, she looked away, and he reluctantly released her. "Here, eat your breakfast." She handed him the cup and plate, and he came to sit beside her on the log.

"It's pretty here." She looked out at the wide green swath of the Pecos.

"Enjoy the water while you can." He stabbed at a piece of pork. "It's the last we'll see for a while—until we get to El Paso."

"And when will that be?"

He heard the weariness in her voice. How difficult this hot, dry traveling must be for a woman who had grown up in England, which he had heard was filled with green hills and lakes. Not to mention she probably wasn't used to having to ride miles on horseback, cook her own meals, and pack and unpack her own camp every day. She'd probably had servants to do everything for her back home. Yet she hadn't uttered a single complaint—something he couldn't say for most of the other women, and a good many of the men, traveling with them. "A few more days," he said, continuing to watch her out of the corner of his eye.

She nodded and squared her shoulders. "The country between here and California, is it similar to what we've seen so far?"

"Worse." He grinned at her dismayed expression.

"Will there be fighting? I've heard talk there's to be a war."

"Relations between the United States and Mexico are shaky at the moment. It seems likely there'll be a war, but maybe not for months. We're being sent to California to secure U.S. holdings there." He shrugged. "Other than the chance of encounters with guerillas, I imagine the trip will be pretty dull."

She hugged herself. "I'm glad I didn't try to make the trip alone, or with other civilians."

"This is definitely the safest way to travel." He winked at her. "After all, you've got yours truly at your side to protect you."

She did not answer right away, her eyes sweeping over him in a slow, considering look that made him grow warm from his boot soles up. "Just remember," she said, picking up the empty plate and standing. "Even Samson lost his strength." She smiled over her shoulder as she turned to leave. "And to a woman."

He stared after her, open mouthed. Then his shoulders began to shake with silent laughter. So Ellen had spotted his weakness already. The riddle now was what was she—or he—going to do about it?

Ellen smiled to herself as she rode through miles and miles of dismal South Texas desert that afternoon. She did not notice the barren countryside, remembering instead the look on Michael's face when she'd left him that morning. She blushed when she recalled how brazen she'd been, flirting with him so openly. She hadn't been able to resist that remark about Samson, not since she'd learned some of the women in San Antonio had referred to him that way because of his long curls.

If only he knew that *she* was the one in danger of losing what willpower she possessed to *him*! Watching him by the river this morning, she had not been able to stop looking at him. As he'd pulled the razor across the taut skin of his throat, she had imagined her own fingers following the blade, stroking the smooth flesh. And when he had cut himself, it was almost as if she'd felt the pain herself.

She had thought for a moment that he might try again to kiss her and she had waited for his touch, welcoming it. But at the last moment she had lost her nerve and turned away.

Was it only that she knew she could not have him that

made her want him so? Or was it just her nature to want to give herself to a man, and this man happened to be the one who was currently available?

"Now wouldn't I give a picayune to know what put that look on your face." Katherine rode up alongside Ellen and grinned at her.

She flushed and looked away. Did her expression betray her thoughts so clearly?

"I swear, if I don't get to look at somethin' besides dirt and cactus and the backside of the horse in front of me soon, I'll go plumb crazy." Katherine settled her hat, a man's battered Stetson, more firmly on her head. "Though I may go batty before that out of sheer boredom."

"I imagine the men are as bored as we are," Ellen said, "though I can't say there's much comfort in that thought."

"Well, they ought to be used to it. A general once told me the soldier's life is made up of long stretches of absolute boredom, with an occasional moment of stark terror thrown in for variety."

"When you put it that way, I don't know why anyone would want to be a soldier."

"Some men are just born with a taste for adventure, I guess. Others are in it because they want to prove themselves." She shrugged. "Some ended up in the Army because they didn't have anyplace else to go."

Ellen looked out over the line of troops in front of them. "I suppose you could say that's how I came to be here," she murmured. "I had no place else to go."

"I signed on for adventure, I guess." Katherine made a face. "But I ain't seen none of that yet." She winked at Ellen. "Why don't you and me go find a little fun of our own?"

"Where are we going?" Ellen asked as she turned Fly to follow Katherine's mule.

"You'll see."

She was surprised when they drew up alongside the ambulance. "Afternoon, Solly." Katherine nodded to the doctor, who was seated next to a young private in the wagon seat.

"Why, if it isn't Katherine the Great!" The bearded man stood and made a mock bow in Katherine's direction. He turned to Ellen. "And I see you're looking lovely as ever, Mrs. Trent."

Ellen might have blushed, but the wagon hit a bump just then, and Doc Solly was forced to sit down, hard. So she found herself smothering a laugh instead. "What brings you two ladies back to see me?" he asked, making a show of rubbing his supposedly injured backside.

"I was hankerin' after a game of cards and thought you might oblige," Katherine said. She winked at Ellen. "And maybe we could give my friend here another lesson in how to play."

"You should be ashamed, corrupting an innocent." Solly grinned at Ellen. "What do you say, Mrs. Trent? Do you want to learn to gamble? Perhaps you can move on from there to swearing and drinking and other pursuits at which Katherine here is equally as talented."

"Blazes, Solly, I just want to teach her a simple game of cards. You make it sound like the devil's own pastime."

"Some would say that it is." He turned to the private. "Whoa, soldier. Let's let these ladies climb aboard."

Solly met them at the rear of the wagon, where they tied their mounts. He extended his hand to help Ellen climb in, and she handed Bobby up to him.

"What's this?" he asked, frowning at the squirming dog.

"This is Bobby." She pulled herself into the wagon and took the dog, cradling him to her chest. "He goes where I go."

"Yes, well, wouldn't we all like that?" Solly muttered, turning away.

She followed him toward the back of the wagon as the vehicle lurched forward once more. They stepped carefully around the soldier who lay along one side of the wagon bed. "Don't mind Private Alexander here," Solly said. "His horse took objection to a rattler in its path and threw him yesterday. He'll be up walking on that leg in another month or so."

"And here I was feelin' sorry for myself," the young man said, propping himself up on one elbow. "Nobody told me ladies were comin' to call."

Solly cleared a space in the middle of the wagon, then laid out a folded blanket as a kind of table. Onto this he dropped a packet of cards, then sat cross-legged beside it on the floor. Katherine plopped down across from him, and Ellen arranged herself with her back against the side of the wagon, Bobby next to her.

The sun was less oppressive here inside the wagon, but the heat more stifling, with little breeze to move the air, which reeked of sweat and the strong odor of camphor. Ellen could feel perspiration soaking the back of her shirt, pooling at her waistband.

Her traveling partners seemed oblivious to the heat. Though, she thought ruefully, none of them was wearing a velveteen riding habit. Indeed, Private Alexander was stripped to a sleeveless undershirt and trousers, and Doc Solly wore a full linen shirt open at the throat, revealing a thick mat of gray hair. Katherine's usual attire of a short-sleeved, gathered blouse, divided skirt, and boots seemed perfectly suited to the oppressive temperatures.

"You look a little woozy there, Mrs. Trent," Solly observed, looking up from shuffling the cards. "Don't go taking the vapors on me. Here." He reached back behind him and rummaged in a wooden crate. "This'll put some of the starch back in your collar." He pulled out a bottle of amber liquid and a smudged glass and poured out a hefty dose. "Drink this." He shoved the glass into Ellen's hand. "And shuck that goldurned jacket before you melt away."

She sniffed at the liquid that sloshed in the glass with each turn of the wagon wheels over the rough road and wrinkled her nose. "Go on, drink it up," Solly ordered. "Just what the doctor ordered." As if to demonstrate his own good advice, he upended the bottle and took a long swallow.

"Hey, pass some of that over here," Katherine said, holding out her hand.

"If I share my whiskey, what will you give me in return?" he asked, a wicked gleam in his eye.

Katherine made a swipe at the bottle, but he pulled it away. "What's a drink worth to you, Katy dear?"

"I'll give you a knock upside the head if you don't quit foolin' with me, Solly *dear*. We'll see how you like that." But she smiled as she said the words.

"We'll settle the debt later," Solly said, relenting and handing over the bottle.

Katherine took a long swallow. "Ahhh!" She wiped her mouth with the back of her hand. "That'll clear out the dust."

Ellen closed her eyes and gulped a large mouthful of the foul-tasting "medicine," which immediately sent her into a coughing fit. She gasped for breath, feeling as if the lining of her throat had been burned away. Katherine took the glass from her and slapped her on the back. "Don't worry," she said. "You'll feel better in a minute."

She helped Ellen out of the jacket, then returned the glass to her. "I'm gonna teach you to play five-card draw," she said. "It's lots of fun, you'll see."

"Oh-ho! What's going on in here?" Ellen looked up to see Captain Gregory Dunleavy peering over the tailgate of the wagon.

"Come on in, Captain!" Solly motioned him inside. "We could use another player."

The captain swung into the wagon and crouched just inside, frowning, hands outstretched to balance himself against the constant swaying. "Cards? I saw the ladies headed back this way and feared one of them might be taken ill." He nodded to Ellen. "I haven't forgotten your close call the other day."

Ellen looked away, face flushed, though whether from the liquor or from the fact that the whole time Captain

Dunleavy was speaking his eyes were fixed on her chest, she couldn't say. She was uncomfortably aware of the thin blouse she wore, the lace of her shift evident through the fabric, which clung to her in the heat. Picking up Bobby, she held him close, as if for protection.

"We're teaching Mrs. Trent the finer points of poker," Solly said. "Care to join us?"

"I suppose she thinks if she learns the game she can keep her husband away from the saloons." He crawled forward to take a seat between Katherine and Ellen. In the cramped space his shoulders brushed her own, and she moved away. He smiled at her. "Though the man must be insane to ever leave such a lovely lass alone."

"You're wasting your charm," Katherine said, leaning over to cut the cards. "Pipe down and let's play poker."

After a little initial confusion, Ellen caught on to the game quickly. The painted cards fascinated her, and the names of the suits and their values were easy to remember. Every card had its position in the "family" and its ranking—just like life in a castle. The king and queen came first, and their ne'er-do-well son the knave, or jack. She saw the picture of the Jack of Clubs, with his elaborate mustache and leering grin, and thought of her cousin Randolph. Bobby, no doubt, was the shiny black two of spades, the marks reminding her of his pricked-up ears. Her father, the earl, would have been the King of Diamonds; her mother a lovely but anonymous five or six.

She took another sip of whiskey, which wasn't so bad now that she was used to it, and tried to decide on a card for herself, wavering between the four or five of diamonds, or maybe hearts. She studied her hand, and her eyes fell on the Jack of Hearts, blond hair curling to his shoulders, and she smiled. Yes, Michael was definitely the Knave of Hearts.

"Ellen, you've got to learn not to let your face give away your cards like that," Katherine said. "The way you're smilin', I know I might as well fold right now."

"What?" Katherine's teasing brought her mind back to

the game at hand, and she surveyed her cards again. Her smile broadened. She had four jacks!

"I'm out." Private Alexander threw down his cards and leaned back against the wagon's side. "It's a good thing we ain't playin' for money. Mrs. Trent would have cleaned us out."

"Beginner's luck, I suspect," Captain Dunleavy said, frowning at Katherine. "And I imagine it helps to be a friend of the dealer."

"Don't get yourself all in a pucker." Katherine shoved the cards toward him. "Let 'er rip."

They played all afternoon, until Ellen lost count of the number of hands. Someone refilled her glass, and a little later they began playing for money, using bits of paper instead of cash, with Solly keeping account in a ledger of how much was owed to each player.

She began to grow drowsy with the heat and the constant rocking motion of the wagon. Bobby curled beside her and slept, and she closed her eyes, tempted to join him. "You can't go quitting on us now," Captain Dunleavy prompted, his voice close to her ear. "We're just beginning to win the money back that you took earlier."

By the time they halted to make camp, the sun had set, and Ellen was unsure whether she had lost $10 or $100. When she tried to stand and follow the others out of the wagon, her legs had fallen asleep and refused to support her.

"Let me help you, lass." Before she could protest, Gregory Dunleavy gathered her into his arms and lifted her out of the wagon.

"I'm fine, really." She turned her face up to gulp the fresh air that wafted over her. "Please, put me down."

The captain did as she asked, and she clung to the back of the wagon, swaying slightly. She'd just stand here a few more minutes and let the fuzziness in her head clear.

"This'll never do," Captain Dunleavy said. "You'll fall off your horse, for sure." He put his arm around her shoulders and pulled her close. "We'll just have to walk, then." And so she found herself headed toward camp in the company of Captain Gregory Dunleavy, whom she decided deserved to be known as the Knave of Spades, a card with an expression that led her to believe he was up to no good.

Chapter Seven

Michael unsaddled Brimstone, brushed him down, then fed him a measure of barley and turned him loose in the makeshift corral. All he wanted was a cup of coffee and a hot meal. He smiled to himself as he walked toward the campground. No more cold beans and bread for this soldier. Not with Ellen looking after him.

She usually had camp set up by the time he found her each evening. But as he moved among the wagons today, he saw no familiar red hair or blue-clad figure. He saw the baggage wagons and the other women hurrying to claim their belongings. But no Ellen.

A dozen possibilities raced through his mind, none of them comforting. Had she wandered off from the wagons and gotten lost? Had she fallen from her horse and been hurt? Had she been bitten by a snake or captured by Indians?

A shout went up, and he turned to see the ambulance approaching, the last to make camp. He gaped as he saw Katherine Roberts astride the lead mule and Doc Solly at the reins, the two of them bellowing an off-key rendition of a singularly bawdy song. Then his eyes wandered to the horse tied behind the wagon, and he felt as if he'd been punched in the stomach. If Ellen's horse was tied to the ambulance, that could only mean she was inside, hurt.

A crowd surged around the wagon, and he had to fight to make his way to the front. "Where's Ellen?" he asked Solly, shouting to make himself heard over the chorus of the song, which others had joined in singing.

The doctor shrugged, then stood and made a show of scanning the crowd for the missing Mrs. Trent. He grinned and pointed behind the wagon, then collapsed in his seat once more with a salute.

What the hell was that about? Michael fumed as he shoved his way to the back of the wagon. He was even with Ellen's mare when he saw the woman in question, jacketless, hair in disarray, lolling in the arms of Captain Gregory Dunleavy.

The sight of Michael's face, ruddy with ill-concealed anger, was enough to make those around him shrink back. He moved to block Dunleavy's path. "Let her go!" he demanded.

Dunleavy halted, one arm still clutching Ellen to his side. She smiled up at Michael. "Hello, there."

Michael glared at Dunleavy. "Let her go!" he commanded again.

Dunleavy chuckled. "If I do that, the lass is likely to fall over in a heap."

Michael frowned at the vacant expression on Ellen's face, then leaned closer to her, inhaling the sharp aroma of alcohol. "She's drunk!" He grabbed Dunleavy by the collar and jerked him forward. "My God, Dunleavy, what have you done to her?"

Dunleavy released Ellen then, sending her staggering back while he grabbed Michael by both shoulders and pushed him away. "I'll not take the blame for the condition she's in," he growled. "As for what you're insinuating . . ."

"Gentle . . . men!" Ellen stood before them, arms crossed in front of her. "I inswish . . . inshist . . . I *demand* you stop fighting."

They stared at her as she swayed, as if pushed from side to side by an invisible breeze. She looked at Michael and put one hand to her head. "I . . . I don't feel very well."

They both rushed to catch her, but Michael was quicker. He sent a warning look in Dunleavy's direction and gathered Ellen to his side.

"What have you been doing?" he asked as he guided her through the crowded camp, unable to disguise the irritation he felt. "Besides hanging all over Dunleavy like a common camp follower?"

She tried to draw away, but he held her fast. "Well, that's what I am, isn't it?" she said, glaring at him. "After all, I agreed to marry you so I could *follow* you to California."

"What were you doing?" he asked again. "Who gave you the liquor, and where's your jacket?"

She succeeded in freeing herself from his grasp, stumbling back, almost tripping over Bobby who, as usual, followed close at her heels. "I don't have to tell you!"

"Damn it, you're my responsibility! I've got enough to worry about without trying to keep track of you, too," he snapped. "The least you could do is stay out of trouble!"

"Why are you shouting at me?" She moaned, cradling her head in her hands.

"I'm not shouting!" He reached out to take her hand, but she jerked away and ran, stumbling past the groups of soldiers making camp, who stared after her with open curiosity. He started to follow, then saw Katherine Roberts come up and take her hand, and lead her to a seat by a campfire.

He turned away. His stomach felt as if he'd swallowed lead. Frowning after Ellen, he started back toward the wagons in search of Doc Solly. If anyone was in need of medicine, it was him, though he wasn't sure even whiskey would cure the sickness that ailed him.

He found the doctor lounging on the tailgate of the wagon, a mug of coffee in one hand, a ham sandwich in the other. "Well, Lieutenant, what brings you here?" he asked.

Michael leaned against the wagon. "How about a shot of brandy for a tired soldier?"

Solly shook his head. "Sorry, can't do it."

Michael raised one eyebrow in surprise. Solly had never refused him before. "Why not?"

The doctor looked at him and grinned. "That wife of yours and her friend drank it all."

He blinked. Ellen and Dunleavy, drinking Solly's whiskey . . . His stomach churned at the picture that formed in his mind. He clenched his hands into fists. He lunged for the doctor, but Solly deftly moved to one side. "What did you think you were doing, giving whiskey to Ellen and that barbarian . . ."

"Well, I can think of a lot of words to describe Katherine, but I wouldn't have used *barbarian*. Amazon, maybe, or magnificent, or . . ."

"Katherine?" Michael felt as if all the breath had rushed out of him. "Ellen was drinking with Katherine?" He might have known Bear Roberts' wife had something to do with this.

"Well, I might have shared a drop or two with them, just to be sociable," Solly said. "After all, what's a card game without a little whiskey?"

"Cards?" Michael had to sit down. "Ellen was playing cards?"

"Damn well, too, for a beginner." He grinned. "Katherine decided she should learn to play, as a way to pass the time." He took a bite out of his sandwich. "God knows it's boring enough out here. I'll settle for any amusement I can get. Including gambling with women."

"Solly, you got her drunk!"

He shrugged. "I may have overestimated her capacity for strong drink."

"The hell you did! She's an earl's daughter. She's probably never had more than a glass of claret in the drawing room."

"She's from England. I thought they gave whiskey to infants in their bottles over there."

Michael frowned. "How did Dunleavy get involved in this? She was with him when I found her."

Solly nodded. "He happened to stop by, and we invited him to join us. I reckon he was just escorting the lady home—or back to camp, as the case may be."

He groaned and put his head in his hands. "I never thought . . ."

"Common problem among young men, I've found," the doctor said. "Some older ones, too. Especially when there's a woman involved." He patted Michael on the shoulder. "You don't need a drink, Trent. What you need is to quit pretending this marriage of yours isn't as real as the next fellow's and make an honest woman out of that gal. I can't promise you any less grief, but you'll have a hell of a lot more fun, I can guarantee it." He winked and climbed up into the wagon.

Michael turned away, thoughts whirling in his head. The picture was becoming clearer now: Katherine and Solly cheerfully plying the ever-agreeable Ellen with drinks while Dunleavy looked on, waiting for his chance.

What had he done? He'd all but accused Ellen of acting like a whore, when she probably hadn't even realized Dunleavy had had his hands all over her. . . .

Campfires glowed across the prairie like fireflies in the tall grass as Michael made his way through the encampment. He paused now and then to scan the groups around the fires, looking for Ellen. Words of apology formed and reformed in his head. If only she'd listen to him . . .

Bobby drew him to her. He heard the dog barking and followed the sound to where she sat alone in the darkness, her back against their stacked bedrolls. She looked up when he stopped before her. "Come to tell me again how ashamed you are of me?" she said, then looked away.

He fell to his knees and gripped her shoulders. "Ellen,

listen to me." His voice was gruff. He swallowed and tried again. "Ellen, I'm sorry. I didn't know. . . . I talked to Doc Solly. He told me what happened, how it wasn't your fault . . ."

She shook her head. "It doesn't matter. I already know what you think of me." She sniffed. "I asked Katherine what a 'camp follower' is. She t . . . told me it meant a p . . . prostitute!"

"Oh Ellen, Ellen . . ." The pain in her voice wounded him more than any lance or saber could have. "I'm just a stubborn, foolish man. Sometimes men say things we don't mean." He stroked one finger along her cheek, feeling the dampness of her tears, then let his thumb trail to her chin. Raising her head, he bent his lips to hers, wanting to kiss away her sorrow, to erase even the memory of her pain.

He tasted salt and felt the sting of her tears against his tongue. He caressed her gently, so gently, stroking his hands up and down her arms, asking for forgiveness with the firm pressure of his kiss.

He pulled her closer, and she let out a sigh, easing against him and parting her lips slightly. He slipped his tongue between her teeth, groaning with pleasure at the sensation. Tenderly he coaxed her own tongue into his mouth, delighting in her furtive explorations.

She trembled in his arms, and he pulled her still closer, so that the length of their bodies from chest to knee were clasped together. He stroked the sides of her breasts, eliciting from her a gasp of pleasure. How long he had waited to hold her like this! His arousal strained the front of his trousers, and he trailed his hand to her buttocks to press her against him more fully.

Some sound startled her, and she gasped and pulled away. "It's all right," he soothed, trying to draw her to him once more. "No one will see us here in the dark."

She blinked at him, as if coming to. She looked around at the darkened prairie and the distant glowing fires. "What am I doing?" she cried, and wrenched away.

"Ellen, wait . . ." He reached out, but she slipped his grasp and struggled to her feet.

"I won't do this!" she sobbed, and turned and ran.

He started to follow, then sank back on his heels, aching and angry. He'd only meant to kiss her, and he'd ended up treating her like the kind of woman he'd accused her of being. Of course he'd frightened her, almost throwing himself on her, here, in the open, without so much as a blanket beneath them.

He ran a hand through his hair and groaned. He'd certainly been no gentleman tonight, and Ellen knew it. Instead of taking Solly's advice and making an honest woman of her, he'd only succeeded in pushing her further away.

He lay back on the ground, staring up at the starlit sky. Solly was right about one thing, though. All the whiskey in the world wouldn't make up for the fact that what he really needed was Ellen. Not just for one night, or until they reached California, but forever.

Ellen stared at the biscuits and bacon on her plate and swallowed hard. Her stomach protested at the very sight of food, and the smell was almost more than she could bear. She didn't want to think about what might happen if she went so far as to attempt to eat.

She eased the plate away and took another sip of the heavily sugared coffee Katherine had pressed on her. Her head throbbed, and every inch of skin was tender. Oh, why had she let Solly talk her into drinking?

"Well, if you're not going to eat it, give it here, and we'll save it for noonin'." Katherine picked up the plate and wrapped the contents in a piece of sacking. She smiled down at her friend. "Not feelin' too pert this mornin', are we?"

Ellen shuddered and shook her head. "Why do people ever drink if it feels so bad afterward?" she asked.

"Oh, you get used to it after a while and then you don't always feel so terrible." She shrugged. "Or maybe it's just that when you're drinkin', you forget the punishment that's ahead."

"I'm never going to do it again." Rising slowly, she followed Katherine toward the baggage wagons. She looked down the row of waiting horses and wagons and let out a groan. The thought of riding all day in the heat and dust was enough to make her want to curl up and cry.

"Come on." Katherine took her by the arm. "I've got a job that'll help take your mind off your misery."

She followed Katherine past the baggage carts and mules, toward the rear of the train. "Oh, no," she said, balking as they approached the ambulance. "I don't want anything to do with that place."

"Solly has promised there'll be no drinkin' and no cards. He's asked for our help rollin' bandages and restockin' medicines."

Ellen shook her head and stood firm. Arms folded across her chest, she stared at the ground, unable to meet Katherine's eyes.

"You're embarrassed, aren't you?" Katherine said.

The rush of warmth to her cheeks betrayed her.

"Well, don't be. Solly was in no shape yesterday to be makin' judgments on anybody's behavior." Katherine slipped her arm around Ellen's shoulder. "Besides, I'll have you know I've never seen such a . . . a *ladylike* drunk in all my born days—and I've seen my share of folks with a brick in their hats." She patted Ellen's back and released her. "Besides, wouldn't you rather rest in the shade and nurse your sore head than try to ride a horse in this heat?"

Even the thought of being in the saddle made her feel queasy. She sighed and let Katherine lead her to the ambulance.

Solly bowed low at their approach. "Good morning, ladies. Climb aboard, and we'll get this ship under sail."

It was still relatively cool under the wagon canvas. Ellen sank down on an upturned crate and gripped the handhold at the side of the wagon as the team lurched forward.

Katherine settled herself cross-legged on the floor beside her. "Where's Private Alexander?" she asked.

"I judged him sufficiently recovered to drive one of the baggage wagons." Solly moved past them and began rummaging in an ancient trunk, its leather blackened and cracking. "The Army doesn't like its soldiers lollygagging around any more than necessary."

"But then, the Army doesn't approve of drinkin' and gamblin' either, now does it?" Katherine asked, winking at Ellen.

"And how are you feeling this morning, Mrs. Trent?" he asked, pulling a bundle of linen from the trunk.

She frowned. "Your 'medicine' seems to have done more harm than good, Doctor."

He nodded and turned on his heels to face her. "Yes, well, I apologize for not warning you of the possible side effects. Your husband has already pointed out that I was remiss in my duties." He dumped the linen in front of her, then turned back to the trunk. "I will now attempt to redeem myself by mixing up a restorative that should ease your discomfort. In the meantime, you can occupy yourself tearing those sheets into bandages."

Ellen picked up a sheet and tore off a strip. The activity revived her somewhat, and soon she was ripping at the linen with such fierceness that Katherine looked alarmed.

"Whoa there, now. Doc said tear it, not shred it." Katherine put a hand on her friend's arm. "Or is it somebody you're wishin' you could tear apart like that?" She winked. "Should I tell that handsome husband of yours to be careful when he turns his back on you?"

Ellen shook her head and turned to rolling the strips of material she'd torn into tight balls. She didn't want to harm Michael. What else was he to think when she showed up in such a deplorable condition? She'd as good as proven the truth of his accusation by being willing to give herself to him out in the open, without even a blanket to cover them.

Her mind had known what they were doing was wrong, even as her body betrayed her. When his lips met hers, she'd started to tremble, despite the warmth that spread over her and pooled in her loins. She'd clung to him, drawing strength from the hard planes of the muscles of his arms and chest, and the other, warm hardness pressed against her stomach. Her body longed for him to touch her everywhere.

Longed for him still. She dropped the roll of bandages and hugged her arms across her chest, as if to squeeze out the aching in her breasts and in her heart.

She knew she had been right to stop what had been happening. But then why did she feel so miserable? She'd wandered the camp for hours afterward, walking and thinking. Lingering in the darkness, she'd watched the groups around the campfires, talking and laughing. She'd seen couples walk away together. Would there ever be a time when she wasn't alone?

After a long while, she had made her way to her bedroll and fallen asleep, Bobby curled beside her. This morning she had carefully avoided Michael. Now she was doubly grateful to Solly and Katherine for seeing that she was occupied and hidden from sight for the rest of the day.

"Here you are, my dear. Drink it all up."

She studied the glass of milky-looking liquid Solly held out to her. "Well, go on," he said. "It will make you feel better, I promise."

"As long as it doesn't contain alcohol."

He shook his head. "Though some swear by a hair of the dog as the cure for a hangover." He waited until she had downed the chalky-tasting drink, then retrieved the glass. "Your husband was quite upset with me yesterday," he said. "A lesser man might have run me through, or at least beaten me to a pulp for my part in your unfortunate condition."

She looked away. "Michael was only looking out for me. He's a good man."

Solly narrowed his eyes. "So you think he's a good man, do you?"

She bristled. "Of course he's a good man! He's brave, and kind, and polite, and . . ."

To her dismay, the doctor began to laugh. He shook his head. "Oh, I believe you, Mrs. Trent. Lieutenant Trent is no doubt a good man." His laughter faded, and he leaned close to her. "The trouble is—does *he* believe it?"

He turned away, moving toward the back of the wagon, and Ellen stared after him. What a strange man. And what a strange thing to say about Michael.

Michael considered a day of hard riding in the unrelenting heat and dust fitting penance for the mistakes he'd made the night before. Tonight he'd try once more to set things right with Ellen. The drudgery of the day's march would give him time to sort out his thoughts and come up with the right words to say to her.

Colonel Peabody had other ideas, however, and summoned the lieutenant to his side. "Trent, I want you to select a small detail to escort the Rangers to parley with a couple of the local *rancheros*. We want permission to cross their land undisturbed."

Michael couldn't hide his distaste. "Begging your pardon, sir, but do you think the Rangers are the ones to negotiate with anyone? They don't strike me as having much, well, finesse."

"If I needed *finesse,* Lieutenant, I'd send a damned diplomat. What I need is somebody who speaks Spanish and understands the way the locals think. Dunleavy and his bunch fill the bill." Peabody speared Michael with a sharp look. "I'm sending you along to see to it that things don't get out of line."

Michael straightened and snapped a smart salute. "Yes, sir."

But as he made his way back to his men, he felt anything but obedient. Of all the ways he'd thought to spend the day, he'd never have chosen to pass the time in the company of the man he was growing to hate.

He chose Bear Roberts and Simon Ward to accompany him. They met up with Dunleavy and his bunch and muttered greetings, then set out from the column. Dunleavy maneuvered his mount alongside Michael. "Just so we understand things, Lieutenant, *I'll* do the talking here."

Michael nodded. "As you wish."

"As you wish, *sir*." Dunleavy scowled. "I don't like your attitude, Trent. As your superior officer, I deserve your respect."

Michael tightened his hand on the reins. He avoided looking at the captain, and spoke through clenched teeth. "Begging your pardon, *sir*, but while you may command my obedience, a man has to earn respect."

"Ah, so you don't think I'm respectable, do you?" He leaned toward Michael, so close he could smell the stink of onions on his breath. "I'll catch you out alone one day, Trent, and there won't be enough of you left for the buzzards to clean up. Then you can respect *that*." He spat in the dirt. "Then I can show that pretty wife of yours what a real man's made of."

Michael blinked to see past the red haze that filled his vision. His jaw ached from clenching his teeth so tightly, fighting the urge to lash out. "Stay away from Ellen!" he said. "You've harmed her enough already."

Dunleavy straightened and managed to look offended. "I had nothing to do with her unfortunate condition yesterday."

"You did nothing to prevent it," Michael countered.

The captain shrugged. "I was merely trying to assist her, since *you* were nowhere to be seen."

"I was seeing to my duties. I don't have time to waste my days playing cards and drinking."

"Quite the model soldier, aren't you?" Dunleavy sneered. "I know all about you and your exploits, Lieutenant. You've been in Company Q so often they've got a cell there with your name on it."

Michael knew enough to recognize the captain was trying to goad him into a fight. He forced himself to relax in the saddle and meet the ranger's gaze with a cold look. "Stay away from my wife, *sir*."

Dunleavy slouched in the saddle and regarded him with a half-smile on his face. "I might stay away from her, Lieutenant, but she owes me twenty dollars."

"Twenty dollars! Why would she owe you money?"

The captain's smile became a full-fledged grin. "Mrs. Trent is not the best card player in the world, I'm afraid. You can ask the doctor if you don't believe me. He kept the books."

Michael pulled his money purse from his tunic. "I'll pay it." Twenty dollars was a small price to pay to be rid of the ranger.

"Not so fast, Lieutenant." Dunleavy's meaty hand stayed him. "Maybe we should settle the debt in another way."

Michael shook off his hand and opened the purse.

"I don't want your money, Trent." Dunleavy waved away the proffered coins. "What I lack most is entertainment. Why don't you and I play a little game for stakes?"

"What sort of stakes?" He didn't trust the ranger as far as he could throw him. There had to be a catch here.

"Double or nothing. You win back your wife's losses, or pay me double."

Michael had no doubt Dunleavy had something up his sleeve. Common sense told him to pay Ellen's debt and stay as far from the ranger as possible after that.

But he'd never claimed to have an overabundance of prudence, and the chance to even the score was too great a temptation. He slipped the purse back into his tunic. "All right. Best two out of three games."

Dunleavy nodded. "Tonight, when we make camp. We'll meet at the doctor's wagon."

Michael nodded. "I'll look forward to it."

Dunleavy grinned, showing a mass of yellowed teeth. "I certainly will." Then he spurred his horse and shot ahead, galloping out across the prairie like the very devil in pursuit of an errant soul.

Chapter Eight

Rancho San Sebastion rose up out of the arid plains like a mirage. As Michael and his men followed the Rangers across a dry wash to the massive wooden gates marking the entrance to the ranch, he rubbed his eyes and blinked. Stone towers flanked the gates, and beyond them a ten-foot-high adobe wall stretched as far as the eye could see. The gates parted at their approach, revealing a castle of gleaming white adobe, complete with crenelated towers and high stone parapets. Pennants flew from the towers, snapping in the breeze. Who would have expected such grandeur in the wilderness?

A well-dressed Spaniard rode out to meet them, flanked by a trio of heavily armed guards. "*Bienvenidos a Rancho San Sebastion*," he said. "Welcome to San Sebastion Ranch."

"*Buenos diãs, señor*." Dunleavy reined in his horse before the Spaniard and nodded in greeting. "Captain Gregory Dunleavy, Texas Rangers."

The Spaniard looked Dunleavy up and down, sharp eyes seemingly making note of every wart and weapon. Then he turned to Michael and asked in richly accented English, "And you, *señor*? You are not a Ranger, no?"

Michael snapped a smart salute. "Lieutenant Michael

Trent, First Dragoons, United States Army, sir, at your service." He bowed low in the saddle.

The Spaniard looked pleased. "I am Don Carlo. What brings you *gentlemen*"—he glanced at Dunleavy—"to my home?"

"We intend to cross your ranch on our way to Santa Fe." Dunleavy's tone held no room for negotiation. The lines around Don Carlo's mouth deepened, and the men at his side brought their hands closer to their weapons.

Michael glared at Dunleavy. He might have known the man wouldn't handle this properly. "What the captain means to say is that we would like to request permission to cross your ranch, Don Carlo. It is not our intention to inconvenience you." With a gesture, he indicated the great house. "You have a magnificent place here."

If looks could have killed, Michael might have keeled over in the saddle from the scowl Dunleavy was directing his way. Don Carlo, at least, had relaxed some. "Rancho San Sebastion has been in my family for more than a hundred years. Our land grant was awarded by King Felipe himself."

Michael's family had never lived in one house more than a few months before being forced to move on, either because Dapper Dan had grown restless, or, later, because Michael's mother was unable to pay the rent. What would it be like to know that your father and your father's father and his father before him had occupied the same home? It must have been like that for Ellen, growing up in a castle that had been part of her family for hundreds of years. How poor Army life must seem to her in comparison.

"How many are in your party, Lieutenant?" Don Carlo's question brought him back to the present.

"Three hundred soldiers and thirty supply wagons, sir," Michael spoke quickly, before Dunleavy could upset things further. "Except for water and grazing for the horses and mules, we are completely self-contained."

"And your destination is Santa Fe?" Don Carlo asked.

"Our destination is California. Santa Fe's just the next

stop." Dunleavy regained the floor. "All we want is permission to water our stock and set up camp for one night." He looked grim. "My guess is, if we hadn't bothered to tell you we're here, you'd never have known the difference."

"Then you would have guessed wrong, Captain." Don Carlo returned his attention to Michael. "In fact, I have known of your approach since yesterday." He nodded. "I had expected you to try to slip by without the courtesy of paying me a call. So you see, I find your presence here now to be a pleasant surprise."

Michael might have grown up on the street, but he recognized a true gentleman when he met one. Don Carlo lived on the edge of nowhere, but he had the bearing and manners of royalty. He bowed again. "My commanding officer, Colonel Peabody, sends his regards. He also requests you dine with him this evening." The colonel had requested no such thing, but Michael would convince him of the wisdom of the gesture. Men like Don Carlo—true gentlemen—appreciated such things.

"On the contrary, your colonel shall dine with me this evening." Don Carlo snapped his fingers, and one of the men at his side turned his horse and galloped back toward the castle. Michael hoped he was going to tell the cook and not to call in reinforcements. "In fact, we shall host a *fiesta* in your honor," Don Carlo continued.

Dunleavy muttered something about wasting time, but had sense enough to keep his complaints to himself. "Then I take it we have your permission to cross," he said.

Don Carlo nodded. "You have my permission. But first we must celebrate together."

Dunleavy answered the Spaniard's smile with a scowl. "What are we celebrating?" he asked.

Don Carlo's smile broadened. He extended his arms, as if to embrace all around him. "Life, my friends. We will celebrate life."

A trio of guitar players serenaded the company as they filed through the tall wooden gates, voices calling out in

Spanish and English with all the excitement of a crowd at a fair. Ellen and Katherine rode into the courtyard behind the last of the soldiers and sat gaping at the sight before them. "Would you get a load of that?" Katherine asked, standing in her stirrups to take it all in.

To Ellen, the gleaming white structure before them resembled an elaborate sand castle, a thing of fantasy come to life. Red and purple pennants popped in the stiff breeze, while masses of bright pink flowers climbed trellises on either side of the veranda that stretched across the front of the house. Men in white pants and tunics and women in brightly colored dresses milled about the plaza, some carrying baskets of food or large earthen water jars. A trio of children chased one another across the veranda, their laughter carrying over the noise of the soldiers' arrival. Everywhere she looked she saw busy, happy people. She felt the sharp pang of homesickness. Life at her father's castle had been just like this, except that there, every face had been familiar to her, and she had had her own part in all the activity, no matter how small.

"*Buenos dias, señoras.* Welcome." A dark, handsome man rode up to greet them. "Please, rest yourselves. Have some refreshment. Ernesto will see to your horses." He snapped his fingers, and a boy arrived to take Fly and Katherine's mule.

Ellen and Katherine followed the man, who told them his name was Don Carlo, into the main hall of the house. There, he turned them over to an older woman, who gave them coffee and cakes made of dried figs and nuts. They sat in painted wooden chairs along one wall and watched people hurry by them in all directions.

Katherine ate the last of the little cakes and drained her cup, then set the dishes under her chair and stood, brushing crumbs from her skirt. "That little tea party was fine and dandy," she said. "But I'm not one to sit around all prim and proper-like for long. What say we take a look around?"

Ellen glanced toward the doorway where the old

woman had long since disappeared. Wandering around unescorted would have been frowned upon in her father's castle. "What if someone sees us?" she asked.

"They invited us in, didn't they?" Katherine crossed her arms over her chest. "The problem with being a lady, as I see it, is that you get to thinking you have to be good all the time. Haven't you ever wanted to be bad every once in a while?"

"I think getting drunk and losing money at cards would qualify as being bad." Ellen smoothed her hands over her skirt, trying to hide her smile from her friend.

"And you'd have never done either if I hadn't convinced you, would you?" Katherine grabbed her arm and pulled her from the chair. "Come on now. You strike me as the type who's spent her whole life being perfectly proper. To my way of thinking, that means you've got a lot of catching up to do before you've had even half as much fun as a normal person ought to."

Ellen laughed and followed Katherine without protest. It was fun breaking the rules every now and then. Others had made choices for her all her life. Who was to say the time hadn't come for her to make her own decisions, even if they weren't the expected ones?

They hurried through high-ceilinged rooms filled with heavy carved furniture and came to one that was empty save for a row of benches along one wall. Workers stood on ladders tacking paper streamers to the ceiling, and women wove bright paper flowers around pillars in the center of the room. "I heard someone say they're going to have a *fandango* tonight," Katherine whispered as she and Ellen crouched behind the doorpost. "Looks like this is the place."

"What is a *fandango*?" Ellen asked.

"A dance." Katherine grinned. "They're lots of fun. Everybody will be there. You'll see."

Would Michael be there? Would he dance with her in public, as he had danced with her in the clearing that night? She smiled, remembering the feel of his arms around her, holding her as if she were a woman to be treasured. For that moment, at least, she had believed it was so.

Her smile faded as she remembered all that had happened since then. Things were still unsettled between them, and though she knew he was no longer truly angry with her, any closeness they had once enjoyed had vanished. If anything, he now avoided her as much as possible. Would she ever find a way to rekindle the friendship that had once blossomed between them, a way to make him see her, not as a burden, but as a woman?

"Are we invited to this dance?" Ellen asked. If an invitation had been issued to her, she had not heard of it.

Katherine shook her head. "Not exactly." She glanced back at Ellen. "The Don sent the invitation to the colonel and left it up to him who to invite. He's such a stick in the mud, he probably thinks it wouldn't be proper for a white woman to attend. I mean, heaven forbid we dance with one of these handsome Spaniards."

Ellen's spirits sank. She wasn't interested in dancing with Spaniards, only a certain tall, blond lieutenant.

Katherine led the way through the ballroom, down a passageway and out the door, toward a long log building from which drifted much noise and a mouth-watering array of aromas.

"Talk about enough food to feed an army!" Katherine lifted the lid on a cast-iron kettle that bubbled with some sort of stew, then moved on to sample a tray of pastries an apron-clad woman was removing from a stone oven.

All around them women smiled and nodded and murmured in Spanish. Katherine answered them in their own language, and soon they swarmed around her. With her dark hair and tan skin, she might have been one of them, while Ellen felt singularly out of place. She shrank back against the wall, hoping no one would notice her.

Katherine would have none of that, however. She dragged Ellen forward. "Ellen, this is Pepita and her sister, Rosa. Alicia, Carmen, Michaela, Juanita. They'll all be at the *fandango* tonight."

The woman smiled and nodded. "*Si, si, fandango*," they murmured.

"These ladies are going to help us get into the party tonight," Katherine said. She looked as excited as a child at Christmas.

Ellen began to feel uneasy. "Just what are they going to do?" she asked.

Katherine pulled her closer. "They're going to help us play a little trick on the men." She conferred with the women in excited Spanish, then translated for Ellen. After a moment Ellen couldn't keep back her own smile. What Katherine proposed was definitely irregular, and possibly even illegal, but it might be just the thing to capture Michael's attention and put things right between them once more.

A hundred wax candles in iron sconces cast golden light over the Rancho San Sebastion ballroom. The smell of beeswax and hair pomade and the sharp tang of tequila hung heavy in the air, and the twang of guitars and bleat of trumpets was loud enough to drown out thought as Michael made his way farther into the room. Though the hour was still early, people crowded the room: soldiers in dress blues, Mexicans in white trousers and colorful *serapes*, Don Carlo and his family in black suits with short, tight jackets trimmed in silver braid. And women, dozens of Mexican women in multicolored skirts composed of layer upon layer of ruffles, their white blouses worn off the shoulder, drawing attention to their smooth flesh and full breasts. They danced barefoot or in little satin slippers, with flowers in their hair and tucked into their sashes. More than once, Michael had fallen under the spell of such women, their dark eyes and supple bodies speaking to him in a language that needed no translation.

Even now, as he made his way across the ballroom, a comely *señorita* in a red dress with white flowers in her hair plucked at the sleeve of his tunic and gestured toward the dance floor with her lacy fan.

He smiled and shook his head. Some other time, perhaps, but for now his heart was not in dancing. To step out onto the floor now would only recall the last time he had danced, with Ellen in the clearing, before he had made such a mess of things between them.

He'd been looking for her all day but had been unable to find her in the mass of people crowding Don Carlo's home and spilling out into the courtyard. He told himself he only wanted to make sure she was well settled for the evening, but he knew that was merely an excuse to see her against this backdrop of wealth and privilege, the sort of surroundings where she belonged.

He spotted Solly coming toward him and raised a hand to hail him. "Quite a show they've put on for us, isn't it?" Solly sipped from a stoneware mug and surveyed the twirling figures on the dance floor.

"Have you seen Ellen?"

"What was that?" Solly put a hand to his ear. "Can't hear a damned thing over the music."

"Have you seen Ellen?" Michael was practically shouting, and more than one person turned to glare at him.

Solly shook his head. "She wouldn't be here, anyway," he said. "She's probably back at camp, all settled in for the night."

Michael followed Solly's gaze to the dance floor and the dark-eyed beauties twirling there. Of course Ellen wouldn't be here. What had he been thinking? This wasn't a quiet, respectable ballroom in some nobleman's home. This was a *fandango*, a colorful, chaotic celebration filled with all manner of people. In San Antonio all sorts of men had frequented the dances held every Saturday evening in the old part of town. He couldn't recall ever seeing a white woman in attendance. No respectable woman would even think of such a thing.

"So, gentlemen. Why do you not dance? A *fandango* is for dancing." He felt a firm hand on his shoulder and turned to see Don Carlo at his side.

"Don Carlo, you have been a wonderful host," he said. "We cannot thank you enough."

Don Carlo bowed his head in acknowledgment, then looked up, a twinkle in his black eyes. "But you have not answered my question, Lieutenant. Why do you not dance?" He swept a hand toward the dance floor.

"You'll have to forgive the lieutenant, Don Carlo." Solly saluted Michael with his mug. "The truth is, he developed quite a reputation with the *señoritas* in San Antonio. It's made him so incredibly vain that not just any woman will do for him."

Don Carlo laughed. "Ah, yes, I can see the lieutenant is a man who can afford to be particular as to dance partners." He clapped Michael on the shoulder once more. "Do not worry, sir. I will find the perfect woman and send her to you."

Don Carlo made his way past them and began to greet other guests. Michael glared at Solly. "What do you think you're doing? He'll probably send me his sister or something, and I'll have to dance with her."

Solly laughed. "Would that be so bad?" He took another drink from his mug. "I don't know what's gotten into you, Trent. Married life has made you as dull as dishwater."

Michael scarcely heard his friend's last words. His attention had shifted to the doorway across the room and the woman entering it now.

Actually there were two women: a tall, slender girl dressed all in white, and her black-clad *duena*, or chaperon. The girl moved into the room, layer upon layer of ruffles making little whispering noises as she walked. The full skirt of the dress belled out from a tiny waist, and her breasts, though demurely clad in a high-necked bodice, swelled against the gown with promising fullness. Her hair was gathered up in white netting, so heavily encrusted with jewels it was difficult to tell what color the locks might have been, and this was covered over with a white lace mantilla. More white lace formed a veil concealing her face, except for her eyes, which were heavily outlined in kohl, dark and shining.

"Now that's not your run-of-the-mill peasant girl." Solly spoke in his ear. "Wonder what she's doing here."

"Probably a daughter of the house," Michael said. Chaperon at her side, the girl would be permitted to view the festivities without actually taking part. Don Carlo must have a lot of confidence in his personal security force to show off such a beauty to a bunch of soldiers who were already heavily into the tequila. Not to mention Dunleavy's bunch of Rangers.

As he watched, the Scotsman spied the girl and made his way through the crowd toward her. Michael hurried to cut him off. Not only did Dunleavy risk insulting the woman in question with one of his coarse remarks, he could very well set off a minor battle if he offended a daughter of the house.

He'd underestimated the *duena*, however. Before Michael could reach him, she'd descended on Dunleavy. Black shawl and veils flapping about her like the wings of a crow, she berated him in harsh tones, until he was forced to retreat.

Michael started to withdraw also, but the next thing he knew, the *duena* had spotted him and latched on to his wrist with an iron grip. Still chattering in Spanish, she dragged him forward, directly to the beauty.

Though he might have expected the sheltered miss to be shy in his presence, she studied him intently from behind her lace fan, eyes sparkling with some emotion akin to mischief. In the flickering candlelight, he was unsure of their color, but surely it was not black or brown.

Solly was right. This was no ordinary peasant girl. Everything about her spoke of breeding and refinement. He could not remember ever meeting anyone like her—certainly not at a *fandango*.

She fluttered her eyelashes at him in what could only be described as a flirtatious gesture. He found himself drawing up to his full height, wanting to present himself to the best advantage. Nothing would come of it, of course, but what man would not be flattered by the attentions of one such as this?

The band struck up a lively tune, and all around them couples left their chairs and the refreshment tables to take to the floor once more. The beauty in white looked longingly toward the gathering dancers, then pointedly at him. No one but a cad would refuse such a silent invitation.

Still, he had to tread carefully. He glanced toward the corner where he had last seen Don Carlo standing. He didn't want to cause trouble with their host by dancing with a favored daughter. Sure enough, Don Carlo was still holding court with his armed guards around him. Michael caught his eye, and the Spaniard smiled amiably. Then Don Carlo's gaze drifted to the woman at Michael's side. He raised one eyebrow as if surprised, then smiled broadly. To Michael's astonishment, he winked, and made a motion with his hand as if Michael should indeed lead the beauty onto the floor.

Needing no further encouragement, he turned to the fair maiden and bowed low before her. Though the rest of her remained hidden behind the veil, her eyes smiled at him. He offered his hand, and she took it, her gloved fingers as delicate as glass against his palm.

"Tell me your name, *señorita*," he said as he led her into the first figure of the quadrille.

Her eyes remained blank, and she shook her head, mute. Did that mean she would not reveal her name or only that she did not speak English? Most likely the latter. He wished now he'd paid more attention and learned more of the Spanish language than the words to order a beer and locate the latrines.

She danced gracefully, her hand clasped firmly in his own, his hand fitting neatly to the curve of her waist. He could not take his eyes from her, and found himself wondering about the color of her hair and what her lips would be like if the veil were removed. Would they be full and moist, the kind of lips that begged to be kissed, or would her mouth be small and unschooled, wanting only the right man to coax her into an arduous response?

While they danced, her eyes scarcely left him, searching, memorizing his features, speaking to him in the silent language of a woman who feels an attraction for a man that she dare not name. Perhaps she did not even know the name for her feelings. One so young and delicate, living so far from society, must be as virginal as her white gown and veils would indicate.

She moved closer, her skirts brushing against his legs, and the pressure of her hand in his increased. He realized abruptly that the music had changed. The measured notes of the quadrille became the vibrant strains of the *mesemba*, floating around them, the sultry rhythms driving them closer still.

Michael knew they should leave the floor. This was no proper dance for an innocent maiden—or for a married man. This was a dance of seduction. A dance that brought bodies closer and closer together. A dance whose very beat and rhythm mimicked the act of making love. He tried to move away, but she pulled him back.

She mesmerized him with her virginal dress and voluptuous body and teasing eyes. Her rich perfume filled his nostrils, and the feel of her hands sliding down his arms sent heat curling through him. When had a woman moved him so, and why must it happen now, when he had pledged himself to another?

She beckoned again. To refuse might cause a scene. Best to soldier on with as much dignity as possible.

He clasped her waist and drew her closer still. Any moment now the *duena*, or Don Carlo himself, would be upon him, dragging them apart.

The music grew louder, guitars strumming in furious rhythm, horns soaring in cries of passion. Eyes locked together, man and woman danced. They drew apart for a moment, then came together again, closer still, the ruffles of her skirt crushed against his legs, the tips of her breasts brushing against the braid of his tunic. He eased his hand lower, shaping his fingers to the curve of her back. Her eyes widened, and she let out a small gasp.

Then he knew.

He stared at her intently, losing the rhythm of the dance altogether. "Ellen?"

The rosy blush that washed over her was all the answer he needed. As couples jostled around them, he continued to stare. "Why?"

"It was the only way I could come to the party," she said, her voice filled with anguish. "I so wanted to dance with you."

Her voice trembled when she spoke, and set up a like trembling inside him. Unable to give words to his emotions, he swept her into the dance once more.

Servants circled the room, extinguishing every other candle. One by one, couples slipped into the shadows. The music grew softer, but no less intense. Michael slid his hands up from her waist to brush the undersides of her breasts and inserted his leg between her thighs. She could have no doubt what he was feeling now, no doubt of the passion she had kindled. Her heart pounded, reverberating against his palm, and her eyes grew dark and heavy-lidded. He raised his hand, intending to rip aside the veil and kiss her the way she deserved to be kissed.

A heavy hand on his arm jerked him back to reality. He steeled himself to face Don Carlo or Colonel Peabody, but instead stared into the ugly scowl of Gregory Dunleavy. "I'll take over from here, Lieutenant," the captain said. The odor of tequila hung in a cloud around him, and his clothes were more disheveled than ever.

Michael glanced at Ellen. Veil still in place, it was unlikely Dunleavy had guessed her identity. She stared at the Scotsman with a look of distaste. Son of a noble or no, Dunleavy certainly didn't look like a gentleman now. "Leave us be, Captain," Michael said, and gathered Ellen into his arms once more.

"I said I'm cutting in." Dunleavy grabbed his arm once more. "That's an order, Lieutenant."

"The lady doesn't wish to dance with you," Michael said, struggling to keep his temper.

"I'll let her be the judge of that." Dunleavy shoved Michael away and took Ellen's arm. "Leave us be, before I have you arrested for disobeying an order."

Rage fogging his vision, Michael stared as Dunleavy dragged Ellen away. He'd like nothing better than to pound the Ranger Captain into the floor, but men had been hanged for less. There was even one story of a colonel who had desired a sergeant's mistress for himself. When the sergeant refused to give the woman up, the colonel had the man court-martialed.

"There you are, Captain! I've been looking all over for you!" Still in her black *duena*'s costume, minus the headdress and veils, Katherine descended on Dunleavy and grabbed him by the arm. "I hear you and Lieutenant Trent have a date to play cards and wondered if I could sit in. I wouldn't want to miss that for the world."

As Katherine led Dunleavy away, Michael started for Ellen, but Solly intercepted him. "Oh, no, you don't," Solly said, steering Michael toward the door. "The lady can wait. Besides, from what I saw on the dance floor, it would do you good to cool off a bit."

"Where are we going?" Michael asked as Solly led him out into the cool night air.

"You heard the lady. You've got a date to play cards with Captain Dunleavy."

Chapter Nine

The laughter and music of the fiesta receded as Michael and Solly made their way out into the courtyard, gradually replaced by the murmured conversations of the groups of Mexican workers who gathered around campfires inside the compound walls. The dry mesquite wood popped and crackled as it burned, sparks flying upward like fireworks, filling the air with the pungent aroma of wood smoke and the green smell of agave roasting in the coals. The two friends slipped through the gate in the wall and onto the prairie where the company had established camp.

A sleepy sentry demanded the password, which Solly supplied, then the doctor grabbed Michael by the wrist and dragged him on toward another campfire, where half a dozen soldiers lounged like spectators waiting for the start of a show.

Michael shook free from his friend. "You don't have to drag me like some prisoner," he said, straightening his tunic. "I'm ready enough to beat Dunleavy at his own game."

"Just be sure you settle for besting him at cards." Solly stopped on the edge of the circle of light and sent Michael a searching look. "The look on your face on the dance floor was murderous."

Michael stared across the fire, where Dunleavy and his Ranger cronies had gathered. "There's no love lost between us, it's true. But I know enough not to throw everything away for the sake of the satisfaction of punching him out."

"A good soldier knows when to retreat, remember that." Solly clapped him on the back. "Ready?"

Michael nodded. "I'll have more than Ellen's debt paid before the night's over."

"Ah, Trent." Dunleavy rose to meet him. "I hope you've come with money in hand, Lieutenant. You're going to need it."

"We'll see about that, Captain." He nodded to the others in the circle—three Rangers and Bear Roberts. They'd agreed that each man would choose two others to join in the game. Michael had selected Roberts and Solly, while two of the Rangers took their places alongside Dunleavy.

A corporal produced a new packet of cards, and when they were all satisfied the cards were indeed new and unmarked, they drew straws and the first turn as dealer fell to the Scotsman.

Five cards landed facedown on the blanket in front of Michael. He raised them to his eyes, his expression bland, though inwardly he frowned at the cards before him. Nothing much to work with here. He discarded two cards and signaled to Dunleavy to deal him two more.

"Two to the lieutenant," Dunleavy announced. "One to the doctor. As for me, I like the looks of my cards well enough."

Michael thought the Scotsman looked entirely too pleased with himself. The hair at the back of his neck rose in warning. Dunleavy was up to something.

"I can't believe you boys started without me!" Katherine, dressed once more in her usual outfit of skirt and peasant blouse, sauntered into the ring of firelight, followed by Ellen, who had also forsaken her ballgown for her red wool dress. "I know you fellows won't mind if we watch, will you?" Katherine plopped down next to Bear and gave Dunleavy a look that dared him to try and make her leave.

Ellen made her way over to Michael. "May I sit by you?" she asked.

He moved over to make room, the cards all but forgotten as he breathed in her spicy fragrance and felt his body grow feverish from the recent memory of her in his arms.

"Are you going to play cards or sit there gaping like an idiot?" Dunleavy laughed as if he'd made an excellent joke. Michael scowled and studied his cards. Nothing here. Should he try to bluff? He glanced across at Dunleavy. The man positively beamed at his cards. He might be bluffing himself, but no . . . something told him to cut his losses now and wait for a better opportunity during the next hand.

"Fold," he said, and lay his cards on the blanket before him.

The other players did the same. Dunleavy laughed. "Three jacks," he announced, displaying the cards in one hand while dragging his winnings toward him with the other.

Solly was next as dealer. A lone queen gazed out from Michael's cards amid a mixed batch of spades and hearts. "Let me see," Ellen whispered, and rested her chin on his shoulder.

He let her see the cards, conscious of the curve of her breast against his back. A second queen joined the first in his next round of cards, and he began to grow hopeful. When a third queen appeared in the last deal, he had to fight to hide a smile. Only when he gathered his winnings at the end of the hand did he allow his pleasure to show.

"You won!" Ellen threw her arms around him and kissed his cheek, and every nerve in his body responded.

"You must be good luck," he told her. This game could not be over soon enough for him. He'd take her back to their tent and show his appreciation properly.

One of the Rangers, a man known only as Red, was next to deal. He passed the cards with silent efficiency, but gave Michael nothing he could use. "You lose again, Lieutenant," Dunleavy said as he once more collected the pot.

Solly threw his cards onto the blanket in disgust. "With the cards you're dealin', ain't none of us good players tonight."

"*Somebody* should be more careful how they play their cards," Katherine said, looking up into the sky, at no one in particular.

"Are you suggesting someone is cheating, madam?" Dunleavy's voice rose with indignation.

She pursed her lips and shook her head. "I'm just saying I'd hate to think there was anything *irregular* in this game."

Michael began watching Dunleavy more closely. He lost the next hand, but was back to his winning ways for the fourth round. What was he doing?

Ellen leaned closer, her lips grazing his ear. He almost dropped his cards and had to shift position to accommodate the swelling in his groin. "I think Red is helping him," she whispered, her breath warm against his neck.

He swallowed and forced his mind to the matter at hand. This time he kept his eyes fixed on Dunleavy and Red throughout the game. Dunleavy leaned forward to poke at the fire, sending a shower of sparks heavenward. There! Had Red passed him a card?

"Maybe Red would care to give his place to Mrs. Roberts," he said with feigned casualness.

"Why would I want to do that?" Red said.

Michael narrowed his gaze. "You wouldn't want to disappoint a lady, would you?"

Red grinned at Katherine. "If she's a lady, I'll be hanged for a polecat."

This brought both Bear and Katherine to their feet. "Apologize to my wife!" Roberts bellowed.

"I'll make you eat those words." Fists clenched, Katherine started toward the hapless Ranger.

Dunleavy stood and forced his way between the warring parties. "What's this *really* about, Trent? Why are you so interested all of a sudden in getting Red out of the game?"

Michael remained seated, cool as ice. "Let's just say I think he may have been giving you a little too much help."

"Are you accusing me of cheating?" Dunleavy drew his heavy brows together in a thick line.

Michael slipped the Bowie from its scabbard and made a pretense of cleaning his nails. "My father always said the pig that squeals the loudest is the one who's spilled the feed."

Dunleavy frowned, as if unsure if he'd just been insulted or not. Michael watched the Scotsman's right hand, wondering if he could throw the knife fast enough to keep from being shot. Not that he intended to risk court-martial, but if he pleaded self-defense . . .

Dunleavy's scowl changed to a sneer. "I might have known the likes of you couldn't be expected to play a *gentleman's* game. If you've proof I'm cheating, out with it, man. Enough with riddles."

"Are you boys gonna fight or play?" Katherine stepped onto the blanket and faced them, hands on her hips.

Michael replaced the Bowie in its scabbard and rose to his feet. "One hand of blackjack," he said. "All or nothing." He nodded to the doctor. "Solly deals."

Dunleavy's mouth pinched to a thin line, and his hands clenched and unclenched from around the grip of his pistol. After a glance around the circle, at those who might brand him coward or cheat if he refused, he nodded. "All right. One hand. A hand you'll lose."

They sat across from each other on the blanket, Solly kneeling between them. The others ranged around them, watching. Michael could feel Ellen behind him, though she was no longer close enough to touch him.

The cards made a sighing sound as Solly shuffled them

together. Dunleavy cut the deck, then Solly dealt two cards, first to Michael, then the Ranger captain.

Michael looked down at the eight of spades showing on the blanket. Dunleavy had the jack of diamonds. Heart pounding, he lifted the corner of the face card and saw the six of hearts. "Hit me," he said.

He didn't miss the look of amusement at his words. *Laugh all you like,* he thought. *Under different circumstances, we would go at each other with fists. And I would not let you win.*

"I'll stand," Dunleavy announced.

Solly dealt Michael a third card. The six of clubs. Did Dunleavy have an ace for his down card? Or another face card to tie the score?

"Would you like another card, Lieutenant?" Solly prompted.

Michael shook his head, his eyes fixed on Dunleavy. The ranger grinned and flipped his down card, showing an ace of spades. "*Vingt y un*," he crowed. "You lose, Lieutenant."

He reached for the stack of coins between them, but Katherine's foot on his wrist stopped him. "Not so fast, Captain." She bent and scooped up the cards before him. With a ripping sound, she peeled the ace from the backing, revealing a second card, a deuce of spades, beneath it. "The ace card has glue on it," she said. "All he had to do was slip it in place, over the deuce, when he thought no one was looking."

"This is preposterous!" Dunleavy leaped to his feet and slapped the cards from Katherine's hand. "This is your fault, you meddlesome whore! And yours!" He stabbed a finger at Michael. "You've made a fool of me tonight, but I'll have my revenge."

Michael went for the Bowie once more, prepared to defend himself and those around him, but Dunleavy whirled and stormed away.

Everyone stared after him, scarcely daring to breathe. Wordlessly Ellen slipped up behind Michael and put her hand on his shoulder. Katherine shook her head and flipped the torn cards into the fire. "That's what I call a sore loser," she said.

Yes, Dunleavy was a sore loser. And not a man to forget an insult. For once Michael was grateful for his youth on the streets. Those years had taught him to deal with men like Dunleavy. As long as they traveled together, Michael would be careful to watch his back.

Ellen had thought Michael would take her somewhere private, where they could finish what they'd begun on the dance floor. But privacy was an elusive quality in an army encampment. No sooner had Captain Dunleavy departed than soldiers descended on Michael, demanding a recounting of the evening's events. And then Captain Peabody's aide appeared, ordering them to prepare to move out at sunrise. In the end, she found herself spreading her bedroll with the laundresses beneath the supply wagons while Michael oversaw the repair of a cannon casson whose iron wheels had come loose from the frame.

The next morning she loaded her belongings into the supply wagon and she and Bobby mounted Fly and waited for the orders to move out. All around her, men and mules and horses stirred. Mule drivers shouted in Spanish, over the jangle of tent poles being collapsed and the braying of their animals. Soldiers shouted in English, hurrying to and fro, weapons clanking against them as they rushed across the compound.

The air sizzled with excitement, evident in the ring of men's voices and the speed of their footsteps as they rushed to get ready to march. This was the last stretch of hard travel before they reached the oasis of El Paso. From there, they'd move on to Santa Fe, and then California, a land that the campfire talk painted as a true paradise.

She absently stroked Bobby's soft fur and thought of California. She ought to feel happier about reaching her goal, the promised land where family and welcome waited. But those were mere fantasies she'd conjured to give herself courage on the journey. True, she had written Uncle David and requested a place in his home, but she'd had no answer. She couldn't be certain he'd welcome her or that she'd even be able to find him.

She clenched her hands into fists, willing herself not to give in to the panic that threatened. Reaching California meant leaving Michael. He had promised a temporary arrangement; she had no right to expect more. No right to long for fulfillment of the silent promises she thought they'd made on the dance floor. No right to hope that an officer and a gentleman would see her as more than a temporary inconvenience to his ordered life.

She took a deep breath and forced herself to think of other things. California was still weeks away. Plenty of time to decide what to do with her life.

The order went up to move out, echoing down the lines to the baggage carts and women at the rear. "Move out! Move out! Move out!" With the jangle of harness and creak of leather, the column began to move forward, slowly at first, then at a brisker pace, dust boiling up around the horses' hooves and wagon wheels.

They had not been traveling far when Michael appeared at her side, harness gleaming, shako set at a rakish angle. "I came to see how you were faring," he said.

"I'm fine, thank you." Better still, now that he was here. She didn't see nearly enough of him these days on the road. He turned Brimstone to ride beside her. She was conscious of him so near to her, his shadow mingling with her own, until they appeared to be one person, moving together. Silence stretched between them, recalling moments when words had not been needed. "Tell me about El Paso," she said abruptly.

"I've never been there, but reports are it's a beautiful, green place, with many orchards and vineyards. The city is known in these parts for the fine quality of its wine."

"Green." She looked out over the expanse of desert, at

a landscape painted in shades of brown. Wheat-colored grass rustled in a hot wind, dry washes cut across the landscape like slashes of brown crayon, and even the sky was tinted a dull tan by the dust their wagons raised. "I never thought I'd long so for shade."

"There'll be shade in El Paso."

"And a market?" she asked hopefully.

"Yes, there's a market."

"That's good." She looked down at her riding habit, faded almost white by the unrelenting sun. "I would like to do some shopping."

His expression grew solemn. "Promise me you won't go out alone. Always take someone else with you, one of the privates or another woman. There are bandits in the area, and a woman alone would be easy prey."

She nodded. "I promise." She grinned. "Besides, I have Bobby to protect me."

Michael looked down at the little dog, who trotted beside them, nose and ears alert to every scent and sound. "Better keep an eye on him, too," he said. "Someone might decide he's a tasty little morsel."

She gasped, then relaxed as she saw the smile playing across his lips. "Don't you dare joke about a thing like that. I'll sic Bobby on you."

"Too late. He already likes me." He grinned. "I feed him tidbits from the table when you're not looking. I've learned the way to a dog's heart is through his stomach."

"I thought that was the way to a man's heart."

"Then you've won me heart and soul, ma'am." He was still grinning, but the light in his eyes was more serious.

She tried to answer him in a teasing manner. "You're much too easy a conquest."

"Only for the right woman," he said, his voice softening. "I might learn to enjoy surrender."

She looked away from his searching gaze. *Oh, Mother,* she thought, feeling her heart pound. *Is this what you felt when you met the earl? All this power and weakness whirled together, sucking you in, making you let go of all the rules and proprieties, until you were lost altogether?*

She could feel herself letting go, all the morals and proverbs and catechisms slipping from her grasp. When her hands were free, what would she have to hold on to but this man?

Riding near the head of the column, Michael looked back over his shoulder at the long line of troops headed west toward El Paso. If he squinted, he could barely make out the line of supply wagons trailing them, over a mile in the distance. The women rode even farther back, with a small contingent of soldiers to defend them in case of attack by Indians or the bandits who were said to prey upon travelers in this region.

He fought the urge to ride back and check on Ellen once more. She was perfectly safe, and his place was here at the head of the column. But reason and duty had nothing to do with his desire to be near her. Traveling had left little enough opportunity for moments alone with his wife, but had provided plenty of opportunities to study her. Some nights he would sit by the fire, watching her as she sewed, mesmerized by the play of her slender fingers over the fabric, or the thick golden lashes that framed her eyes.

He ought to take advantage of the time to be with her now, while he had the chance. Soon they'd be in California, where they'd pledged to part. There, in the arms of her family and countrymen, she'd have little use for a ragtag soldier from the wrong side of the tracks.

A shout pulled him from his reverie, and he looked up to see a contingent of Rangers riding down the line. Captain Dunleavy led the way, and as he passed, Michael did not miss the hate-filled look Dunleavy directed at him. The captain had lost no opportunity to express his disdain for "that yellow-livered lieutenant," and Michael had no doubt they'd come to blows before this campaign was over.

When they stopped at noon, Michael rode back until he found Ellen, seated under the makeshift shade of a tarp stretched between four tent poles. He stopped a little ways from her, enjoying the chance to observe her in secrecy.

She knelt on a blanket, tearing off bits of tortilla and feeding them to Bobby, laughing as the dog did tricks for the treats. The sound of her laughter floated to him, like bells, sending a shiver of pleasure down his spine.

Katherine brought her a plate of food, while a private adjusted the tarp to keep the sun from her eyes. She smiled up at them all, like a queen surrounded by adoring subjects. How like her to look regal even here in the middle of nowhere.

Blood will tell. Wasn't that how the expression went? Anyone looking at Ellen would know she was of noble birth. Just as, no doubt, anyone who knew him very long would spot him for the counterfeit gentleman he was.

He started to turn away then, not wanting to spoil her pleasant afternoon with his dark presence. But she spotted him as he gathered the reins, and waved him over.

"Michael, how are you?" she asked, smiling up at him, a look that left him breathless. "How long will it take us to reach El Paso?"

"Let the man eat before you pepper him with questions," Katherine said. She handed Michael a plate of beans and tortillas, then picked up the iron bean pot. "If that's enough for you, I'll take the rest over to Solly."

Michael stared after her. "Solly?" He gave Ellen a puzzled look.

She nodded and moved over to make room for him beside her on the blanket. "He and Katherine seem to have renewed their old friendship."

He settled down beside her, aware of her legs almost touching him, beneath the layers of skirts and petticoats. She set aside her plate for Bobby to lick clean, and stretched her arms over her head in a lazy gesture.

Michael almost choked on a mouthful of beans, staring

as her breasts rose, straining the fabric of her jacket. Innocent of her effect on him, she smiled and put a hand on his arm. "It's good to sit here in the shade, isn't it?"

He nodded, mesmerized by the single droplet of sweat making its way down her throat to the hidden cleft of her breasts. He imagined the taste of that salty drop, the feel of her satiny skin against his tongue.

He shifted on the blanket, wanting to hide the evidence of his sudden arousal. But then, it seemed he was in a state of constant excitement around Ellen. She had merely to look at him and his body responded.

She reached behind her for her canteen and unscrewed the cap. She raised it to her lips, then drew it away, frowning. "That's odd."

"What is it?"

She handed him the canteen. "This was full this morning. And I've hardly drank any."

He examined the metal flask and found the leak by the telltale dampness in the cloth covering around it. "It's rusted through here." He slipped his own canteen over his head. "Here, you take this one."

"Nonsense. We'll share. I can get another one from Solly before we leave. I know he has extras." She unscrewed the lid from the flask he offered her and lifted it to her mouth.

He watched the action of her throat as she drank, his breath quickening at the sight. When she returned the vessel to him, her fingers brushed his, like a current running through him. Eyes still fixed on her, he raised the canteen to his own lips and drank.

He imagined he could taste where her mouth had touched, and he wondered at the direction her own thoughts were taking as she watched him, breathing rapidly through parted lips. He longed for just one kiss, to quench the thirst in him no water could slake.

Setting aside the canteen, he leaned toward her, and she tilted her head up, as if directed by an invisible hand. Her lips were still damp from her recent drink, rosy and inviting as fresh fruit. Michael swallowed hard and bent his head, eager for the feel of her against him—

The blare of the bugle startled them both, and they pulled away. Ellen held a hand to her breasts and gasped. "What is it?"

Michael was already on his feet, the familiar strains of "Boot and Saddle" filling his ears. "Get behind the mules," he ordered. "Stay down."

He turned and ran for his horse, mounting in one swift movement and spurring him toward the front of the line even as he saw Ellen take cover behind the line of pack mules.

All around him, men shouted and ran for their mounts. Brimstone thundered toward the front of the lines, dust billowing at each strike of his hooves against the dry earth.

He found Peabody at the head of the caravan, spyglass raised to his eye. Michael stared at the immense cloud of dust rolling toward them. Even at this distance, the earth shook with the rumble of charging horses. "Trent, lead a group on a flanking movement. See if you can size up what we're up against."

Michael led twenty men in a wide sweep around the left flank of the approaching force. He braced himself for enemy fire, but the troops seemed ignorant of his approach. Emboldened, he drew nearer, ordering his men to hold their fire.

They rode within a hundred yards of the troops when he began to realize he could make out no uniforms or Indian buckskin. No sabers or arrowheads glinted in the sun. In fact, this army had no men at all!

He halted his troops and began to laugh. "What is it?" Bear Roberts asked, drawing up beside him.

"Watch this." Michael spurred Brimstone forward. He rode to within an arm's length of the charging force, coughing in the clouds of dust that boiled around him. The ground shook beneath Brimstone's hooves, vibrating through the horse to him. It was like being caught in some great cannon battle, with smoke and thundering shot. But he had no fear of being hurt. Covered in dust now, ears ringing, he wheeled and raced back to his waiting men.

"Horses!" a man cried as the cloud approached. "It's a herd of wild horses!"

As they sat and waited, the mustangs galloped past, the ground trembling. Michael pulled his kerchief over his nose and squinted at the hundreds of horses moving past. They were black and red and spotted, manes and tails flowing in the wake of their passing.

Brimstone raised his head and whinnied, and Michael leaned forward to pat the animal's neck. "Do you wish you were running with them, old fellow?" he said softly as he stroked the velvety black pelt.

When the mustangs were gone, with nothing left of their passing but acres of churned-up ground, Michael ordered his men back to the main body of troops. He reported to Colonel Peabody, then made his way down the line, intending to check on Ellen.

"All ready to fight those mustangs, weren't you, Trent?"

He frowned as Dunleavy rode up alongside him, laughing, a sound that made Michael grip his reins until they cut into his gloves. "Just following orders, Captain."

"Some soldier you are," Dunleavy taunted. "If a cloud of dust on the prairie strikes fear in your heart now, you'll be less than useless when there's real fighting to be done."

"I'll fight when the time comes."

Dunleavy nodded. "Aye. Well, watch your back, Lieutenant."

Michael stiffened. "Is that a threat?"

"Cowards always die shot in the back. Running away." Dunleavy gathered his reins. "That's how they'll find you, no doubt." He turned his horse and rode away.

Michael stared after him, a chill sweeping over him. Was it fear or hatred that made him grow cold whenever the Scotsman was around?

Chapter Ten

El Paso looked like a city made of sugar cubes set on green velvet. As the troops skirted the town, Ellen craned her neck to study the flat-roofed houses tucked against the mountains. Flowers bloomed in the courtyards, and birds sang in the trees. Fields of corn and orchards heavy with fruit stretched out around them, and clear streams flowed down from the mountains. The blue-tinged peaks and verdant fields reminded her of England, and a sudden homesickness gripped her. Would she ever see her homeland again? Had she been foolish to leave a place where she had been, if not happy, at least secure, for an uncertain future among strangers?

She was still feeling sorry for herself when she reined Fly to a halt in the middle of the shaded grove where they were evidently to make camp. All around her the wagon drivers were unloading their beasts and dumping the packs on the ground, while soldiers milled among them in an attempt to claim their belongings. She frowned at the chaos. How would she ever find her own possessions?

"Don't worry about them," Katherine said, coming up beside her. She held up her hand. "Get down from there, and let's go. While they're all arguin' over whose tent is whose, we'll pick you out a good camp spot."

She slid from the saddle and set Bobby on the ground,

then led Fly past the scattered tents and bedrolls, toward a stand of tall trees draped in moss. A narrow stream gushed from the rocks beneath the trees. Katherine led her across this, to a level spot surrounded by brush. "How's this?" Katherine asked, sweeping her hands around the area. "Will you sleep like a princess, or what?"

Ellen smiled. The grass felt springy beneath her feet, and the gurgle of the stream pulled the tension from her body. Bobby scampered along the brook, barking at dragonflies hovering over the water. "I'll leave Fly here to stake our claim, but how will we get our tents?" Ellen asked.

"Oh, I won't be putting my tent here," Katherine said. "Bear and I'll set up with the other enlisted men. I just thought you might like it here."

Of course. Even here, half a world away from her father's castle, society dictated who could associate with whom. A private couldn't set up his tent next to a lieutenant, any more than a gentleman's son could marry an English nobody.

Only Katherine disregarded such regulations so openly. She made friends with everyone, never mind their background or rank. Impulsively Ellen stepped forward and hugged her friend.

Katherine pushed her away, blushing. "Oh, go on now. You get Fly staked out over there, and I'll send somebody over to set up your tent. Then you'll want to cut some of this Spanish moss to make a nice mattress." She winked. "Be sure not to mix in any twigs. You don't want anything pokin' you in bed but the lieutenant."

Ellen blushed to the roots of her hair, sending Katherine into gales of laughter. She waved and hurried away, while Ellen turned to tend Fly.

In another hour the tent was in place, and she had shed her jacket and pulled enough moss from the trees to stuff two makeshift mattresses. During the day they could rest on the bedstead, when anyone walking by might glance into the tent. At night, they could be pulled apart so that she and Michael would each have their own couch.

She smoothed the sheets and wished she were making only one bed. She still recalled the illicit pleasure of lying in Michael's arms.

"Good, you're all set up." She turned to find the man who occupied her thoughts standing in the door of the tent. He removed his cap and surveyed her work. "Looks nice." He smiled at her, and her longing to cling to him increased.

It's only the long journey that makes me feel so weak, she told herself. She busied her hands rearranging some violets she'd placed in a jar on a crate.

Michael moved toward her, but stopped a few feet away. "I thought you might like to take a bath," he said. He looked around the tent again. "Some of the women are going upstream to find a secluded place."

After days of dusty traveling, a bath would be heavenly. Even a cold stream in the company of others would be far better than the sponge baths she'd had to content herself with until now. "As soon as I gather my things I'll go with them," she said, already turning toward the trunk to fetch soap and towels.

Michael coughed, and she looked up to see a flush creeping up his neck. "No doubt some of the enlisted men intend to follow and spy on them."

It was Ellen's turn to blush. "Then I'd rather not—"

He nodded. "That's what I thought. If you don't mind heating the water, I've persuaded one of the general's cooks to lend a washtub. You could bathe in here, in privacy."

She smiled, but he was avoiding her eyes. "I'd like that very much."

He nodded. "I'll send it over for you right away, then." He went to the trunk and began unpacking a fresh uniform. "I'll go downstream with some of the men."

When he was gone, she sank down onto the trunk, all the strength going out of her. Michael was so good to her, so thoughtful, so kind . . . She curled her hands into fists at her sides. Why had she been cursed to fall in love with a gentleman?

Michael was glad of the cold water to temper the feverish thoughts he had of Ellen in her bath in their tent. He would have given a pretty penny to join her there, rather than dodging the horseplay of several dozen rough-edged men. How sweet it would be to run his hands across her satiny back, or to watch water cascade from her full breast . . .

He grabbed up the soap and scrubbed his skin until it burned. He had neither money nor background to indulge such idle daydreams. Hadn't he learned that lesson well enough in his younger days, when the fairest flowers of San Antonio society had refused to dance with Dapper Dan's son? "He's handsome enough," one young lady had been heard to remark. "But no matter how well you might dress him up, he'll never quite be able to shake the stench of the gutter, will he?"

The words had wounded then, but he'd learned to laugh them off. What did it matter if the society maidens snubbed him as a suitor? There were plenty of women who welcomed his attentions, and he didn't have to worry about their mamas' expectations of marriage and a future. After all, he was his father's son, as restless as those wild horses they'd seen on the plains. He didn't have it in him to settle down in one place. That truth had never bothered him much before . . . until now.

By the time he returned to the tent, he felt he had his emotions well in check. Even the sudden quickening of his heartbeat when he first spotted Ellen as she tended a campfire might easily be attributed to the brisk march along the creek bank.

"Hello." She smiled when she spotted him. "Did you have a good bath?"

"Just what the doctor ordered." He sniffed the air appreciatively. "What smells so wonderful? I'm starved." He came to look over her shoulder at a bird spitted over the fire.

A Husband by Law

"Roast chicken. Bobby's already been sampling it for us, and he thinks it's good." She pinched off a bite and turned to give it to the dog, but before she could toss it, Michael bent and captured the morsel in his mouth.

She gasped as his lips met her fingertips, and all thought of the chicken vanished as hunger of another kind took hold of him. Her skin was like velvet against the slick hardness of his teeth, and she tasted of the salt and spices she'd used to season the chicken, and of the sweet oil she must have rubbed on her body after her bath. He swept his tongue across her fingertips, wanting to capture every sensation of taste and touch. Everything in him leaped at the contact, warming and quickening in a dizzying rush.

She turned her head and met his gaze, burning into him, stripping away all pretense and artifice, leaving only raw emotion. Lips parted, she swayed toward him, and he would have drawn her to him, crushing her into his arms.

But something in him held him back—the memory of those society belles who had turned him away, or of the tavern wenches and dancing girls who had not. He had pledged to protect and keep Ellen, and to deliver her safely to her family in California. That included protecting her from himself, keeping her safe for a man who could give her the name and status, and commitment, she deserved.

Trembling with the effort, he released her and turned away. "I'll wash up before we eat," he said, moving to the bench by the door, where she'd placed a bucket of warm water, soap, and a towel. Never mind that he'd just come from his bath. He needed to do something with his hands, to keep them from reaching for her once more.

By the time he entered the tent, she'd arranged the chicken and some roasted potatoes on a table she'd fashioned from the inverted washtub, draped with her shawl. He removed his cap and jacket and dropped them onto the bed, along with his saber. She hurried to fill his plate with chicken and potatoes, avoiding his gaze.

She'd spread quilts on the floor for them to sit on and set a lamp on a crate, along with the violets she'd picked earlier. He marveled once again at her ability to add beauty to the humblest of surroundings.

She sank to the floor on one side of the washtub, the skirts of her red dress swirling around her, her still-damp hair twisted into a single braid and trailing over her shoulder.

"Everything looks wonderful," he said. *Most of all, you,* he silently added, but dared not speak the words out loud.

"Come, sit down." She indicated the space across from her. "We're having an indoor picnic."

He sat cross-legged on the blanket and accepted a filled plate. "This is a fine campsite, isn't it?" He hurried to fill the silence with small talk. Here, alone with her, he didn't want the opportunity to think.

She nodded. "It's so cool and green. And it's nice to have water so close." She picked at the food on her plate and looked at him through veiled lashes. "Thank you again for arranging the bath for me."

He nodded. "I didn't think you'd want to join the others out in the open . . . I mean . . ." His collar felt too tight, and he hurriedly took a drink of water.

"Well, it was very thoughtful of you." She smiled at her plate. "Did some of the soldiers follow the women?"

He nodded, and swallowed the chicken he'd been chewing. "They paid for it, however." He grinned. "Katherine crept up behind them and fired off a musket almost in their ears. Those who didn't jump into the water, she pushed, and the women all ran away."

She laughed. "Oh, I wish I could be like Katherine. She always knows what to do."

He frowned. "Katherine may be amusing, and even good-hearted, but she'll never touch you when it comes to grace and intelligence and beauty and . . . and cooking."

"Need I guess which one of those attributes you appreciate the most?"

He looked away but did not answer. If she could guess the truth of his thoughts of her, she'd no doubt slap his face.

"Your hair is getting quite long," she said.

He looked up and realized she had been studying him. He pushed an errant curl behind his ear. "I'm thinking of cutting it. It's getting to be a nuisance, always falling in my eyes and—"

"No! Don't cut it!" She blushed. "I mean . . . why don't you tie it back?"

"With what?"

She set aside her plate, rose, and went to her bag. Taking out a comb and a gold cord, she came and knelt behind him. "Here, let me show you." She gathered the long curls in her hand and used the comb to tease the locks into smoothness.

He tensed, determined to hide the effect she had on him. The sweet lavender and soap scent of her filled his head, and each brush of her fingers sent tremors of sensation through him. Over and over, she pulled the comb through his hair, gliding from scalp to shoulder in smooth strokes, shaping the curls around her fingers. Drawn by a force he could not fight, he found himself leaning toward her, until his back rested against her legs and torso as she knelt behind him.

Taking the cord in one hand, she gathered the hair in the other and tied it at the nape. She rested her hands on his shoulders, the warmth of her touch seeping through the wool tunic. "There. That looks much neater, and it won't be in your way."

She started to move away, but he reached up and covered her left hand with his own, wanting to prolong the contact. If only things could have been different. . . .

They sat this way for a long time, not speaking. Then he took a deep breath and shifted away from her. "Why don't I try this dessert? It looks wonderful."

She sighed and moved around in front of him once more to serve the peach duff. He ate without tasting the food, unable to fill the emptiness inside him that had nothing to do with hunger. In his years as a soldier he had never fought a fiercer battle, this war between desire and duty.

No matter what the outcome, he stood to lose. He could only hope to stand firm, to keep Ellen from ending up a casualty as well.

The long trek from San Antonio had created a mountain of dirty uniforms, so that the camp soon resembled a giant laundry, with steaming kettles and dripping garments everywhere, the smell of soap and starch heavy in the air. Ellen and Katherine worked together, Katherine stirring the boiling wash pot while Ellen draped wet shirts and trousers and underclothes on nearby bushes.

"It's clear to me the Army never gave a thought to the likes of us when they trimmed these uniforms with all this yellow that's the devil to wash," Katherine complained as she scrubbed at a stubborn stain. "If they'd asked me, I'd have told them to make every uniform a mottled brown. Then a bit of dirt wouldn't matter."

Ellen laughed and straightened one of Michael's tunics across a shrub. "An Army dressed all in brown wouldn't look nearly as handsome as the men do in their blue and yellow, would it?"

"Some of the best-looking men in this outfit don't even wear a uniform." Katherine tossed the scrubbed garment into the wash pot and prodded it with a wooden paddle.

"Do you mean the Rangers?" Ellen frowned. She wouldn't care to call that bunch of bearded ruffians handsome, though perhaps a woman like Katherine . . .

"I was thinking of Doc Solly." Katherine wiped the sweat from her brow and grinned. "Now there's a man who can fill out a pair of trousers."

"Katherine, the things you say!" Ellen shook her head. Her friend never ceased to shock her. She supposed most women thought such things from time to time, but Katherine was the only one she'd met who would actually say them.

"Tell me if it ain't the truth."

"I suppose the doctor is a very nice-looking man," she demurred.

"You should have seen him when we fought the Seminoles." Katherine leaned against the paddle, a dreamy expression on her face. "He cut a fine figure, I tell you. He saved my life in Florida, did you know that?"

Ellen shook her head. "How did he do that?"

"I came down with malaria there in the swamps, and Solly nursed me back to health." She sighed. "If I'd have been smart, I would have stuck with him then, instead of being so all-fired anxious to see the world."

"I'd forgotten you and Solly knew each other before." She picked a shirt from her basket and shook it out. "Isn't it funny you'd meet up again so many years later?"

"Maybe it's fate that brought us together." She turned to Ellen, bright-eyed. "Maybe I'm getting another shot with Solly."

"Another shot?" She frowned. "What do you mean?"

"I mean, maybe now that I'm older and wiser, I've got another chance with a really *good* man."

Was Katherine saying she was attracted to Solly? "But . . . you're already married to Bear."

"Oh, not really." She waved her hand as if swatting a fly. "Not like you and the lieutenant. No priest ever said any words over us."

Ellen thought back to her marriage ceremony, in a language she didn't understand, with guests who were all strangers to her. Is that what Katherine thought constituted a real marriage? She looked at her friend again. If only Katherine knew how wrong she was about her and Michael. In many ways, Katherine and Bear were more married than they would ever be. "People think you're married," she said. "Solly thinks you're married."

"I could change his mind about that, I'm sure."

"And what about Bear? Don't you think he'd object to your going after another man?" Katherine's giant of a husband didn't seem like a person you'd want to make angry.

She shrugged. "He'd get over it. We have kind of an understanding that way." She plopped down on an overturned wooden tub, chin in her hands. "No, the real problem is that Solly's too much of a gentleman."

"You mean he wouldn't entertain the attentions of another man's wife."

Katherine gave her a puzzled look. "Who said anything about throwing a party? And I told you my arrangement with Bear is just a little problem to overcome. The big trouble is that Solly is too fine by half for the likes of me."

Ellen considered the rather roguish camp doctor. "Well, he is older than you," she began.

"Fifteen years!" Katherine said, as if this were a lifetime.

"And he seems very well educated."

"I left school when I was twelve."

"And he certainly has the manners and speech of a gentleman."

"His father is some high Boston muckety-muck." Katherine sighed. "I'm nobody from nothing."

Nobody from nothing. The words might have described Ellen herself and the educated gentleman Michael. She sank down onto the washtub beside her friend.

"It's hopeless," Katherine said. "No matter how much I love him, what would a man like Solly see in me?"

And what would a man like Michael see in me? Ellen thought.

They sat in silence for a while, each lost to her own thoughts, then suddenly Katherine jumped to her feet. "By gum, he ought to be *glad* to have a woman like me hankering after him."

Ellen blinked. Was Katherine still talking about Solly?

Hands on her hips, Katherine turned and faced Ellen. "I may not have a fancy name or education, but I reckon if Solly was after those things, he wouldn't be here in the Army. I've got a lot to offer a man like him. I'm healthy and strong." She flexed her arms, then hefted a basket of laundry on one hip. "I know a lot of good jokes and card games and I'm a good dancer, so he'd never lack for entertainment. I can cook and clean with the best of them and . . ." She dropped the basket of laundry, sending clothes tumbling out, and held up one finger, her mouth spread into a wide grin. "And once he'd welcomed me into his bed, I'd see to it that he'd never want me to leave."

"Do you really think it's as simple as that?" Ellen couldn't keep the doubt from her voice.

Katherine's grin never faltered. "Men are simple creatures, Ellen. Doesn't matter if they're a Boston banker's son or the village idiot, they all want the same things." She bent and picked up a freshly washed shirt and shook it out with a snap. "Solly probably doesn't realize right now all I have to offer him, but I'm going to make sure he finds out as soon as I can."

Ellen helped her friend gather up the scattered laundry, marveling at Katherine's boundless confidence. In her experience, life wasn't as simple as Katherine made it out to be, but maybe that was because she'd been making things too complicated for too long. Was it possible a poor English orphan was just what Michael needed—and all she had to do was open his eyes to the possibility?

Michael was grateful for the drilling and guard duty that kept him away from camp for much of each day. Being near Ellen in such close quarters would try the will of even the strongest man. In his free hours he volunteered for extra duty or visited among his friends at camp, avoiding his tent, and Ellen, as much as possible.

"If you're going to make such a nuisance of yourself, you can at least ride with me into town," Solly said one afternoon when Michael was hanging around his tent.

"I didn't realize you found me such a nuisance," Michael said. "But yes, I'll ride with you."

"Ever been to El Paso before?" Solly asked as he and Michael left the army encampment on the outskirts of town.

"No. Have you?"

The doctor nodded. "Came out here for a while in

thirty-eight. I'd had enough of swamps back in Florida, thought the desert would be a nice change."

"What were you doing in Florida?"

"Same thing I do here—handing out hangover remedies and stomach medicine and patching up soldiers who were fighting the Seminoles."

Michael nodded. Army life caught and held some men that way. They signed up when they were young and eager, thinking to go adventuring for a few years before settling down to real life, and the next thing they knew they were grizzled veterans and the military was a job like any other, with the same duties from year to year, only the location changing.

"I met Katherine there, you know."

"What was that?" He forced his attention back to his companion.

"I met Katherine when I was in Florida."

"Katherine Roberts?"

"She was going by the name of Katherine Edwards then." He shook his head. "You know, in camp now they call her Katherine the Great. It suits her, don't you think?"

Michael wasn't certain what he thought of the big, brash woman who had befriended Ellen. On one hand, Katherine seemed too coarse to be Ellen's companion; on the other hand, Ellen seemed to enjoy her, and who was he to dictate whom she chose as friend? "Has she changed much since Florida?" he asked. Or had Katherine always been as bold and bawdy?

Solly shook his head. "Hardly a hair. If anything, she's finer than ever."

Michael blinked, uncertain he had heard correctly. He studied his friend more closely. There was something about his expression . . . "You're attracted to her, aren't you?"

Solly flushed. "I may be older than you, Trent, but I'm scarcely in my dotage. I can appreciate a fine figure of a woman as well as the next man."

The blustery response confirmed Michael's suspicions.

"I think your feelings for this particular woman might be more than simple appreciation." He leaned toward his friend. "Plan to try your luck at taking her away from Bear, do you?"

Solly glowered at him. "Bear Roberts doesn't have her. No man ever will. If she's with him now, it's because she chooses to be, and I predict it won't last long."

"And then she'll be with you, is that it?" He grinned.

Solly saw no humor in the matter, though. He shook his head. "No, I'm too old and stable for her. She's not the type to settle down with one man for long."

"People can change," Michael said.

"I'm not sure they can."

Michael thought of his father, who could never stay in one place for long. His mother always told him he was just like him. He had taken it for granted this was true. He had never even been tempted to stick with one woman before now. Did his past, his character, doom those dreams to failure?

They turned onto a narrow side street leading into town. Solly glanced over at him. "All this talk of women has me in need of a drink. What say we inspect one of the cantinas?"

Michael laughed. "All right, Doctor. As long as you're buying."

They rode slowly down the street, watching for a likely building. Daylight had faded fast, and already men were lighting torches and lamps in the houses and stores around the main square. Michael and Solly tied their horses to an iron ring set in a post in front of one of the buildings and went inside.

Conversation faded as they walked past the groups of old men gathered at the small tables filling the one room of the bar. Michael studied each face as they passed, watching the eyes, seeing the hostility there. Whether it was his uniform, or the fact that he and Solly were strangers, they weren't welcome here. He draped his hand casually over the hilt of the Bowie and pushed the sash of his uniform down just enough to show the butt of the pistol held tucked there. He didn't want trouble, but he wanted the men around him to know he was prepared.

"*Dos tequilas*," he ordered from the short, brown man seated behind the wooden bar. He dug in his pocket and flipped a two-bit piece onto the counter.

The bartender eyed the money, then scooped it up and deposited it in his shirt pocket. He reached under the bar and pulled out a bottle and two glasses.

"Not exactly a friendly reception," Solly observed, turning to survey the sullen crowd. A few of the old men had returned to their game of monte in the corner, and the others resumed drinking, but their eyes never moved from the soldiers.

"Maybe they don't like the way we're dressed." Michael tossed back a shot of tequila, savoring the rush of warmth down his throat to his stomach. "Next time maybe we should wear our dress coats."

"No, it's you." Solly held his own glass out for a refill. "Your reputation has followed you from San Antonio. They're all afraid for their women." He sipped the liquor and grinned. "Should I tell them their *señoritas* are safe, now that you're a happily married man?"

Happily married. If Solly only knew. He set aside his empty glass. "Maybe we should leave. Find some place where we're more welcome."

Solly looked around. "What's wrong with these people? Usually they welcome the boys in blue with open arms. And they damn sure don't mind taking our money."

"Come on." Michael jerked his head toward the door. "Let's leave."

They were halfway across the room when the loud report of a gun stopped them in their tracks. Michael drew his pistol as he turned toward the back of the bar. "Is there an alley behind this place?" Solly asked.

"That or a back room." Michael nodded toward a door in the back wall.

The other patrons of the bar scattered as he and Solly

made their way to the door. Standing to one side, Michael listened to sounds of a struggle on the other side of the wall. He looked across at Solly. "We'd better find out what's going on here."

The doctor nodded, and together they threw themselves against the door. It burst open, and they stumbled into a darkened storeroom.

"Get out!" a voice ordered.

As Michael's eyes adjusted to the light, he could make out three figures crowded into a corner of the room. A man and woman cowered before a larger man who loomed over them, threatening.

"I said, get out of here, Trent. This is none of your business."

The larger man turned toward them, thrusting his face into the light from the open door. Michael gripped the pistol tighter. "Dunleavy! What are you doing here?"

Chapter Eleven

Dunleavy straightened. He looked Michael and the doctor up and down, then relaxed his stance and gestured toward the other man with his pistol. "The saloon keeper and I were just discussing his donation to the soldiers' benevolence fund."

"I've never heard of the soldiers' benevolence fund," Solly said.

Dunleavy's eyes narrowed. "Maybe that's because it's a fund set up by the Rangers." He glanced at the saloon keeper. "We're always very grateful to anyone who makes a donation and make it our personal business to see that they and their families aren't harmed."

Michael tightened his grip on the butt of the pistol. "And just who do you think would harm this man and his family?"

Dunleavy had the gall to grin. "Well, now, Lieutenant, you know how rowdy these soldiers get sometimes. Men on leave drink too much, fights break out, women are molested. . . . One night's revelry can do a great deal of damage to a small business such as this one."

The saloon keeper glared at Dunleavy. "I do not pay extortionists."

"You'd be a disgrace to the uniform if you wore one."

Michael moved closer and motioned with his pistol. "Step aside."

"Who are you to order me around?" Dunleavy sneered at Michael, then returned his attention to the saloon keeper. "As for you, this gun says I'll take whatever I damn well please, and you'll be quiet about it." He eased back the hammer of the pistol, and the woman screamed.

"*Qué Dios!* No!" She launched herself at the Scotsman, who laughed and held her off with one hand.

"I like a woman with spirit," he said, wrapping his hand around her arm and pulling her toward him. "Maybe you'd like to come with me when I'm through here. We could get to know each other better."

He ignored the woman's struggles and covered her mouth with his own, while his pistol in the saloon keeper's chest kept the man frozen in place.

Michael's vision blurred with a haze of anger. He'd had his share of run-ins with men like Dunleavy, who thought power and position gave them the right to trample the world. He wouldn't stand by and watch this time, as he'd been forced to before. He brought the butt of the pistol down hard on the back of the Scotsman's head, feeling the crunch of metal on bone.

Dunleavy raised his head and bellowed, and Michael drove his fist into the Ranger's nose, shoving him back off the woman. She ran to the saloon keeper, and the two of them retreated behind stacked barrels of beer.

"You son of a bitch!" Dunleavy drew a knife and slashed out at Michael. The blade sliced across Michael's wrist, drawing blood.

Michael hit the Scotsman again, a blow to the stomach that bent him double. He brought the pistol down once more, laying Dunleavy out on the floor, blood running from a gash on the back of his head.

Solly caught Michael's hand, stopping him from striking again. "He's out. No sense killing him."

In the sudden ringing silence, Michael stared down at

his enemy. Dunleavy lay sprawled like a stuffed dummy, face slack, limbs splayed. The gravity of what he'd done descended on him like heavy chains. He shoved the pistol back into his sash. "What's the penalty for striking a superior officer these days?" he asked. "Hanging or firing squad?"

"If he's got the nerve to admit you bested him, it would still come down to his word against yours." Solly looked toward the saloon keeper and the woman. "I don't think those two would testify in his defense." He moved around to stand in front of Michael and looked him in the eye. "And let's not forget who would hear the charges—a bunch of regular Army, fellow West Pointers and all." He clapped his friend on the shoulder. "You don't have anything to worry about."

Michael stepped over the unconscious captain to the couple by the beer barrels. "Are you all right?"

The woman nodded and clung to the man. "Go now. Leave us." The man made a shooing motion toward the door.

"What will you do with him?" Solly asked, glancing back at Dunleavy.

The saloon keeper shook his head in disgust. "We will drag him into the gutter where he belongs."

"When he wakes up, he'll be too mortified to ever admit this happened," Solly said.

Michael looked back at the Scotsman. Even unconscious, he wore a look of disdain. "All the same, I'll be watching my back." He moved in front of Solly, across the bar, and out into the torchlit street.

They said nothing on the ride back to camp. Michael's wrist began to ache where Dunleavy's knife had slashed him, but the pounding in his head was worse.

"Go on, now, forget about Dunleavy and the whole nasty business," Solly said when they reached the Army encampment and dismounted. "Give that beautiful wife of yours a kiss for me and have a thought for men like me who have to watch the woman they love head off into the night with another man."

If you only knew the truth, my friend, Michael thought as he left the corral to make his way to his tent. *Would you think me as big a fool as I sometimes feel I am?*

He made his way back to the tent, anxious to reach that sanctuary and at the same time reluctant to return. The lighted canvas beckoned him—as close to a home as he'd had in years. Inside, Ellen would be waiting, her very presence adding warmth and beauty to the lonely surroundings.

He was going to miss her when she was gone. The thought descended on him like a black cloud. When they reached California, he'd surrender her to the love and protection of her family and go back to his old way of living with no one to care for or be responsible to. At one time he'd cherished that freedom, but it held little appeal for him now. How long would it take him to grow accustomed to his former life, or had he lost forever the contentment he'd once known?

He paused outside the canvas and took a deep breath, mustering the courage to act as if nothing troubled him in the least. Then he pulled back the flap and ducked inside.

Ellen looked up from her seat at the table, the lighted lamp casting a halo about her unbound hair. A pile of sewing lay before her, and across from that a covered plate.

"I saved you supper," she said, rising and uncovering the plate.

He hung his hat and sword belt on the bed, then pulled out his chair at the table. "You didn't have to do that. I'd have found something at the mess."

"I wanted to do it."

He had thought his appetite had deserted him, but the aroma of the stew she set before him made his mouth water. He picked up his spoon and began to eat.

"Michael! What happened to your wrist?"

He frowned at the gash Dunleavy's knife had opened. A thin trickle of blood had run down to soak his sleeve.

"Let me see." Ellen rushed to his side and gently cradled the injured hand. "How did this happen?"

"A minor disagreement with a man in a saloon." He shrugged and would have pulled away, but she held him firmly.

"It needs tending to," she said. "I have some things in my bag."

She relinquished his hand then, but only long enough to fetch a towel, a roll of linen bandages, and a tin of salve from the trunk. She poured water into a basin and brought these things to the table. She folded back the cuff of his tunic and shirt and knelt beside him.

"Here, take my chair—" He started to rise, but she pushed him down.

"I can tend you better this way. Now sit still." She dipped the cloth in the basin and began to bathe the wound, her forehead creased in concentration.

He stared down at her, transfixed. The lamplight shimmered on her hair and shadowed the valley between her breasts. Her long, elegant fingers probed the wound with exceeding gentleness, her touch relaxing him. Her very presence had a healing quality, powerful as any medicine.

When she had finished cleaning the wound, she opened the tin and began to dab on a salve. It smelled like mint and spread a soothing warmth through his skin.

"Why must men fight?" she asked.

"Sometimes it's the quickest way to settle things." *Or the only way,* he added, thinking of Dunleavy threatening the saloon keeper and his wife. He didn't want Ellen to know the seriousness of what had happened tonight, though. "I've been in various scrapes since I was a boy," he said. "I suppose in a way it's become habit to seek justice with my fists."

"What was your first fight about, do you even remember?" She picked up the roll of bandages and unwound a long strip.

He could not swear it was his first fight, but certainly the one that had made the biggest impression. "I was ten," he said. "A boy at school teased me."

"He teased you? What did he say?" She began winding the bandage around his wrist.

The boy in question had been named Adam Bowman, son of one of the richest men in town. He had taunted Michael on any number of occasions, criticizing everything from his hand-me-down boots to his blond curls. But on that particular day, Adam had gone too far. He had called Michael's mother a whore, an insult young Michael could not let go unanswered. "Just the things boys say," he told Ellen. "He went on and on until I'd had enough."

"So you hit him." She sounded disapproving, but then again, he'd have been surprised if she hadn't. Women were disdainful of such things, even when done to defend their honor. They didn't understand that there was a time for talk and a time to stop talking and take action.

"I hit him," he admitted, "and he promptly beat the tarnation out of me."

"Oh, my." Ellen looked at him, eyes filled with concern. For him, or for the boy he'd been? "You would think an incident such as that would teach you not to fight."

He shook his head. "No. It taught me that I never wanted to be that helpless again. It made me learn to defend myself and others." He had developed a reputation as a champion of the underdog. He knew too well what it felt like to be a target. He forced a smile to his face and adopted a cheery tone. "You could say that fight was the making of me in other ways."

"How is that?" She tied a neat knot in the bandage and clipped the ends with her sewing scissors.

"The father of the boy came by to see my mother the next day, to apologize for his son's behavior. He took an interest in me, and years later was my sponsor into West

Point." Stephen Bowman had in reality taken an interest in Polly Trent, who was still pretty despite her years of struggle and poverty. After a time she became his mistress, and he assumed the role of benevolent uncle to the children. His own son had no desire to follow his father's footsteps into the military, so when Michael expressed an interest, Bowman was only too happy to help him.

"Odd how things work out sometimes, isn't it?" She looked at him a long moment, her eyes full of unspoken questions. Michael wondered how things would work out for them when these long weeks of travel had ended.

She gathered up the medical supplies and put them away, then sat back down across from him and resumed her needlework. "How long will we be in El Paso, do you think?"

"A few more days. Why?" He began to eat, scarcely tasting the food.

"I'd like to go into town tomorrow to do some shopping."

A picture of Dunleavy, and others like him, roaming the streets flashed into his mind. "Promise me you won't go out alone."

She looked up, puzzled. "All right. But why?"

"It's not safe. There are . . . rough men in this place. There have been reports of attacks on some of the citizens." He reached out and touched her wrist. "Promise me."

She nodded. "All right, I promise."

He had a sudden inspiration and shoved back his chair and went to the trunk, at the end of the bed.

"What are you doing?"

He threw back the lid and began pushing aside the dirty clothes and blankets, spare harness and books and old boots. "I know it's in here somewhere . . . Aha!" He held up a slender knife encased in a tooled leather scabbard. "I want you to start carrying this," he said, bringing the weapon to her. "Keep it with you all the time."

When she didn't reach for the knife, he laid it on the

table in front of her. She stared at the scrolled leather. "Do you really think the locals are that dangerous?"

"It's not the locals I'm worried about."

The words themselves were fearful, but words alone would not have raised the knot of fear that rose in Ellen's throat. The look in Michael's eyes, and the flat way he spoke, sent a tremor through her and made her reach for the knife and slip it into her pocket.

Later, as she moved about the tent, clearing away the supper dishes, she was conscious of the weight of the weapon, brushing against her leg. When everything was scrubbed clean, she took out her mending and sat at the table once more.

"The chaparral was hard on all our clothes," Michael observed as he watched her take up a pair of his trousers.

She nodded, carefully aligning the yellow stripe that ran the length of the blue fabric. "I noticed the Rangers wear some sort of leather leg protectors to guard against thorns."

He frowned. "They're called chaps. Too awkward, if you ask me." He leaned across the table, studying the fine stitches. "Where did you learn to sew like that?"

"My mother taught me. She was the best seamstress in Lanesmore." She smiled at the memory of her mother sitting in the doorway of their little house, yards of silk and satin spread around her as she fashioned a fine gown for one of the ladies of the castle. Margaret's ability with the needle had kept them well fed and clothed, so that they did not have to rely on the vagaries of the earl's generosity.

Michael's frown deepened, and he leaned back in his chair, arms crossed on his chest.

Though her eyes were on her work, Ellen was acutely aware of the man across from her. She had spent many hours riding beside him, seated across from him around a campfire, or even lying next to him in her bedroll. But now the canvas walls of the tent lent a new intimacy to their time together, as if by separating them from others, the tent drew them closer.

She glanced at him from time to time, studying the handsome profile from beneath veiled lashes. The sun had bronzed the skin of his face and hands and bleached the ends of his hair almost white. He'd shaved this morning, but already new bristles dusted his chin.

Her eyes lingered on the full lips, and with a sudden jolt she remembered the feel of them against her fingers. What was she coming to, that even her thoughts could set her to trembling this way? She forced herself to look away, to concentrate on making tiny, even stitches.

She heard the chair scrape back and looked up to see Michael putting on his coat. "Where are you going?" she asked as he buckled on his saber.

"I'm going out for a while."

He moved past her, toward the door, and a longing rose within her, to call him back, to ask him to stay with her. "Michael."

He paused in the act of pulling back the tent flap, a frown still etching lines around his mouth. "Yes?"

She sighed and shook her head. What right did she have to ask him to stay if he didn't want to be with her of his own accord? "Be careful," she said, echoing his own warning to her. "Just . . . be careful."

Careful of what? Michael thought as he walked away from the tent. *Careful of these thoughts and feelings I can't control when I'm around you?*

Just when he thought he had reined himself in, to deal with Ellen as a gentleman ought, she would unwittingly remind him again that he was anything but the well-mannered, high-born dandy he played at being. Some word, or action, or look, would bring back a flood of memories he'd thought long since put away for good.

Watching her sitting by the lamp, so upright in her chair, long fingers skillfully plying the needle, he'd had a sudden picture of her seated in a parlor at her castle. She and her mother and the other ladies would have worked at delicate embroidery, while servants brought tea and added logs to the fire.

His own mother had never had time for such pursuits. She had been too busy scrambling for food, her hands too raw and work-roughened to handle delicate fabrics or hold a needle. The clothes Michael and his sisters had worn were old and ill-fitting, castoffs that came to them through the dubious charity of their betters.

He groaned and put his hands to his head, as if to squeeze out the pain that swelled there. He increased his pace as he moved through the streets, toward town.

He spied a cantina ahead and started to cross the street toward it, but his way was blocked by a hand shoved into his chest. Scowling, he raised his head and stared into the angry, blood-shot eyes of Gregory Dunleavy. He groaned. Of all the people he didn't want to see right now, Dunleavy was at the top of the list.

"I'll have a word with ya, Trent," Dunleavy growled.

"I don't have anything to say to you." Michael tried to move past, but Dunleavy laid a heavy hand on his shoulder, fingers digging in.

"That's right, but you'll damn well stand and listen, and that's an order—*Lieutenant*." He pushed his face close to Michael's, his hot, sour breath washing over him.

Michael clenched his jaw and drew himself up to his full height, emphasizing the fact that Dunleavy was several inches shorter. "Yes, *sir*, Captain," he said, his voice heavy with contempt.

Dunleavy shoved him back, sending him staggering, but he quickly righted himself. "You had no business interferin' with me in that saloon earlier today," the Ranger captain growled. "And if you so much as lay a hand on me again, I'll be wearin' those curls of yours on my belt, because you won't be needin' them anymore."

Michael's hand dropped to the Bowie at his side, but Dunleavy was quicker, brandishing a wickedly curved blade and waving it under his nose. "That's right. Go ahead and try it. I'd relish carving you up properly."

Michael took a deep breath and eased his hand away from the knife. "I don't have time to waste with you, Dunleavy."

"You're just like all the rest of these lily-livered regulars, aren't you? With all your fancy uniforms and polished sabers and high-steppin' Kentucky thoroughbreds—but when it comes to a fight, you don't ken the meanin' o' the word." He shoved the knife back into the sheath at his belt. "That lass you're married to must not be the lady I mistook her for, else she'd not be wastin' her time with a coward like you."

He spat into the dirt at Michael's feet and turned to go, but Michael grabbed him by the shoulder and whirled him around, landing a bone-crushing blow to his left cheek.

Howling, Dunleavy pulled out his knife and slashed at Michael's chest, ripping the fabric. Michael jumped back, jerking the Bowie from its scabbard, all the frustration and anger of the past twenty-four hours swelling within him. He thrust upward with the blade, slicing into his enemy's shoulder.

Dunleavy dropped his knife and staggered back, clutching the wound, blood bubbling up between his fingers. "You'll pay for this, Trent."

Michael stared at him, trembling. He was dangerously close to the edge, straddling the line between reason and rage. One more word from Dunleavy would be enough to send him over, and he'd plunge his knife into the Scotsman's breast and leave him lying in the street. He replaced the knife in its sheath, struggling to slow the racing of his heart.

Dunleavy glared at him. "That's the last smart decision you'll ever make," he said. "By God, I'll see you hang. . . ."

Michael could listen to him no more. He jerked the pistol from his belt and raised it, as Dunleavy's eyes widened in fear.

He brought the heavy barrel down on the ranger's head with a solid thud, and Dunleavy sank in a heap in the street.

Michael stared at the gun in his hand as if it had acted apart from him. Heart pounding, he struggled against the panic clawing at his chest. To strike Dunleavy once had been foolhardy. To fight him a second time was tantamount to suicide.

With shaking hands, he shoved the pistol back in its holster and glanced around them. The distant sounds of music and laughter from the cantinas along the street filtered to him, but here in this passageway, the only noise was the labored sigh of Dunleavy's breath.

At least he was still breathing. Michael stared down at the Scotsman. Blood trickled from the gash on his forehead. He'd have a nasty headache when he woke, and more than enough evidence to bring charges against the man who had hit him.

Michael backed away. He didn't want to be around when Dunleavy awoke. Given the choice, he'd have left the country rather than face down the enraged Scotsman. He turned on his heel and began walking back toward the encampment, of half a mind to pack his kit and leave. He could lose himself in California or Oregon Territory, and no one would be the wiser. Better to leave behind a reputation as a deserter than to swing from an Army gallows.

As he walked, his head began to clear. Of course he couldn't leave. What would Ellen do without his protection? She wouldn't be allowed to travel with the Army and she'd never reach her family in California. Unless, of course, she chose to marry someone else. Someone like Dunleavy . . .

He could scarcely breathe at the thought. He'd be damned before he'd abandon Ellen to the likes of the

Scotsman. He halted and turned toward headquarters. There was only one thing to do. He'd turn himself in to Colonel Peabody and plead self-defense. If he got to the commander first with his side of the story, he might weaken the force of Dunleavy's charges and get off with a stint of hard labor, or at worst a public flogging.

Even at this late hour the commander's tent glowed with light. Aides hurried in and out, and he could make out the old man himself, seated at a desk beneath a lantern, scratching out a letter. Michael stopped a respectful distance away and stood at attention. After a moment Peabody looked up and recognized him. "Lieutenant! Do you still have that devil of a horse of yours?"

Michael blinked at the question. "Yes, sir, Brimstone is in fine health, last I checked."

Peabody nodded and laid aside his pen. "Then I have an errand for you." He shook sand from a silver flask over the freshly written letter. "I need you to take this message to General Kearny in Mesilla."

Michael stepped forward. "Sir, I . . . There's something I need to discuss with you."

"Whatever it is can wait until your return." Peabody folded the paper in thirds and sealed it with wax. "This information must reach Kearny before we arrive." He shoved the letter into a leather dispatch wallet and held it out to Michael. "Well, don't just stand there gawking, Lieutenant. Get a move on!"

"Yes, sir." Michael took the wallet and shoved it into his tunic. He swallowed and tried again to say what he'd come to say. "Colonel, about Captain Dunleavy—"

"Leave the damned Texans out of this," Peabody said. "They've been nothing but a thorn in my side since they were assigned to me." He made a dismissive gesture with his hand. "Go, Lieutenant. There's no time to waste."

Michael clicked his heels and gave a smart salute. He'd wanted to flee from Dunleavy; here was his chance.

Maybe on the long ride to Mesilla he'd think of some way to save his skin and to protect Ellen.

Michael's hasty departure in the middle of the night alarmed Ellen. Riding alone all the way to Mesilla sounded dangerous to her, but he assured her he would be well armed, and Brimstone could outride any other horse. She scarcely had time to rise from bed and pack what food she could find before he kissed her cheek and was out the door.

She had lain awake a long time afterward, one hand to her cheek, as if to hold in the warmth where his lips had touched her.

The next day the announcement came that this was their last day in El Paso, so she and Katherine headed to town to do what shopping they could. She found material for a dress and some white linen that would make a fine shirt for Michael. She also bought sugar and chocolate, and other delicacies that might prove difficult to find further west.

The two women were unpacking their purchases at Ellen's campsite when a pounding shook the frame. "Trent, come out here!" a familiar voice bellowed.

Bobby began barking furiously and raced toward the door. Startled, Ellen turned to her friend, but Katherine had already jerked back the tent flap. Hands on hips, she confronted the man on the other side. "Didn't anybody ever teach you any manners, Captain?"

Ellen grabbed Bobby by the collar and gathered him into her arms, where he trembled and growled. She peered over Katherine's shoulder and saw Captain Dunleavy confronting them. He had an angry gash on his forehead, and his shoulder was bandaged. "Captain, what happened?" she asked.

His scowl grew fiercer. "Your husband tried to kill me!" he bellowed. "And I'll see that he pays for it."

Ellen felt dizzy. She started to protest that Michael

wouldn't kill anyone, but then, he was a soldier. Killing was what he was trained to do, wasn't it?

"Lieutenant Trent isn't here." Katherine folded her arms over her chest and studied Dunleavy's wound with a critical eye. "I'd say if the lieutenant intended to kill you, he'd have done a better job. That blow wouldn't do anything but give you a nasty headache."

If Dunleavy looked like this, what did Michael look like? When he left last night, had he been hiding wounds he didn't want her to see? It had been dark, and she'd been half asleep. What if he was hurt and needed her?

"How do I know you're not hiding him?" Dunleavy demanded. "It'd be just like Trent to hide behind women's skirts."

"He isn't here!" Anger was fast overtaking Ellen's fear and worry. "Colonel Peabody sent him on an errand."

"An errand?" Dunleavy raised one eyebrow in question. "Where did he go?"

Ellen clamped her lips together. What if Dunleavy went after Michael and tried to intercept him? "It was Army business," was all she'd say.

"Maybe I'd better have a look around just in case." Dunleavy tried to shove past them. Bobby erupted with furious barking, and Ellen struggled to contain him. Katherine stepped between the captain and the entrance to the tent. "You don't really think I'm going to let you in to ransack my friend's private quarters, do you?"

"Move out of my way!"

Katherine held her ground. Ellen looked around for help. She wished she had a gun. The knife in her pocket seemed little enough defense against the angry Ranger.

"Having some trouble, ladies?"

She breathed a sigh of relief when she saw Doc Solly riding toward them on his horse, Pepper. He stared down at Dunleavy. "Are you bothering these women, Captain?"

Dunleavy glared up at the doctor, but Solly held his gaze. Ellen half feared one or the other of them would draw a weapon and begin firing, but after a long moment, Dunleavy backed away.

"That's a nasty gash you have there, Captain," Solly said. "Would you like me to take a look at it?"

"Stay the hell away from me!" Dunleavy whirled and strode away.

Katherine ran to the doctor. "Solly, you were wonderful," she said. "A regular knight come to rescue us."

The doctor's expression was dour. "I doubt very much you really needed rescuing," he said. "I imagine you would have used that Bowie you keep strapped to your leg if you'd needed to."

Katherine looked coy. "And how do you know about that knife?" she asked.

"I knew a great many things about you at one time, didn't I? And I haven't forgotten a one." He touched the brim of his hat and nodded, then turned his horse and rode away.

Still holding Bobby, who had finally grown quiet, Ellen came to stand beside her friend.

"I think that's just about the most romantic thing a man ever said to me," Katherine said with a sigh.

Ellen cradled her cheek against Bobby's soft fur and tried to make sense of everything that had just happened. "Do you really think Michael tried to kill the captain?" she asked.

Katherine shrugged. "Men fight all the time. Over booze. Over cards. Over women." She gave Ellen a pointed look.

Ellen's eyes widened. "Over wom— You don't think they were fighting over me, do you?"

"I don't know what they were fighting over. From what I've seen, some men don't even need a reason." She patted Ellen's shoulder. "There's no call for you to worry yourself any. The men are just bored, staying in one place too long. An army likes to be on the move. Tomorrow we'll be on the road to Santa Fe, and everyone will be in better spirits, you'll see."

Ellen doubted another dry, dusty trek across the desert would put her in better spirits, especially since she'd be making the trip without Michael. She thought of him, alone on the road to Mesilla, and said a silent prayer for his safety. She only wanted for them to be together, never to part again.

Chapter Twelve

The road shimmered in the harsh sunlight, mirages of water appearing and disappearing on its surface. Clouds of powdery dust rose as Brimstone's shod hooves struck the ground. Michael pulled his forage cap lower to shade his eyes and tried not to think of the heat or his own weariness.

He had stopped early this morning in a village near the border to feed and rest Brimstone and to steal a few hours' sleep for himself. By nightfall, he'd be in Mesilla, where he could sleep all he liked and wait for the rest of his company to catch up.

Would they come with manacles and orders for his arrest? He rubbed his wrist, as if he could already feel the bite of the steel bonds. Dunleavy had looked in a bad way when he'd left him. He supposed he could hope the blow had been enough to erase his memory, but he doubted the chances of that were good. The odds were much higher that he *would* be arrested.

Peabody, who hated the Rangers, might side with him, but would that be enough? If he could convince the Army that he was more valuable to them than the captain of the irregulars, he might escape with his life, though he'd be lucky if they didn't buck him all the way down to private.

He sighed and squinted out at the vacant landscape.

He'd heard bandits frequented this route, ready to attack lone travelers, but thus far he'd had the road to himself. A man could disappear out here, and no one would be the wiser. At the next crossroads he could turn off the main road and lose himself in some little village. The Army might brand him a deserter, but then again, they might think he'd fallen victim to a highwayman. He wouldn't hang, wouldn't have to stand trial. He could make a new life for himself, maybe a better one.

The prospect pulled at him like a strong river current, but he might as well have been tied to the bank. He'd pledged to protect Ellen, to accompany her safely to her family in California. He wouldn't abandon her.

He tightened his hands on the reins and cursed himself for a fool. What would that fine family of hers think of her marriage to a soldier with no money and no name? Would he be able to convince them that their union had been one of convenience only, and that his bride remained as pure and untouched as when she came to him?

Here, alone in the desert, the very idea struck him as ridiculous. What kind of man would agree to such an insane scheme? As for insanity, he might very well lose what mind he had if forced to continue in this charade. He wanted Ellen more than he had ever wanted a woman before. Should he take what she offered, as a temporary pleasure, and let her go to meet her family in California without him? They wouldn't have to know about her temporary liaison with a man who was not her equal.

She'd forget about him soon enough, and he'd go on with his life somehow, though he knew her memory would burn in him for years to come. At least if he welcomed her into his bed he'd have memories to savor on long nights alone.

He straightened in the saddle, weariness fading. As soon as he was able, he would go to Ellen and make her his wife in the truest sense. First he would tell her the truth about himself. He wanted her to come to him freely, knowing fully what she was about. If she still wanted him then, they would enjoy what time they had together, and when they reached California, he would somehow find the strength to let her go.

Dust devils whirled on the horizon, and Brimstone's ears arched forward, alert. Michael tensed as the figure of a man appeared in the dust, a man dressed in black, riding a bay horse at a fast clip toward them.

He slowed Brimstone to a walk and removed the pistol from its holster at his side. Resting the weapon across his thigh, his finger near the trigger, he approached his fellow traveler.

The man slowed a good distance away and hailed Michael. "Hello, Lieutenant!" he called. "How fare you this day?"

As they drew nearer, Michael found himself face-to-face with a ruddy-faced fellow about his own age in a dark homespun suit and battered derby hat. "Simon Leland, late of California, on my way back East," the man said when they were close enough to touch.

Michael took the hand he offered and shook. "Lieutenant Michael Trent, First Dragoons. What brings you to this lonely road?"

"I might ask the same of you, Lieutenant." Leland sat back and surveyed the desolate landscape. "I traveled this way last year with a scientific expedition out of Washington. When time came for my return, I could persuade no other parties to travel with me, so I chanced a trip alone."

"You must be anxious to return East."

Leland grinned. "That I am. I have a lovely young woman who has waited to be my bride this long year. I dare not keep her waiting longer."

Michael thought of the woman who waited for him and returned the man's smile. "You say you were in California. What part?"

"All parts, really. My last stint was with a group of Englishmen who were working to establish farms in the San Joaquin Valley."

Michael's heart quickened. "Englishmen?"

"Yes. Nice bunch, really. I would have stayed with them, but I'd promised Patricia . . ."

"Was one of them named David?" Why hadn't he paid more attention when Ellen talked about her uncle? He couldn't for the life of him remember the man's last name. "David Winthrop, or something like that?"

Leland rubbed his chin. "There was a fellow they all called Davey. Don't think his name was Winthrop, though."

"I'm not sure on the Winthrop part. Listen, would you consider doing me a large favor?"

"I suppose that depends on what it is."

"My wife is from England, and she's trying to locate her uncle David, who's somewhere in California. It could be he's one of the people you were with. Or maybe they know where to find him."

"So what is it you want me to do?"

"Would you consider coming back to Mesilla with me—just for a day or two? My wife will be arriving with the rest of my company, and you could talk to her, tell her what you know. It would mean a great deal to me."

Leland looked doubtful. "I don't know if I could tell your wife anything useful."

"I'm sure you could. And if you're willing to wait, I could arrange for you to travel as far as San Antonio with some of the freighters who will be returning that way after delivering supplies to Santa Fe."

"I'll admit I've been a little nervous about traveling alone." Leland nodded. "All right. I'll do it." He turned his horse and fell in alongside Michael. "Your wife wouldn't by any chance be a good cook, would she?"

Michael grinned. "Ellen is an excellent cook."

"Ah, well, then I'll be happy to stay with you a few days. There aren't very many women out here, and fewer still who can cook. You're a lucky man, Lieutenant Trent."

Luck. In his current position he wouldn't have said he was particularly lucky. Maybe that was about to change. In spite of everything, with Ellen at his side, how could a man feel unlucky?

Ellen peered out from the narrow slit in the veil of linens swathed around her. A line of men and horses stretched in front of her as far as the eye could see, shimmering in the heat. They traveled in a cloud of dust, the steady tramp of the infantry and plod of the dragoons' horses sending new particles into the air, coating them all in a white film.

She looked down at Bobby, riding on the saddle before her. His once shiny coat was gray with a coating of dust, and he panted in the heat. She smoothed the fur along his sides and rearranged her makeshift coverings so that they provided him a measure of shade.

If only she could find such shelter. Inside her cocoon of linen, she could feel sweat sliding down her skin, sticking her shirt to her back. The thought of green trees, or cool water with which to bathe her face, was enough to bring her close to tears of longing. The lush fields and woods around her home in England seemed a lifetime away, a childhood memory.

She sighed and pushed such thoughts away. They'd be in Santa Fe soon, where they'd have a few days' rest and another chance to wash their clothes and themselves. And before that was Mesilla, where she'd see Michael again. She longed for that as much as she longed for water. A dozen times a day she found herself thinking of something she wanted to tell him, and during the night she'd wake up, unsettled to find him missing from his usual place near her bedroll. That he could have become such an important part of her life in so short a time amazed her.

On those long sleepless nights, and during the endless dreary days, she'd had time to think—about her life and about her relationship with Michael. When she saw him again, things would be different. She would tell him she wanted more than a marriage in name only. Even if he didn't have it in him to promise her forever, she wanted to love him as long as he would let her. She was through with waiting for her life to begin and was ready to make things happen. She would take Michael as her lover, come what may.

Bobby turned in the saddle and barked, and began to wag his tail. She looked back and watched Katherine riding toward them from the rear of the train. Unlike most of the other women, Katherine refused to cover herself against the dust and sun. As a result, the skin of her arms and face and neck was now golden brown, and her clothes and hair were powdery with dust. She sat slumped in the saddle on the back of the mule, scowling at the ground. She might have ridden right past if Ellen had not called out to her.

"Katherine! Are you all right?"

She looked up, still frowning. "No," she said with a sigh. "I'm not all right."

"What is it? Are you ill? Perhaps we should find Doc Solly—"

"I don't care if I was at death's doorstep. That old quack would be the last person I'd call on!"

Ellen drew back in surprise.

Katherine let her mule fall in step beside Ellen, but her downcast expression put an end to all conversation. After a long while, she raised her head. "I've got myself in a real fix, and I need your advice."

"My advice?" Ellen frowned. "What advice could I possibly give you?"

Katherine glanced about her, a blush creeping up her neck to flood her face in crimson. "How do you know for sure when you're in love?"

The question startled Ellen. Why did Katherine think that she, of all people, would know the answer to that question? "Well, I don't know—"

Katherine maneuvered closer. "I don't mean just hankerin' after a fellow, or thinkin' he's good-lookin', or wantin' to climb under the covers with him," she said. "I mean weddin' ring and babies, death-do-us-part kinda love . . . the kind you have with the lieutenant."

Ellen felt as if all the breath had been knocked out of her. "What makes you think I . . . that we . . . ?" she stammered.

"It's plain as the nose on your face," Katherine said. "The way you two are always lookin' at each other." She smiled. "You just light up like a Christmas tree when he shows up."

A warmth spread through Ellen as Katherine spoke, a heat that had nothing to do with the desert sun. Some inner light glowed and expanded in her chest, until she felt she could not possibly contain it.

Did she dare believe that Michael loved her? Could Katherine really see what her own eyes had been blind to? She looked at her friend. "Do you think you're in love?"

"I don't know what else it could be." She twisted the reins around her hands. "I get this quivery feelin' inside whenever he's around, and if he so much as looks at me, I'm just floatin' on a cloud for hours. But if he ignores me, I'm madder than a wet hen the rest of the day."

She nodded. "Quivery" might properly describe how Michael sometimes made her feel, and more than once she'd been put out with him when she'd felt ignored. "I take it you're not talking about Bear."

Katherine shook her head. "Not him. I've had my fun with him, but he can't hold a candle to the man I'm talkin' about. I can't think about nothin' but him, my food tastes like cotton, I don't half sleep at night—I tell you, I'm plumb miserable!"

Ellen suppressed a smile. "Well, you're certainly coming down with something. Maybe you should see a doctor."

"Who said anything about him?" She glared at Ellen. "That old fool wouldn't know love if it bit him on the ass!" She kicked the mule and rode away in a cloud of dust.

Ellen stared after her. Katherine was usually so easy-going. What had upset her so? She absently stroked Bobby's rough coat. If only they'd reach Santa Fe soon. The heat and dust were wearing them all down.

When the company arrived in Mesilla, Michael reported to Colonel Peabody, half prepared to be clamped in chains, but the commander dismissed him without comment. Careful to keep watch for Dunleavy, he set out in search of Ellen and found her with the other women, sorting through piles of baggage.

He paused on the edge of the melee to watch her, his heart quickening in anticipation of holding her once more. But first he would indulge himself with this silent perusal. Even in this coarse setting, she shone like a jewel, her clothes, though much faded from the sun, still elegant in line, her hair perfectly coiled beneath the campaign hat. While the other women shouted and shoved, arguing with the teamsters in charge of the baggage, Ellen smiled and spoke softly, indicating with a nod of her head which trunks and bundles were hers. The wagon drivers hurried to retrieve her things and vied for the honor of carrying them to her campsite.

She turned to lead the way and spotted him. "Michael!" All reserve vanished; she ran to him, arms outstretched. He gathered her close and happily surrendered to the kiss she planted on his cheek. When they were alone, he would show her how very glad he was to see her, but here, with others watching, he would settle for this more innocent greeting.

"I'm so glad you're safe," she said, drawing back just enough to speak. "I was so worried."

"Of course I'm safe." He patted her back, touched by her concern, unsure how to respond. Best to keep things on a polite level until he'd told her all he had to say about himself and his humble background. Then, if she wished, they could continue with a more intimate relationship. "Have you picked us out a good campsite?" he asked.

She frowned. "As good as was offered. I hope California has more trees than this."

They walked together across the compound, two teamsters trailing with their baggage. Michael took her elbow to assist her over the rough ground, but mainly because he relished the feel of her so near. "I believe there are plenty of trees in California," he said. "Speaking of which, I've invited a guest to dinner. A man from California. I believe he may know your uncle."

"Uncle David?" She turned to him, eyes wide in an expression of delight. "Really? This man knows him?"

"Maybe. He knows a group of Englishmen in California. He's coming tonight to tell you all about them." He'd hoped to please her, but now that he saw her excitement, he felt bereft. Was she really so anxious to leave him?

"I'd better see about finding something to make a good dinner. Someone said there's a market in town, I'll check there." She reached up and straightened her hat. "Do you think I look all right?"

"Ellen, darling, you could manage to look elegant in rags." He released his hold on her reluctantly. "Go on and do your shopping. I'll see that camp is set up and everything's unpacked."

"You will? Oh, bless you. I have so much to do." She whirled and hurried off in the direction of the village. Belatedly he thought he should have accompanied her. But it was broad daylight, after all, and the market was near. He doubted any trouble would come to her. In the meantime, he'd see their camp established and visit the company barber for a bath and a shave. He wanted to look his best for tonight.

Simon Leland was suitably impressed with the meal of roast chicken, corn dumplings, beans, and apple tart Ellen spread before him. "Best meal I've had all year, Mrs. Trent," he said. "If you're ever of a mind to go into business in California, you could open a restaurant. Many a man would pay good money to eat like this."

"Why, thank you, Mr. Leland. Though I daresay I'd never thought to go into business for myself." She smiled and poured more coffee. "I'll keep it in mind, however."

Though she seemed to enjoy cooking for him, Michael had a hard time imagining Ellen overseeing meals for a bunch of strangers. At her uncle's house she wouldn't have to worry about such things anyway. She'd no doubt have servants to cook and serve her. "Mr. Leland worked for a group of Englishmen in California," he said. "In the San Joaquin Valley, was it?"

"That's right." Leland nodded. "They were setting up a farm to raise vegetables and fruit. Apparently they'd done that sort of thing back in their home country."

"I'm thinking your uncle might be in this bunch," Michael said.

Ellen looked doubtful. "I don't think Uncle David had ever done any farming."

"Of course not," Michael said, "but he would have owned farms, wouldn't he? As part of his estate?"

"Estate?" Leland looked from Michael to Ellen. "I take it your uncle is a man of some means."

"Ellen is the daughter of an earl," Michael said.

"But my uncle doesn't have a title," she blurted. She shifted in her chair and looked away. "I mean, he's my mother's brother, and a middle son, and . . ." Her voice trailed away.

Michael frowned. He certainly hadn't meant to embarrass her. What did it matter, after all? The man might not have a title, but that didn't make him any less noble.

"What's his name?" Leland asked. "Could be I know him."

"It's David. David Winthrop."

"Winthrop. But that's your name." Michael glanced at Leland and cleared his throat. "Or rather, it was."

Ellen blushed. "It . . . it's a very common name where I'm from."

Leland shook his head. "Can't say as I know a David Winthrop. There was a Davey Winters in this bunch, but he wouldn't have been related to you. Common as dirt this fellow was, though a nice enough chap and a hard worker. But no royal blood in his veins, I'm sure."

Ellen nodded. "I'll just have to ask around when we arrive in California," she said. "I'm sure someone will have heard of Uncle David."

"Sorry I couldn't be of more help, ma'am. But thank you for the meal. It's one I won't soon forget." He rose and picked up his hat. "Now, if you'll excuse me, I'd better get some rest before I head out with the teamsters tomorrow. Good night, Lieutenant, Mrs. Trent."

When he was gone, Ellen set about clearing away the dishes. Michael helped her, puzzled by the way she'd withdrawn into herself. "I'm sorry Mr. Leland didn't know your uncle," he said. "But I thought it was worth a shot."

"Oh, yes. I appreciate that." She stacked cups in a basin and poured water from a kettle over them.

He took the kettle from her and set it aside, then took her hand and led her back to the table. "Are you sure your uncle really is in California?" he asked.

Eyes downcast, she nodded. "His last letter was from there."

"And how long ago was it written?"

"About . . . eight months ago, I suppose."

"So he might not even be there." The realization stole his breath, and he sat back a moment, trying to recover. She said nothing, her hand limp in his, eyes focused on the floor. "Ellen," he said softly.

She raised her head and met his gaze. He saw the fear in her eyes, mixed with desperation. "Ellen, why did you come all the way from England and agree to marry a man you'd never met, if you weren't even sure there'd be someone to welcome you in California?"

"I had to leave England," she said. "There . . . there was nothing for me there."

"What do you mean nothing for you?" He leaned toward her, wanting desperately to ease her pain. "Surely your father provided for you."

"Yes, he provided for me." Did he imagine the bitterness in her voice? "But the others . . ." She swallowed hard and began again. "I have a half-sister, Gennette, and a cousin, Randolph. They were . . . responsible for me. Gennette decided to marry me off to Randolph."

Understanding ebbed over him. "And you ran away rather than agree to the marriage."

She nodded. "Randolph is a horrible person," she said. "And when . . . when he looked at me, I felt horrible, too."

The last words came out as a whisper, tearing at Michael's heart. He pulled her close and laid her head on his shoulder. "I didn't know you, but I knew you were a good man," she said, her breath warm against his chest.

"How did you know that?" He rested his cheek against the softness of her hair.

"I knew it . . . in my heart. I knew I'd be safe with you, that you were a real gentleman."

Except that he was not a gentleman. He was Dapper Dan's son, a reckless and wild wanderer who had as good as lied to her when he'd let her go on thinking he was better than he was.

How could he reveal the truth now and not hurt her? Every vision of a passionate reconciliation shattered. He could no more burden her with that revelation now than he could have cut off one of her fingers. With a heavy sigh, he pushed her away. "We'll find your uncle somehow," he said, patting her hand. "I promise." Then he stood and left the camp, to walk in the darkness and try to master the flood of emotions that threatened to overwhelm him.

Ellen cried herself to sleep, mourning the dream she'd had of their first night together again that had failed to materialize. Was she so inept at communicating her feelings that Michael had no idea of how much she wanted to be with him? Or was he so committed to keeping his freedom that he couldn't wait to be through with his obligation to her? Why else had he brought Mr. Leland to her, to tell her about a group of Englishmen he'd hoped would take her off his hands?

The troops set out again the next morning, wagons loaded with water barrels for the ninety-mile forced march known as the *Jornada del Muerto*, the "Journey of Death" to Santa Fe. For the next three days Ellen scarcely saw Michael as they traveled up to fifteen hours a day, pausing in the hottest hours to dole out precious water to the horses and mules. When they stopped, she would collapse in the shade of a supply wagon and try to steal a few hours' sleep. When the call came to move out again, she would rise and ride on in a stupor.

Michael rode back to check on her when he was able, but most of his time was spent exhorting his men to keep moving, overseeing the care of the horses, and taking his turn riding ahead to scout for water.

Even when they reached Santa Fe, parched and exhausted, Michael was sent back with water for those who had fallen behind. Ellen spent her first night in the city alone, tossing and turning in the bed made for two, wondering if things would ever be right for her and Michael.

"Knock, knock. Anybody home?" Katherine stuck her head into the tent the next morning. "Have I got a surprise for you."

Ellen forced a smile and faced her friend. "A surprise? What are you talking about?"

"Get together whatever you need for a bath, and I'll show you."

"A bath? Does someone here have a tub?" The thought of immersing her whole body in warm water was too wonderful to contemplate.

"Better than that." Katherine grinned. "There's a hot spring just west of town—lots of warm, clean water bubbling up out of the ground in a pool. Grab some soap and a towel, and we'll go treat ourselves to a soak."

"I don't know...." She hesitated, remembering Michael's warnings about going out alone. "Are you sure it's safe?"

"Of course we'll be safe." She smiled down at Bobby. "The pup here will warn us if anyone's coming. And just let anyone try anything on us—I'll settle his hash." She put a hand to the waistband of her skirt, revealing the pistol tucked there, then pulled up her petticoats to show a knife strapped to her thigh.

Ellen thought of the knife Michael had given her, lying heavy in the pocket of her skirt. Would she really be able to use it to defend herself if she had to?

"Come on," Katherine said, coming to stand over her. "How often do you think we're going to have a chance at a real bath?"

The thought of soaking in a tub and being able to wash her hair in more than a bucket won out over Ellen's vague fears. "All right. Let me change into my riding clothes."

"I'll get the horses and meet you back here."

She began gathering fresh clothing, soap, and towels, suddenly anxious to be away from this tent and all the reminders of the man who could not bear to be in it with her. Maybe a bath was just what she needed. She'd wash away the dust of the trip and perhaps some of her frustration as well.

Chapter Thirteen

Ellen followed Katherine west of town, across a desolate expanse of brush and cactus parallel to the river. They rode single file along a narrow track, Bobby trotting between them, until they came to a grove of stunted trees.

"This is it," Katherine said, swinging down out of her saddle. "The woman who told me about this place said to leave the horses here and walk down to the springs. There's a little shelter where we can undress."

Ellen dismounted, tied her horse beside Katherine's mule, and then, carrying her towel, soap, and comb, followed her to a three-sided arbor fashioned of rough posts lashed together with vines. A cane-covered roof jutted out over a rock-lined pool which gave off a strong mineral smell. Bobby walked to the edge of the pool and studied it, wrinkling his nose.

"I can't wait." Katherine dropped her towel and began unbuttoning her dress. "I feel like I could soak a week."

Ellen looked around the little oasis as she unbraided her hair. No sound intruded upon the solitude except the faint gurgling of the spring. After their ride in the morning heat, the shade here was cool and inviting. Stone steps led from the arbor down into the spring, which had room for a dozen or more people to bathe in its waters.

"Come on," Katherine said, kicking out of her dress and bending to unlace her shoes. "You can't take a bath in your clothes."

Ellen laid aside her towel and removed her shoes. Skirt, blouse, and stockings quickly followed. She hesitated over her corset, but having noticed that Katherine did not wear one, she removed it also. At last, clad only in shift and drawers, she turned around to find a naked Katherine laughing at her.

"Don't tell me you're going to take a bath dressed like that," she said as she removed the pins from her hair. "If I'd been blessed with a figure like yours, I'd be showin' it off every chance I had."

Ellen blushed and looked away. She had never actually seen another woman—or any other person—naked before. Out of the corner of her eye, she studied Katherine's broad shoulders and small, round breasts. She dropped her eyes to her friend's flat stomach and narrow hips, guiltily lingering over the mass of dark curls between the long, slim legs. Here was a woman experienced in loving a man, yet except for size and coloring, she did not look any different from Ellen herself.

"Come on," Katherine coaxed. "You don't have anything I haven't seen before. And there's no one else here." She looked around the empty arbor. "Bobby will let us know if anyone comes."

Still blushing, Ellen nodded and lifted the shift over her head, then stepped out of the drawers. Despite the heat, goose bumps raised on her skin at the unexpected sensation of being naked out in the open like this.

Stepping gingerly across the rocks, she followed Katherine into the warm waters of the pool. "Oh, this is heaven!" Katherine said. She ducked her head under the water and came up, shaking like a dog, showering Ellen with droplets. "Aren't you glad you came?"

"Yes!" Ellen lounged back in the water, letting her hair trail in a sheet behind her. The water was slightly warmer than body temperature, heavy with soothing minerals and gently stirred by the action of the springs. Every last bit of tension eased from her body as she soaked.

They lathered and rinsed their hair and bodies, luxuriating in the satiny sensation of the warm water sliding over their clean skin. Then they sat on the bottom of the pool, in water to their shoulders, and soaked, reluctant to leave this pleasant refuge.

"I guess you and the lieutenant had a big reunion last night," Katherine said after a while.

"Oh . . . oh, yes."

"You don't sound too sure about that." Katherine opened her eyes and frowned at her. "Don't tell me there's trouble already in paradise."

Ellen squirmed, avoiding her friend's eyes. "I . . . I'm not sure Michael is . . . happy with me." She swallowed, forcing back tears. She was not going to cry anymore, especially not in front of Katherine.

"Not happy? Hmmm." Katherine leaned back once more, staring up at the sky. "Maybe all you need to do is make things a little more interesting for him. There's nothin' like a little seduction to turn up the heat, make things more enjoyable for both of you."

Ellen scooped water in her hand and let it flow over her shoulders. "I'm not sure I know how to, well . . . seduce a man," she said after a moment.

"Oh, it's easy. And fun, too."

Ellen nodded. She couldn't bring herself to tell her friend that she didn't know the first thing about loving a man. And Michael had made it clear he didn't intend to pursue her. Still, there might come a day when such knowledge would be useful. . . . "Tell me," she said. "Tell me what to do."

Katherine propped her elbows on the rock ledge around the pool and leaned back. "Most men like a woman who lets them know what she wants. They may say they like 'em meek and mild—but not in bed." She studied Ellen through veiled lashes. "Men get all excited by what they see, so wear something pretty—a little revealing. Think of it like a play. You need costumes and scenery—set the stage, so to speak. Candles, flowers, perfume, fresh sheets, whatever you like. That helps you get in the mood, too."

She leaned forward again, brow furrowed in thought. "Try rubbing his back. Or undress him—slowly. Tease him a little. Don't let him have you all at once. Make him wait a little. It drives 'em crazy, but they love it. By the time you make love, you'll both be pantin' for it, and you won't be able to get enough."

Ellen swallowed hard and tensed her thighs against the aching between her legs. That was how she wanted it to be between her and Michael—slow and sweet and satisfying. Maybe if she took the initiative and showed him. . . .

"Whoo, I'm ready to get back to camp now," Katherine said, rubbing her arms. "Bear just don't know what he's in for tonight."

"What about Solly?" She half hoped Katherine had gotten over her infatuation with the doctor.

"I just might have to pay him a visit, too." Katherine reached for her towel, laughing. "Don't look so shocked. I didn't mean it." She shook her head. "The trouble with Solly is he's made up his mind how things are between us and won't even consider any other possibilities."

Ellen rose from the water and joined her friend in drying off and getting dressed. "How do you know that?" she asked. "Maybe if you told him how you feel . . ."

"I know Solly. He wants the white dress and the picket fence and gingerbread in the kitchen, the whole nine yards. That's just not me. Rather than have fun together while we can, he's decided he doesn't want anything at all. That's how he was ten years ago, and as far as I can tell, he hasn't changed a bit. Don't you worry about me." Katherine pulled her blouse over her head and settled it on her shoulders. "You just see to that lieutenant of yours. Try a few of those things I told you, and I guarantee you'll get his attention."

Ellen smiled, warmth spreading through her that had

nothing to do with the summer sun. She would get Michael's attention. After tonight, he wouldn't be leaving her to sleep alone anymore.

Ellen jumped up, thinking she heard someone in the street outside. But whoever it was moved on, and she sank into a chair once more, fingers nervously smoothing the tie of her robe. She glanced about her at the preparations she'd made. Katherine had said atmosphere was important, so she'd arranged candles around the tent, in groups of threes and fours, casting puddles of golden light on the carved wooden table and on the canvas walls.

She swallowed hard when her eyes came to rest on the bed. The linens were as white as she could make them, and she'd sprinkled lavender from her trunk between the sheets. When crushed, the herb would release its sweet scent.

She looked away, thinking how the lavender would come to be crushed. Unable to sit still, she rose and checked the soup simmering in a kettle over the fire. As she bent to stir the broth, she was aware of the satin of the gown sliding over her breasts and the sudden tightening of her nipples.

The almost translucent, embroidered satin gown and robe made her feel more exposed than if she'd been naked. She wore not a stitch underneath the fine garments, and it seemed the fabric clung to every inch of her, leaving nothing hidden.

Well, that was what she wanted, wasn't it, for Michael to look at her and see her as a woman? A woman no longer content to live here side by side with him and pretend she did not have feelings for him. Feelings that frightened her in their intensity sometimes. Even now she was afraid of exposing her need for him, and her lack of shame in pursuing him this way.

She took a deep breath, drawing in the scents of candle wax and lavender and spicy soup. Bobby looked up from his place by the fire, ears alert, attention to the door. She felt her heart begin to race. Michael was here. And she wasn't ready yet . . .

The door opened, and Michael came in, pulling off his cap as he entered. He pulled the tent flap in place behind him, then turned and froze, staring.

She forced herself to meet his eyes, feeling the heat of the blush that swept over her. She gripped the back of a chair to support herself, praying he wouldn't hate her for what she was about to do.

He looked away, fumbling to remove the sword belt and the sash with its pistols and knife. She wanted to go to him, to help, but no, it was too soon. Instead, she turned to the fire and ladled out a bowl of soup. "Did you have a good day?" she asked, trying to control the quavering in her voice.

"Yes. Colonel Peabody is going to Taos for a few days, and Major Sutton will be commander in his absence, so there were things to do to prepare for that." She heard the scrape of a chair as he sat at the table.

She set the soup before him, carefully avoiding his eyes. "I've already eaten, but you go ahead." She brought bread and a cup of water and placed them on the table, then pulled out the chair and sat across from him.

He tried to eat, but his eyes kept straying to her. "I . . . I haven't seen that outfit before," he said in a strained voice.

She ran her hand down the lapel of the robe. "I haven't worn it before now. It's a lady's lounging costume, from France."

He nodded and turned his attention to the soup once more. Was it her imagination, or was his hand shaking as he gripped the spoon?

She smiled, pleased that she was able to break through his usual gentlemanly calm. When she had devised her little plan, she had feared it would be difficult. She hadn't thought it could be enjoyable as well.

"You've spilled something on your tunic," she said.

"Why don't you take it off and let me clean it before it sets?"

Before he could answer, she came around the table and bent to undo the buttons of the long blue tunic. He grew very still, his breathing shallow, and she was aware of his eyes focused on the tops of her breasts where they rose up out of the low neck of the gown. He let her remove the tunic. Now he was dressed in white shirt and blue trousers.

She sat down once more and opened her mending basket. Michael had stopped eating altogether now, intent on studying her. She let the robe slide open further, revealing the rounded outlines of her breasts. As if his heated gaze were a physical touch, her nipples rose, erect against the silk.

She pretended to select a chunk of naphtha soap with which to scrub the stain, but even if she'd wanted to, she doubted her hands would be steady enough to make much of a job of it. Instead, after a few minutes, she laid the jacket aside. "Let me get you some more soup."

"No, really. I haven't finished what I have...."

She took his half-full bowl, as if to refill it from the pot, then pretended to trip, sloshing most of the rest of the cooled soup onto his trousers.

"Oh, I'm so sorry. Look what I've done." She snatched up a napkin and began frantically wiping at the stains, which trailed across his thigh, toward his crotch. As her hand brushed across him, she heard him draw in his breath with a hissing sound.

She stepped back, avoiding his eyes as she surveyed the damage. "You'll have to take them off," she said. "Those peppers will leave an awful stain if I don't soak them now."

She bent as if to help him remove the trousers, and he stood, backing away. "I don't think . . ." he began.

"Oh, come now, Michael. Your shirttails will keep you modest." She was smiling now, watching him from under the veil of her lashes, enjoying his obvious discomfort.

Frowning, he turned his back and began unbuttoning the pants. She busied herself mopping up the spilled soup.

"Here you are." He held out the trousers, and she took them, noting with a flush of pleasure that the front of the long-tailed shirt stood out from his body to the extent of his arousal.

She took the pants and dunked them in a bucket of water by the fire, bending over to do so and feeling the silk shape itself to her naked buttocks.

Michael stared as the silken gown and robe slipped over the smooth curve of her backside. He bit back a groan, imagining his hand following that curve. God, was she so innocent that she couldn't see what this was doing to him?

"Ellen!" The word was almost a gasp.

She turned and smiled at him. "Yes, Michael?"

He stared at the curve of her breasts swelling the gown, the points of her nipples pressed against the fabric. He dropped his eyes to the shadows between her thighs, and felt the blood roar in his ears. "I think you should . . . well . . ." He swallowed, unable to tear his eyes from her. "I think you should put on something a little . . . a little less revealing."

She moved closer to him, and he watched, mesmerized, as the silk shaped itself to her body with each step. "Why? Don't you enjoy looking at me?" she asked.

He shook his head. "I do enjoy it," he said, his voice husky. He licked his dry lips, struggling to regain control. "Too much."

"I want you to look," she whispered, locking her eyes to his. "And touch." She put her hand on his shoulder, and a tremor ran through him, a path of heat radiating to his loins. "I want you, Michael. I've wanted you for so long now."

She raised her lips to his, and with a shudder the dam of his reserve burst. He reached for her, crushing her to him, caressing her silk-clad body as if he feared she might suddenly melt away, a hallucination of his passion-fogged mind.

The lips that met Michael's belonged to no vision. They were flesh and blood, soft and yielding. She sighed, a long, trembling exhalation, and his tongue ventured between her parted teeth, stroking the inside of her mouth, caressing, drinking deeply of the sweetness that had haunted him for too long now.

She pressed against him, rubbing the sensitive tips of her breasts against his chest. He shaped his hands to the soft mounds, thumbs stroking the hard nipples through the silk. She gasped and wriggled against him, driving him almost to distraction. He reached around to clasp the firm curve of her buttocks, guiding her until she straddled his thigh, and she moaned as she gripped him with her legs.

"Oh, Ellen, I'd never have denied you so long if I'd known you felt this way," he whispered, nibbling at her earlobe.

She gasped in response, her whole body quivering at his touch. A new bolt of heat shot through him as he lowered his head and suckled at one nipple through the layers of silk. He clasped her buttocks, pulling her close against his erection. "You don't know how long I've wanted to do this," he said, turning his attention to the other breast.

She pulled at his shirt, hands stroking his back. Raising his head, he looked down into her eyes, dark with desire. The knowledge that he was the one she wanted made his heart beat faster. He scooped her into his arms and carried her to the bed. After lowering her gently to the mattress, he stood back and began to strip off his clothes.

She watched, eyes growing wider as the layers fell away. His hands shook as he pulled off his small clothes. He had waited so long, but he must not hurry. He must take the time to love her as she deserved to be loved.

She looked away as he knelt beside her on the bed. "Don't be frightened," he whispered, pushing back the fall of hair that concealed her face. The red-gold locks felt as silken as her gown against his hands, which suddenly seemed too big and awkward.

She smiled, a slight upturning of her lips, and he felt encouraged. "I . . . I just never imagined . . . what men look like," she stammered.

He put his hand to her cheek and turned her face so that she looked into his eyes. "Men and women are made the way they are to please each other," he said, smiling. He lowered his gaze to the neck of her gown. "And now it's my turn to see you."

Nodding, she sat and slipped the robe from her shoulders. He helped free it from beneath her hips, then sat back as she raised the gown over her head. The smile fell from his face, and he stared, open-mouthed, at the creamy perfection of her breasts. They hung full and heavy, rosy nipples pointing at him, as if begging for his touch.

She crossed her arms over her chest and looked away. "What's wrong?" she asked.

"Oh, dearest girl." He pulled her to him, burying his face in her hair. "You're more beautiful than I'd imagined. More beautiful than anything or anyone I've ever seen."

"I always felt so . . . big . . . and awkward."

"No. No. Just perfect. For me." He bent and cupped her left breast in his palm and took the nipple in his mouth, gently, so gently, savoring the texture of it as he moved his tongue back and forth across it. He let it slide over his teeth as he released it, and she gasped, jerking in his arms. As she writhed against him, he stroked and suckled, first one breast, then the other, until she moaned in agony and begged for mercy.

"Michael, please, please!"

His lips found hers again, silencing her cries, and his hand gently cradled the damp curls between her legs. "My poor, aching darling," he murmured as one finger slid inside her moist passage, sending new tremors through her limbs. "I'll soon ease your suffering."

She groaned as he began to stroke her, first lightly, then

with more pressure, leaving her gasping for breath. He bent his head to her breast once more, and her head fell back; a cry tore from her throat as spasms of release shook her.

Then he kneeled over her, gently spreading her legs and pressing the hot hardness of his erection against her. She opened herself to him without prompting, and he entered her, anticipating the ecstasy of release.

But he had not gone far before he encountered a barrier, a resistance to his shaft. He struggled for control and caressed her cheek. "I don't mean to hurt you," he said. "But it may, just a little, and only at first. Then it will be all better, I promise."

When she smiled she had never looked more beautiful to him. "It's all right," she said. "I trust you."

He pressed on, and she let out a muffled cry. He held her a moment, until her heartbeat slowed once more, then he began to move in a gentle rhythm. Ellen urged him on, arching against him and wrapping her legs around him.

He abandoned himself then to the rhythm that pounded in his heart and his head and his loins. At each stroke, new tremors of sensation shot through him, every nerve alive to the sight and smell and feel of the woman in his arms.

She lifted her hips to meet his thrusts, and her head fell back, her eyes closing and her breath coming in gasps. He gripped her buttocks and thrust deeper, and lost himself to soaring sensation, rising higher and higher, a cry tearing from his throat as he leaped and fell free, Ellen's own joyous shout ringing in his ears as she fell with him.

He lay afterward with his head on her chest, spent, afraid to move or speak lest he break the spell she'd cast over him. For what else but magic could explain what he was feeling? In all his years of bedding women, he had never experienced what he had with Ellen. Always before, sex had been a physical release, enjoyable, sometimes even memorable.

But tonight the physical had been surpassed by the spiritual—a letting go somewhere in his soul. He raised his head to look at her and was surprised to see tears glistening on her cheeks.

"Ellen, did I hurt you?" he asked, alarmed. He rolled to his side and pulled her to him. "I'm sorry. I just wanted you so badly I couldn't stop."

She shook her head. "No. No. You didn't hurt me." She smiled and wiped away the tears with the back of her hand. "It was wonderful. The most wonderful thing I've ever experienced."

"Then why are you crying?"

She leaned forward and kissed him lightly on the lips. "Just tears of happiness." Her smile broadened when she saw his confusion. "You don't have to understand me. Just don't stop loving me."

"I might as well try to stop breathing," he said, gathering her close once more. He lay back on the bed, her head resting in the curve of his shoulder. He made a vow to himself not to let go of her, as long as he had any breath left.

Ellen murmured sleepily and curled her body toward the warmth that beckoned her. Her skin tingled with pleasure, and she smiled at the sensation of happiness that filled her like light, a warm glow from within.

Something tickled her neck, something warm and soft and moist, caressing her, teasing her flesh to new heights of awareness.

She opened her eyes and saw Michael's loose blond hair as he bent to kiss her neck, his tongue flicking back and forth across the sensitive flesh beneath her jaw.

She moved against him, and he lifted his head and smiled at her. "Good morning."

"Good morning." She smiled and put her arms around him, delighting in the feel of her naked body against the muscles and planes of his own unclothed form. How easily she had slipped into the role of wanton woman. How wonderful it felt to be here with him like this, all barriers and pretense gone. This was the joy her mother must have known with the earl, the joy that had made everything else seem of little consequence.

"How are you this morning?" he asked, running his hand along the back of her thigh and bringing her leg up over his hip.

"I feel wonderful." She snuggled closer, feeling his erection, hot and hard against her, creating an aching, throbbing sensation between her own legs.

"You certainly do feel wonderful," he said, shaping his hand to the curve of her backside. He buried his face in her neck once more, nibbling lightly. "Hungry?"

"Only for you," she murmured, trying to press herself more tightly against him.

He pulled away, out of her arms, backing out of bed so suddenly she cried out in dismay. "Don't worry, I'll be right back." He bent and planted a kiss on her forehead, then moved across the room.

She followed him with her eyes, thrilling at the sight of the muscles flexing under the taut skin of his thighs and buttocks. He bent to stir up the fire and move the kettle over the flames. Then he stepped out of her line of sight, and she realized he'd gone out to the latrines just beyond their tent.

She realized her own need to relieve herself, and took advantage of his absence to use the chamber pot tucked behind a screen across the tent. She drew on the translucent robe and was measuring coffee into the kettle when he returned.

"Oh, no, you don't." He rushed up behind her and swept her into his arms. "This morning I wait on you."

He tucked her back into bed, taking his time removing her robe as he did so, his hands lingering over her breasts, stroking her sensitive nipples until her breath came in gasps. Then he grinned and vanished again.

He returned a little later with a steaming mug in each hand, a thick slice of bread, covered in jam, balanced atop each mug. "This is the extent of my skills in the kitchen," he said, handing her one of the mugs. He winked. "But then, I'm more known for other talents."

"And what might those be?" she asked, taking a sip of the strong coffee.

"You don't recall from last night? Perhaps another demonstration is in order." He leaned over and covered her lips with his own, and she tasted coffee and the sweetness of jam.

She smiled when he withdrew and held up her slice of bread to take a bite, but she was more interested in watching Michael than in looking at her breakfast, and a dollop of the grape jam slid off the bread, landing on her breast.

"Now why didn't I think of that?" he said, before swooping down to lick up the errant jam. His tongue trailed over the curve of her breast to encircle her nipple, stroking and teasing, until she set aside her breakfast altogether and surrendered herself to his attentions.

"Don't let me interrupt," he said, raising his head. "Just go on with your meal."

She shook her head and stretched herself out alongside him.

"You don't mind if I do, do you?" He took another sip of coffee before setting it aside, and picked up the bread. A wicked gleam in his eye, he scooped up a fingerful of jam and dabbed it onto her other nipple. "Why did I ever waste this on bread?" he murmured as he licked her.

Ellen arched her body toward him, a tightness growing within her, and a heat that threatened to melt her bones. Michael slid down beside her, dividing his attention between her erect, aching breasts. He slid his knee between her thighs, pressing against the crux of her womanhood until she cried out for relief.

She bent her head to his, coaxing his lips upward until they covered her mouth once more. With newfound skill, she teased him with her tongue, dancing across his teeth and retreating, plying featherlight strokes along the tender interior of his mouth.

She smoothed her hands across his shoulders and down his chest, brushing across the hard brown nubs of his nipples with her outstretched palms.

He leaned back his head and sighed, the sound almost a moan. "Oh, Ellen, I think you've found your true calling," he murmured. "When I think of all the time we've wasted . . ."

She did not have time to answer him or even to think. He rolled her over and slid into her in one smooth movement, holding her hips and guiding her legs around him. He began to move in and out of her, advance and retreat in a steady, intoxicating rhythm.

She clutched her tender breasts, hands instinctively massaging the nipples, and closed her eyes against the onslaught of sensation. Her whole body trembled, heart pounding, breath coming in gasps. And then she felt the tightening, and the tremendous, wonderful release.

Michael gathered her to his chest and plunged deeper, a sigh escaping from him as she felt his seed spill into her.

They lay in each other's arms, unspeaking, as if to make any sound would break the spell that hung over them. Ellen drifted in that state between sleep and wakefulness until a commotion at the entrance startled her.

Michael rolled away from her and pulled on his pants while she drew the sheets up to her neck. But before he finished dressing, the tent flap was thrown back and a trio of soldiers burst in upon them.

Ellen cowered behind Michael and screamed. He threw his jacket over her and whirled to face the intruders, Bowie knife clutched in his hand. "What is the meaning of this?" he demanded.

A bearded sergeant drew his pistol and pointed it at Michael's chest. "Lieutenant Michael Trent, you are under arrest."

Chapter Fourteen

Michael woke with a throbbing pain in his head, the smell of onions filling his nostrils. He struggled to sit up, every muscle protesting, and looked around at the dirt-floored shack to which he was confined. A band of bright sunlight filtered through the narrow slit at the top of the door, illuminating burlap sacks of onions arranged along one wall. He wrinkled his nose at the strong odor and raked his hand through his tangled curls, wincing at the matted feel of drying blood. He had vague memories of a struggle and Ellen screaming, and then everything had gone black.

Ellen. Had he dreamed those moments of ecstasy in her arms? No fantasy could have matched the reality of their night together. How ironic that after finding such heaven he should end up in this hell.

The rattle of keys in the lock distracted him. The door swung open. "You awake, Lieutenant?" a baby-faced private asked. He carried a lantern in one hand, a bundle of keys in the other.

"I want to see Colonel Peabody." Michael stood and struggled to take a step forward, but his leg would hardly move. He looked down to see an iron band fastened around his ankle, a long length of chain connecting it to a rusting ball. Rage quickly replaced his shock. "Damn you, unchain me at once!"

"Sorry, Lieutenant, I can't do that." The private set the lantern to one side and opened the door a little wider. "The doctor's here to check your head, though."

"Get me Colonel Peabody!" Michael roared.

"Peabody's gone to Taos and left Sutton in charge," Solly said, stepping into the guardhouse, medical bag in one hand, a bucket of water in the other. He looked back at the guard. "That'll be all, Private. You can leave us now."

The soldier closed the door, and Michael heard the scrape of the hasp and the key in the lock. "What's going on here, Solly?" he asked. "They've got me chained up like an animal."

"Sit down on these sacks over here and let me have a look at your head."

Michael sat, and the doctor probed at the tender spot on his skull. He flinched as Solly's fingers teased apart the matted hair. "Concussed you good from the looks of things," he said, wetting a cloth and beginning to clean the wound. "You shouldn't have put up such a fight."

"I wasn't about to let some doughboy haul me off without an explanation," he said. "Did they tell you they came for us in bed? Frightened Ellen half to death."

"Well, you made 'em mad enough to half kill you and clamp you in irons." Solly pulled a pair of scissors from his case.

"What are you doing?"

"I'm going to cut the hair away from that wound so I can get a good look at it."

Michael shot out his hand and gripped the doctor's wrist. "I'm already in jail with a cannonball chained to my leg. I'll be damned if I'll be half bald, too."

Solly shrugged. "Suit yourself. That head of yours is so hard I'd be surprised if a mule's kick could do much damage." He pulled out a bottle and began dabbing the wound with a stinging solution.

"Why am I in here, Solly?"

The doctor looked at him thoughtfully. "Why do you think?"

"It's Dunleavy, isn't it?"

"He says you tried to kill him."

"No. I was doing my best to keep from killing him. He was making it damned hard." He pushed away the doctor's hand and looked him in the eye. "So he's charged me with assault?"

Solly shook his head. "Attempted murder."

"Murder!"

"That's why you're in irons. You're considered a dangerous man."

"But why now? What happened between us happened back in El Paso. Days ago."

"I suspect he was waiting to get Peabody out of the picture. Rumor is the old man has a soft spot for you. After all, he introduced you to the lovely Ellen."

"Oh, God, Ellen!" He groaned and buried his head in his hands. "How is she?"

"Right now, she's beside herself, worryin' about you. She wouldn't give me any peace until I promised to take a look at you right away."

"Hmmmph!"

"Don't snort at me. I did come here as soon as I left your tent. You were groggy and mad as a bear, and obviously don't remember a bit of it. I figured it best to leave most of the doctorin' till morning."

Michael bent and picked up the iron ball, then began to pace across the shack, his chains gathered in his arms. "They'll hang me, won't they?" he said.

"That depends on how the court rules. Did he provoke you?"

"No, I was just tired of seeing his ugly face around camp.... Hell, yes, he provoked me."

"How?"

Solly waited while he made two more circuits of his prison. "He insulted Ellen," he said at last.

"Defending a lady. Of course." He stood and clapped

Michael on the shoulder. "Don't give up the ship yet. Those Texans are none too popular with the regular Army officers. When Peabody returns, the odds will shift back in your favor." He paused at the door. "Anything I can get for you?"

He shook his head. "Take care of Ellen."

"Katherine's moved into your tent with her for now." He knocked on the door, the signal for the guard to release him. "She wants to come visit you."

"No."

"I told her I'd ask."

"Solly, no!" He looked around at the shack, at the dirt floor and the onion sacks. "This is no place for a lady like Ellen."

"It might do you good to have visitors."

"No."

"She'll think you don't want to see her." He sighed. "She'll probably cry. I hate it when women cry."

"Tell her . . . tell her I love her."

He shook his head. "No. That's one message you'll have to deliver in person." The guard opened the door, and Solly picked up the lantern and stepped back. "I think I'll just describe the situation and let the lady decide what to do." He smiled. "Not everyone's a hero, Trent. There's a place for us cowards, too."

Ellen straightened the shawl around her shoulders and rearranged the covering on the basket she carried. "I hope Michael likes these tarts I made. The berries didn't look very fresh—"

"Will you quit fussin'? You know good and well that man would eat mud pies if he thought you made them. And from what I've had of your cookin', they might be good at that." Katherine picked up Bobby and cradled him in her arms. "Now get goin'. It's been almost two days since you've seen the handsome lieutenant, and I can tell you're startin' to pine already." She stroked the squirming dog. "Go on now."

Ellen straightened her shoulders and set off through camp, toward the little adobe building they'd chosen as Michael's cell. Whether because he was an officer, or due to the nature of the charges against him, they'd isolated him from the other prisoners. She swallowed the sudden lump in her throat as she thought of those charges. Attempted murder! Not Michael. Why, she'd never met a gentler, kinder man in her life.

But she remembered the wound on Captain Dunleavy's head, that day he'd come looking for Michael. He'd said then that Michael was responsible, though she'd found it difficult to believe. *There has to be an explanation,* she told herself for the hundredth time. *I know Michael is not a murderer.*

The young private on guard duty rose at her approach and stepped out from the shade at the side of the little building. "Morning, ma'am." He touched the brim of his cap.

"I've come to see my husband," she said, the words sending a rush of warmth through her. "Lieutenant Trent."

"Yes, ma'am." The soldier nodded at her basket. "I'll have to see what you've got in there."

"Yes, of course." She removed the cloth from the top of the basket to show the roast chicken legs, potatoes, berry tarts, and lemonade.

The young man's eyes took on a wistful look. "Sure looks good, ma'am."

"Here. Take one of these." She held out one of the tarts, still warm, sugar sparkling across its top.

"Why, thank you, ma'am." He took the tart in one hand and removed the keys from his belt with the other. "If you'll just let me get the door for you."

She'd prepared herself for the worst, so when the guard swung back the heavy wooden door and she saw Michael standing before her, bruised and somewhat dirt-streaked but otherwise unharmed, she let out a sigh of relief. It was only when he smiled and took a step forward that she saw the links of chain and the heavy ball, and felt a fist clench her heart.

"I told Solly to tell you not to come." He took the basket from her and escorted her to a seat on a pile of onion sacks on which he'd spread his jacket. He knelt and lit the lantern that sat on another stack of onions, then looked up at her, his face bathed in the warm yellow light. "I didn't want you to see me like this."

But his eyes told her a different story—that he very much wanted to see her. They fixed on her with a longing, hungry gaze. Her mouth went dry, and her legs began to shake beneath her full skirts. "Michael, I couldn't stay away from you," she whispered.

His arms slipped around her, drawing her mouth down to his. They kissed hungrily, desperately, as if they might condense all their fear and longing into this one embrace.

After a long while they drew apart, and Michael sat beside her on the sacks of onions. His eyes searched her, as if memorizing every ribbon and ruffle of her dress. The air in the small building was stifling and reeked of onions, but she did not think that was the reason for the sudden faintness that swept over her.

"I was so afraid when they took you away," she murmured.

"Shhh. It doesn't matter now." He took her hand in his. She gripped him so tightly she was sure she was hurting him, but she couldn't seem to let go. To think she might have lost him—

She did not know how long they sat like that before he eased away from her and nodded to the basket between them. "What's in here?"

She smoothed her hands along her skirt, regaining her composure. "I brought you some food. Chicken, tarts, and lemonade."

He lifted the cloth and smiled, taking out a chicken leg and the jug of lemonade. "It's a good thing I'm in here by myself. The other prisoners would kill for food like this."

She flinched at his choice of words. Maybe she

shouldn't ask. Maybe it was none of her business, but she had to know. . . . "What happened . . . between you and Captain Dunleavy?"

He laid aside the chicken leg he'd been gnawing and sighed. "He stopped me in the street in El Paso and started calling me a coward. He went on and on."

"And you hit him?"

He shook his head. "I could have stood him insulting me. But then he went after you, and I . . . I guess I snapped."

"Me? What did he say about me?"

"It doesn't matter."

"But Michael, I want to know."

He sighed again. "He said you obviously weren't a lady if you'd chosen to marry me."

She drew in her breath sharply. Oh, how those words stung! *Michael, if you only knew—*

He reached out and awkwardly patted her hand. "It doesn't matter." He picked up the chicken again and removed a glass from the basket. "Would you care to pour?"

She served two glasses of lemonade, but sat with hers untouched, watching him eat.

"Quite the spot for a picnic, isn't it?" he said, looking around the shack.

She tried to smile, but didn't quite succeed, her eyes coming to rest on the iron ball at their feet. Michael set aside his glass and picked up the ball, looping the chain over one arm. "I've been exercising with it," he said, raising it up with one hand. "Soon I'll be the fittest man in camp."

He studied the rusting orb. "I think I ought to polish it, don't you? The chain, too. Then I'll wear it around my neck, as a kind of ornament. I'll start a new fashion. Soon everyone will want one."

He winked, and she felt a laugh bubbling up inside her. "Oh, Michael, I have missed you."

"I've missed you, too."

She wished he would kiss her again, wished she had the

courage to lean forward and kiss him. But perhaps this wasn't the time or place for it, what with the guard right outside the door. . . .

"Solly said Katherine's moved in with you."

She nodded. "I was too nervous to stay alone. I don't think Bear is too happy with the arrangement, though."

He laughed. "I doubt if he had much say in the matter. Katherine strikes me as a woman who does pretty much as she pleases."

"Dr. Sullivan has been very good about checking on us," she said. "I think he mostly stops by to talk to Katherine, though."

"Solly? Do you think he's really interested in her?"

She smiled. "Why not? She's an attractive woman, and they've known each other a long time. They probably have a lot in common."

"Maybe so. I gather from talking to him that they were an item once. Still, Solly's an educated man, comes from a good family and all. What would he and Katherine have in common?" He shrugged. "Besides, he doesn't strike me as the type to settle down. He's pretty much made a career of the Army, and that's a hard life for a wife and family."

How many times had Michael told her how much he enjoyed being a soldier? Were his words about Solly just a subtle warning to her not to ever expect a permanent attachment from him? She looked away. "What will happen to you now?"

"I'm hoping Colonel Peabody will dismiss the charges once he returns and I've had a chance to talk to him."

"And if he doesn't?"

"There'll be a trial—a military trial."

"And if you're found guilty?"

"They could sentence me to hard labor, or to be flogged, or they could drum me out of the service."

He shrugged, a careless gesture, but she saw the lines of tension along his jaw and the worry in his eyes. She reached out her hand and laid it over his where it rested on his thigh. "Or to death?" she whispered.

He nodded.

She took a deep shuddering breath, fighting back tears. "I'll go and speak to the colonel when he returns. I'll beg if I have to. I . . . I'll tell him I need you . . . that I'm expecting your baby."

She felt his hand contract under her own, and his face went gray in the lamplight. "But . . . that isn't true, is it?"

"Of course not. I mean, I don't think . . ." she stammered, blushing deeply. "I just thought . . ."

He sat up straighter, his normal color returning. "Don't worry. I can plead my own case when the time comes." He stood and held out his hand to her. "You'd better get back to camp now." He rapped on the door.

"I'll say a prayer for you," she said as the door swung open. "I'll go to the church in town and light a candle." Then she turned and hurried away, blinking back tears. The sun blinded her, but inside she felt dark, as dark as the interior of that little shack, where the man who held her heart waited.

"Fifty-one, fifty-two, fifty-three . . ." Michael raised the iron ball to his chest and lowered it, again and again, ignoring the burning in his muscles. He needed the pain to distract him from contemplating his fate. If he allowed it, he'd no doubt go crazy from thoughts of the firing squad or the cat o'nine tails that awaited him if found guilty of attempting to murder Gregory Dunleavy.

He'd seen the skin flayed from men's backs for lesser infractions than his, and others shot at dawn, buried with no markers for their lonely graves. He closed his eyes and brought the ball to his chest again.

Thoughts of Ellen, and how he'd let her down, haunted him. He'd more or less left her defenseless while he was here in prison. He never should have let the likes of Dunleavy draw him into a fight. A real gentleman would no doubt have found a way to avoid it. He couldn't imagine why a woman like Ellen wanted anything to do with him. But she insisted on visiting him every afternoon, and he looked forward to those visits the way some men craved liquor.

The scrape of keys in the lock of his prison pulled him from these dark thoughts. He dropped the ball and reached for the shirt he'd discarded in the onion-scented heat.

"What's this, then? Lying around half-dressed while the rest of us sweat ourselves dry in this godforsaken desert?" Solly stuck his head around the door, smiling as he stepped into the shack. "Did you have to pull rank to get these private quarters?"

"And all the onions you can eat." Michael buttoned up the shirt. "Come to examine me again? My head seems much better."

"No, I have the privilege of escorting you to Colonel Peabody. He's returned from Taos and heard you wanted to talk to him."

Michael tucked in his shirttails and reached for his jacket, his heartbeat quickening. So Peabody had finally returned. If the colonel would listen to reason, he might see the charges dropped, and avoid a court-martial altogether. He raked his fingers through his hair and adjusted the forage cap on his head. "What kind of mood is he in?"

Solly shrugged. "I didn't sit down and have tea with him. He just ordered me to deliver you to him, and here I am."

Michael straightened the jacket and brushed the worst of the dirt from the sleeves. Then he picked up the ball and looped the chain over his arm. "I'm ready."

They were silent until they were well away from the guard. "What's Dunleavy looking like these days?" Michael asked.

Solly glanced at him. "As if he had an unfortunate encounter with the kicking end of a mule. His face is all shades of green and brown, with a dab of purple thrown in for contrast." He grinned at Michael. "You've accomplished the impossible—making him even uglier than usual."

Michael nodded, frowning. "He'll howl if I get off with anything less than a court-martial."

"Let him howl. We've a few tales we could tell on him ourselves. Last I heard, it was still against regs to assault the local citizenry."

"Let's hope Peabody sees it that way."

They found the colonel seated in the shade of a tarp stretched between poles in front of his tent. He frowned as Michael and Solly halted before him, and brusquely returned their salutes. "I don't have a lot of time to waste, Lieutenant, so get to the point."

Michael took a deep breath. Peabody didn't look as if he was in the mood to grant his own mother clemency, much less a lieutenant who had been on his bad side more than Michael cared to remember. "I've come to request that the charges against me be dropped, sir," he said, standing at attention.

"Absolutely not."

Peabody looked away, and Solly gave Michael a sympathetic look. "Sir, I did not attempt to murder Captain Dunleavy." He took a step forward. "I did my best to avoid killing him, though he provoked me."

The colonel sighed. "There's no love lost between the Rangers and most of the Army," he said. "But the majority of my officers somehow avoid coming to blows in the middle of downtown."

"He insulted the character of the Dragoons, sir." Michael struggled to keep his voice calm, reasonable. "And he insulted my wife."

"You should have walked away as a gentleman and an officer. Men like Dunleavy aren't worth wasting your time on."

"I'll admit I did not use the best judgment, sir, but it was *not* attempted murder."

Peabody's frown deepened. "You'll have an opportunity to defend yourself at your trial. I can't dismiss the charges."

"Sir, I was with Lieutenant Trent when we came upon

Captain Dunleavy extorting money from an El Paso saloon keeper," Solly said. "Lieutenant Trent literally pulled that Scotsman off the saloon keeper's wife. The captain's been baiting him ever since."

"You can give your testimony at the trial, Doctor." He waved them away. "You're dismissed."

Solly looked as if he were about to protest, but Michael took his arm and pulled him away. "Looks like the old man's made up his mind," Solly said when they were out of earshot of Colonel Peabody.

Michael nodded. "My guess is he doesn't want to risk offending the Rangers. If we're sent into the interior, the Army's counting on the Rangers to act as scouts and interpreters."

"Are you saying they'd sacrifice one of their own to appease the Texans?"

"Not if I can help it." He balanced the ball in his palm. "I suppose if worse comes to worst, I could escape—head to California and change my name."

"And leave Ellen behind?"

The thought pained him. What would happen to Ellen if he left? He'd promised to look after her. How could he betray her? He lowered the ball and tucked it beneath one arm. "I couldn't do that."

"What about appealing to a higher authority?"

Michael glanced at his friend. "Ellen's already promised to light a candle for me in the Mesilla chapel."

Solly grunted. "Not quite that high. But there's a rumor General Kearny intends to inspect the troops sometime soon. Word is he barely tolerates the Rangers. He might be more willing to release a capable young lieutenant with a fairly clean record."

Michael passed the ball back and forth in his hands, thinking. Would General Kearny even waste time with one prisoner—onion-scented and worse for wear at that? He looked down at the rusting ball and the length of chains looped over his arm. Maybe . . .

"Solly, will you do me a favor?"

"Name it."

"Go to Ellen and ask her for a few things for me. I'll give you a list. And then let me know the minute you hear when General Kearny's coming to camp."

Chapter Fifteen

On the day General Kearny was scheduled to review the troops, Ellen and Katherine claimed a choice spot from which to view the festivities. Ellen gazed out over the ranks of foot soldiers lined up on the parade ground. Bayonets gleamed in the early morning sun, and the company band had shined its instruments to a mirror finish. The smell of brass polish and gun blacking filled the heated air around them. Any other time, she might have enjoyed the pageantry, but today nervousness tied her stomach in knots.

Across from the infantry, the Dragoons waited, resplendent in gold-faced blue, shakos standing tall. They had curried their mounts until the black and chestnut coats gleamed and oiled their saddles to a high polish. *Michael should be with them*, she thought. She clenched her hands into fists and sent up a silent prayer that soon he would be.

Colonel Peabody had given the order that everything and everyone was to be in top form for General Kearny's review. Men who had not been seen in complete uniform since leaving San Antonio were now transformed into the very image of an invincible American fighting force.

"Ever seen a finer bunch of fightin' men in all your born

days?" Katherine craned her neck to peer over the crowd. "Makes you proud to be an American, don't it?"

"If I was an American, I'm sure I would be proud," Ellen said.

Katherine grinned. "Well, you're married to an American. That's the next best thing."

"May I join you ladies?" They looked up and saw Doc Solly astride Pepper. He guided the horse to them. "Has General Kearny arrived yet?"

Katherine grabbed hold of Pepper's bridle for balance and raised herself up on her tiptoes. "I don't see the old cuss, but he ought to be here soon."

Pepper snorted at the unfamiliar touch and tossed her head, dancing to one side. Solly brought the animal under control. "Why don't you come up here with me, where you can see better?" he offered.

Katherine gave him a coy look. "I thought you'd never ask."

He maneuvered Pepper over to a mounting block and slipped his left foot from the stirrup so Katherine could swing up behind the saddle.

"Oh, this is much better," she said, putting her arms around him and settling her chin on his shoulder.

"How are you doing down there, Mrs. Trent?" Solly asked. "Should I try to find you a better perch?"

"I'm fine, thank you." She managed a smile for him. He had been a true friend these past days, even if she did suspect that his frequent visits had as much to do with his affection for Katherine as his loyalty to Michael.

"There's Dunleavy and his bunch." Katherine pointed past the rows of Dragoons to the end of the compound where the Rangers waited. Ellen felt a pain in her chest as she studied the Rangers' motley uniforms of buckskin and fur. As if to emphasize their independence from the regular Army, the Texans had not bothered to shave or change their usual dress. Only their weapons were polished, testimony to their readiness to fight.

"The captain don't look so bad now," Katherine said. "You can't hardly tell he had his face stove in."

Ellen nodded. Most of the bruising had faded from Dunleavy's face, so that he appeared more dirty than injured.

The band began to play "O Susannah!" as General Kearny's entourage turned in to the parade ground. Colonel Peabody and Major Sutton flanked the general, followed by his staff.

Kearny rode his horse past the infantry, nodding his head as he reached the ranks of the Dragoons. Ellen followed, easing her way through the crowd, keeping pace with the general's detail. Solly and Katherine rode beside her.

"Where are you going?" Katherine asked.

"I want to be where I can see the general's face when he gets to the Rangers," she said.

They reached the Texans just behind the general. Kearny frowned at the motley group and seemed about to address them when a commotion to his right drew everyone's attention.

A trio of soldiers marched onto the parade ground, the cadence of their boot heels striking the packed earth echoing across the suddenly silent compound. As they drew closer, Ellen recognized Private Bear Roberts in the front, with Corporal Sam Clark at the rear. Between them, head and shoulders taller, marched Lieutenant Michael Trent. The sun struck him with blinding brilliance, as if he were clad in armor. As the three came to a halt before the general and snapped salutes, Solly began to laugh. "So this is what he had in mind," he murmured.

The general and his group stared at the strange sight before them. Michael held the salute, his back ramrod straight, shako perfectly erect on his head. His uniform showed not a speck of dirt, every crease sharp, empty sword belt pipe-clayed to a brilliant white, boots gleaming like obsidian mirrors.

But it was his shackles that dazzled. Somehow he had

sanded every speck of rust from the old cannonball, and every link of the ten-foot chain shone like silver. He had festooned the chain around him like garland and wore the ball like an oversized medal, resting on his chest.

"I'd never have thought anyone could polish up a ball and chain like that," Katherine said.

"Michael's found the way to the general's heart," Solly said softly. "Word is Kearny admires guts and daring more than anything—and he despises a coward."

"Who are you, and what is the meaning of this?" Kearny demanded.

"First Lieutenant Michael Trent, prisoner, reporting for inspection, sir." Michael barked out the words in clipped, clear tones, the way an officer would give orders.

Kearny frowned at Michael, then turned to Colonel Peabody to his left. "What is this man charged with?"

Ellen held her breath, listening, but could not hear Peabody's mumbled words. When the colonel had finished speaking, Kearny turned his gaze on the group of Rangers. Captain Gregory Dunleavy sat astride a spotted Texas pony in the front row. From across the parade ground, Ellen could feel the heat of the angered look he directed at Michael.

"What do you have to say for yourself, Lieutenant?" Kearny asked.

"Not guilty, sir!" Michael glanced toward Dunleavy. "The captain and I had a personal misunderstanding, which regretfully led to blows. But I never intended to kill him."

"What makes you think I should believe that?" Kearny asked.

Michael threw back his shoulders, the freshly pressed uniform and sparkling chain only emphasizing his six feet, two inches of well-muscled manhood, the pride of the United States Army. "I'm a Dragoon, sir. If I'd intended to kill Captain Dunleavy, I certainly could have done so."

Kearny coughed and covered his mouth with his hand. Ellen thought he might be trying not to laugh. She looked again at Dunleavy, who had his reins wrapped around his hands as if he wished he could throttle Michael with them.

The general turned to Peabody again. "How long has this man been in shackles?"

After a brief consultation, Major Sutton answered. "A week, General, sir."

"A week confined in chains seems fitting punishment for fighting," he said, glancing at Dunleavy. He waved his hand at Michael. "Release this soldier and put him back where he belongs, leading men."

The general turned his horse and was riding away as Corporal Clark and Private Roberts led Michael toward the post blacksmith.

Ellen picked up her skirts and ran to meet them, happiness giving wings to her feet.

Michael's heart raced as if he'd run five miles in the Mexican sun, and it was all he could do to hold back a shout as Roberts and Clark escorted him to the horse shed that served as the post blacksmith's shop.

"You did it!" Roberts said, pounding him on the shoulder. "Did you see the look on Dunleavy's face when Kearny ordered you turned loose? He could have spit nails."

The hate-filled glare Dunleavy had directed at him was burned into Michael's memory. "This isn't the end of it between me and Dunleavy, by no count," he said as they entered the steamy darkness of the shed. He handed the gleaming ball over to the man behind the anvil. "Cut her off, and good riddance."

The smithy glanced at Clark, who nodded. "By orders of General Kearny."

Michael sank down onto a stone bench, and the smithy went to fetch a file for the leg iron. "You ought to keep that for a souvenir," Roberts said, nodding to the shiny chain.

"You're welcome to it. I don't ever want to see it again."

"Michael."

He caught his breath at the sound of his name, spoken in those feminine, lilting tones. When he looked over, he saw Ellen framed in the doorway of the shed, a shapely silhouette against the brightness of the day. She seemed frozen in place, as if reluctant to approach, and pain gripped him. Now that he was free again, was she ashamed to be associated with a man who had all but been branded a criminal?

Roberts glanced at Ellen and began backing away. "I know you two want to be alone," he said. "I won't hang around and spoil the reunion." He grinned at them, then left, whistling the tune to "Camptown Races."

Neither of them spoke while the blacksmith filed and sawed at the leg iron. Michael kept his head down, angled toward the smithy, but he studied Ellen out of the corner of his eye.

He could never get enough of looking at her. Sunlight filtered through gaps in the boards of the shed, streaking her hair and her red dress with shafts of gold. The dress fit her perfectly, accenting her swelling breasts, small waist, and full hips.

When he'd put on the new uniform this morning, he'd been conscious of the fact that Ellen's own hands had tailored the fabric for him from the measurements Solly had supplied. The thought had aroused him as if *she* had touched him, instead of mere layers of blue wool.

He wrenched his gaze away from her, fighting a desire that overwhelmed him like a physical force. He closed his eyes, stifling a groan. He'd done it now. In his twisted logic, he'd somehow reasoned that making love to Ellen would make it easier to let her go when the time came. This past week apart from her had proved how wrong he'd been to make that assumption.

"Are you all right?"

Her voice was soft in his ear, her hand gentle on his arm. He opened his eyes and saw that she was bending over him, her face tender with an expression of concern.

The blacksmith was gone, and they were alone in the shed.

Ellen drew back. "Are you all right?" she repeated.

He tentatively moved his leg. It felt too light, liberated from its burden of iron and steel. When he looked at Ellen again, he forced a smile. "Better than all right."

His smile died away as he met her eyes once more. His body was free, but his heart was shackled with the knowledge that she could never truly be his. He turned away, trying to regain control of his emotions, and his eyes came to rest on the discarded ball.

"I couldn't believe it when I saw you," she said. She sat beside him on the bench, filling the air around him with her scent. "How did you ever polish it up like that?"

"I didn't have anything better to do," he said, somehow finding his voice. "It helped to pass the time."

She began to cry. Her quiet sobs shook him, and he could not keep from reaching for her then, drawing her to him. "What is it? What's wrong?" he murmured.

"I was so worried. I was afraid they'd never let you go. Afraid they'd kill you."

"Shhh. Shhh. It's all right." He kissed the top of her head, his fingers trembling as he stroked the silken locks. How could it matter so much to her whether he lived or died? "It's all right now," he repeated. "It's all over with."

He was conscious of her breasts pressed against his chest, of her back, warm and slight beneath his fingers. He longed to kiss her, to feel those velvet lips against his own, but he knew he wouldn't stop with one kiss, couldn't stop until he possessed her fully.

With all the will he could muster, he gently pushed her away, praying she wouldn't notice his distress. She brushed aside her tears and smiled at him. "You must think I'm pretty silly." She stood and brushed her skirts. "I know you must be anxious to get back home. I'll cook a good supper—"

"Isn't Katherine staying at the tent with you?" he asked. "I could find somewhere else—"

Her smile vanished, replaced by a look of confusion. "Why would you want to do that? Katherine was only staying with me until you returned."

He didn't know whether to be glad or upset with this news. He couldn't wait to be alone with Ellen, to love her again as she deserved to be loved, and yet a warning in the back of his mind echoed: why prolong his misery? Why not make a clean break now?

They found Solly outside the tent, standing with Pepper and watching the door.

"Hail the conquering hero!" the doctor exclaimed at Michael's approach. "You've guaranteed your place in legend, Lieutenant. They'll be telling this story around the campfire for years to come."

"Thanks for all your help." He clapped the doctor on the arm and glanced toward the tent. "Waiting for someone?"

Solly cleared his throat. "Yes, well, I offered to carry Katherine and her things back to her campsite."

Michael managed to hide his amusement at this news. He had a hard time picturing the dignified doctor and "Katherine the Great" together, but stranger things had happened. . . .

"She said she wasn't feeling well, so I thought, as camp doctor, I ought to see her back to camp and, um, check her over." Michael had a feeling the sudden rush of color to Solly's face had little to do with the afternoon heat.

"That was very thoughtful of you." Ellen seemed innocent of any ulterior motive on the part of the doctor, but then, she had probably never had a sly thought in her life. "I'll go in and help her finish packing," she said.

Michael watched her leave, lightheaded with a mixture of anticipation and apprehension. Soon they'd be alone. Before he sat down or ate, before he took off his hat even, he was going to kiss her. They'd kiss until they were both breathless and dizzy, and then he'd carry her to the bed . . .

"You shouldn't let your thoughts show so clearly on your face, Lieutenant." Solly grinned at him.

He'd all but forgotten the doctor was there. "I might say the same for you." He glanced toward the tent. "Do you think Bear Roberts is sharp enough to feel which way the wind is blowing with you and his wife?"

Solly's expression grew blank. "I'm sure I don't know what you're talking about."

"You never were much of a poker player."

"Doctor, you'd better come in here." Ellen's head appeared around the tent flap, looking concerned.

"What is it?" Solly wrapped Pepper's reins around a tent stake and started toward her.

"It's Katherine. She's not feeling well at all."

The two men followed Ellen into the tent, where Katherine lay sprawled across the bed. Her eyes were closed, her skin the color of boiled potatoes.

"What's this, then?" Solly bent over her. "Did you eat something that didn't agree with you?"

She opened her eyes and stared glassily at him, but said nothing. Solly put a hand to her forehead. "My God, she's burning up. Hand me a blanket."

Ellen produced a green wool coverlet and helped Solly tuck it around Katherine, who'd begun to shake. "Fetch me my bag," Solly called over his shoulder. "On the horse."

Michael found the leather doctor's satchel tied behind the saddle and brought it to his friend. Then he retreated to the doorway of the tent, feeling useless. Ellen and Solly had all but forgotten him, all their attention focused on Katherine. He had to admit she didn't look good. How could such a strong woman be struck down so suddenly?

"What's wrong with her?" he asked.

Frowning, Solly put a hand to her throat. He lifted her eyelids to check her pupils, then withdrew a stethoscope from his bag and listened to her heart.

"What is it?" Ellen leaned close. "Will she be all right?"

"Malaria." He pulled his bag toward him and began digging through it. "She contracted it when we were in Florida. That's how we met, actually, when they brought her in in very much this condition." He withdrew a wooden medicine case from his bag and began sorting through the bottles nestled in the felt-lined holder. "Now she's let herself get run down and she's had a relapse."

Ellen sat on the side of the bed, holding Katherine's hand, a look of great tenderness on her face. Michael felt his heart contract. How was it that a woman born to such wealth and privilege had such an abundance of compassion for those around her, including him? And how had he been so lucky as to be able to be touched by her caring ways?

"Can you do anything for her?" she asked, turning to watch Solly.

The doctor lifted a bottle to read the label, then replaced it. "Thank God, I can. As soon as I find my quinine, she'll be on her way to recovery." He lifted bottle after bottle, mumbling to himself. "Belladonna, calomel, castor oil, digitalis, ipecac. Dammit, where's my quinine?"

He picked up the case and carried it to the door, where the light was better. "Maybe this will teach her to take care of herself for a change, instead of wearing herself out looking after everyone else. Paregoric, *nux vomica*, tartar emetic . . ." Michael came to stand beside his friend as he pulled a last bottle from its wooden cradle. They heard the scrape of broken glass and smelled the bitter odor of the medicine that had spilled from the shattered vial. Solly's face sagged in despair.

"Do you have any more?" Michael asked.

Solly glanced back at the woman on the bed. Katherine's dark hair was soaked with sweat, her normally animated face shadowed with pain. "No."

"There must be something else you can give her." Ellen rose and came to stand with them.

"Nothing as good." He replaced the medicine case in the satchel. "I'll have to find more. Maybe in town—"

"I'll go." Michael clapped him on the shoulder. "I'll go straight to the local doctors. One of them is bound to have some." Without waiting for an answer, he left the tent, anxious to be active, to be *doing* something. He'd had enough of sitting in the last week. And even riding around Santa Fe in search of quinine was preferable to sitting in the tent with Ellen when there was no chance for them to be alone.

Chapter Sixteen

"Michael will find what you need." Ellen put a comforting hand on the doctor's shoulder. He looked so much older now than he had even a moment before. The dashing, flirtatious gentleman she'd seen on the parade ground had been replaced by a worried old man. "He won't give up until he does."

Solly nodded and turned once more to Katherine. She moaned and tossed her head on the pillow, her hair a tangle around her face. He sank down onto the bed beside her. "The first time I saw her, she was nothing but a skinny girl in buckskin. When they brought her into the hospital, I couldn't believe they'd let a little thing like that into the Army."

"She strikes me as someone who's always been tough," Ellen said.

He pushed the hair back off her forehead. "Even though she was half crazy with fever, I knew she was something special back then."

Ellen came to stand beside him. "She is special, isn't she?"

"Part snapping turtle, part pet kitten," he said. "Sick as she was then, she hung on to life for all it was worth, and when she began to get well, I could see she was one to squeeze everything she could from the moment. Yet she wouldn't so much as step on a fly if she could help it." He glanced at Ellen. "I was old for my age even back then. Grown cynical from years of watching men shoot at each other, expecting me to patch them back together. She made me think maybe life didn't have to be like that."

"You love her very much, don't you?"

He sighed. "There was a time I'd have been too proud to admit it." He shook his head. "It doesn't matter. Katherine the Great wants nothing of it. Why should she? She could have any of these young bucks she set her cap for. Why should she waste her time with an old graybeard like me?"

Ellen put her hand on his shoulder. He made it sound as if his life was over, but she couldn't believe that was true. "I think she does care for you, so much that it scares her. I don't think anyone's ever loved Katherine the way you do, and she's not sure what to do about it."

He took Katherine's hand in his own. "I think we've ruined your plans for a reunion with the lieutenant."

"There'll be time for that later." The one thing she wanted most for herself and Michael was time. Time to learn to know each other as they should. Time to reveal the past and plan a future. That would come later. Now she must see to her friend. "I'll fetch some water," she said. "Maybe a sponge bath will help bring down her fever."

The doctor didn't seem to hear her, so intent was he on studying Katherine's face. "Ah, Katherine," he whispered, lowering his head to kiss her palm. "Whatever is going to become of us?"

The question echoed in Ellen's head as she left the tent in search of water. *Whatever is going to become of us?* She might ask the same question of her and Michael. Would there ever be a time when they could be sure of a future together?

Though Santa Fe had been a major trading center for many years, its distance from California to the West and the cities of the East made certain items in short supply. A man could find buffalo hides or cotton goods to fill a storehouse, but try to locate a bound volume of Shakespeare or a dentist's instrument, and he would remain empty-handed. Michael's search for quinine was met with shrugs and doubtful looks.

"We are so far here from the coast, where the need for malaria drugs is greatest," one man explained. "An occasional traveler comes to us in need, yes. And it happens I sold the last of my supply just this last week."

Michael leaned on the counter, martialing every nerve against the desire to sag with weariness. "When will you have more?"

Again the shrug. "Next week. Perhaps the next."

He thought of the ashen-faced woman lying on the bed in his tent. Katherine didn't look as if she'd last another week. "Is there anyplace else I can try?"

The shopkeeper eyed Michael's uniform skeptically. "The Army usually has these things when others do not."

With a groan, Michael shoved himself away from the counter and returned to his horse. The sun had set by the time he made his way back to the tent. The lamps were lit, and the scattered tents glowed like fireflies come to rest on the high desert. He sat for a moment just outside the circle of light, allowing himself to contemplate for the first time how close he had come to never seeing these lights again, to never feeling the warmth inside him that came from knowing someone waited for him within those canvas walls.

When he was a boy he'd never cried for sweets the way other children did. Candy was such a rarity in his life that he scarcely knew the taste. And then one day a girl on the street had given him a stick of horehound. The intense, sticky sweetness had flooded his senses, so that as soon as it was gone, he wanted more. The realization that there would be no more was worse than any beating. Worse than never having known that sweetness.

He could see now it would be that way with Ellen. He'd never thought to want someone like her, and now that he had her, he could only try to steel himself for the parting to come.

He swung down off Brimstone and led him to the stables, then went to take his sad news to those waiting. Ellen's face was full of hope when she greeted him. He shook his head in answer. "There isn't any quinine to be had in this whole damn town."

Solly wrung out the cloth he'd been using to bathe Katherine's fevered face and let it drop onto the table beside the basin. "I'm wondering if I should move her to the hospital ward and give you folks back your privacy."

Michael sank into a chair at the table. "Don't bother. The private at the stables told me the order's come down for us to head out in the morning."

"Head out?" Ellen looked done in, her face gray with weariness.

"We're off to California." The very mention of the place sent a pain to his heart. He'd hoped for days, weeks even, here in Santa Fe for a honeymoon of sorts with Ellen. Now they were to be denied even that.

"But we can't leave." She twisted her hands together and looked at Katherine. "Surely it isn't safe to move her."

"One ill washerwoman isn't going to change the Army's plans." Solly rubbed the back of his neck and stifled a yawn. "We'll put her in my wagon where I can keep an eye on her. I'll see that she travels as comfortably as possible."

"What about the quinine?" Michael asked.

Solly looked grim. "I'll find some somewhere."

Michael shook his head. "I've looked. There's none to be had."

"Somebody had some. Somebody is hoarding it. Otherwise, you'd have found some somewhere."

Michael rubbed his eyes. It was late, and he felt dead on his feet. "I'm not following you."

Solly jerked out a chair and sat across from Michael. "A war's about to break out, in case you haven't noticed. My guess is that's why we're in such a sudden hurry to get to California."

Michael frowned. "Word is President Polk has already ordered General Taylor to occupy South Texas. General Taylor's making noises like he's prepared to do battle, and Paredes doesn't like it. What does that have to do with quinine?"

"War brings shortages, and the man with the most supplies stands to make the most money. Medicine can be particularly valuable." He leaned toward Michael. "There are plenty of people here with sympathies for Mexico. They're the ones we want to find."

"How will you find them?" Ellen asked. "You don't have much time."

Solly shoved back his chair and stood. "We have an expression in this country, my dear. They say 'money talks.' I'm about to put my money to talking, and see what sort of response I get."

He picked up the jacket he'd discarded at the end of the bed and put it on. "If I'm not back by morning, see to it that Katherine's made as comfortable as possible. I'll catch up with you as soon as I can."

"I'll go with you." Michael stood and reached for his sword belt.

"Stay and rest, Lieutenant," Solly said.

Michael shook his head. "You helped me when I needed it, and now I'll help you. The two of us can cover more ground than either of us alone." He turned to Ellen. "Will you be all right here by yourself?"

She nodded, her face pinched with anxiety. "Be careful."

"I will." He kissed her cheek, then turned away before he was unable to leave at all.

Michael and Solly rode back into town in silence. When they turned onto the main thoroughfare, Michael turned to the doctor. "Where should we go?"

Solly bent and retrieved a pistol from his saddlebag and shoved it beneath his coat. "I suggest we head to the seediest tavern we can find. That's the sort of place the men we want will be."

The streets they turned down were narrow and dimly lit, little better than alleyways, the shabby buildings on either side leaning toward each other like drunkards on the verge of collapse. Michael and Solly chose the worst of these places, a narrow adobe structure lacking even a door. But the inside was packed with men who bristled with an assortment of weapons and eyed each other with suspicion.

The arrival of the well-dressed doctor and the Army lieutenant was met with sullen silence. They made their way to the plank that had been placed across two barrels to serve as a bar, and Solly slapped a gold piece onto the wood. "A bottle of whiskey and some information."

The barkeep, a hulking, bearded man with a scar across his left cheek, set a dusty bottle before them and pocketed the coin. "Whatever you want, I ain't talking," he said.

Solly placed another gold piece before him. "If we wanted to buy something, something in short supply, who would we talk to?"

The bartender's gaze flickered to the gold. "What kind of something?"

"Something the guerrillas might find useful," Michael said.

The bartender palmed the coin and dropped it into his pocket, then grinned. "Why don't you try the Army? That's where I hear the guerrillas get most of their supplies."

Michael curled his hand around the hilt of his sword. He was worn out, nerves stretched taut. He had no patience left for those who would mock him. Solly put out a restraining hand. "Come on." He nodded toward the door. "Let's try somewhere else."

They had scarcely cleared the doorway into the street before a dark shape materialized beside them. "You are looking for information, gentlemen?" A pair of dark eyes stared out from the depths of a gray wool cloak.

"Maybe." Solly pulled back his coat to reveal the pistol

tucked in the waistband of his trousers. "But I'm only paying if the information's useful to us."

The cloaked man nodded. "I believe you will find the one who can help you secure whatever you need at José Ramos's Saloon." He stretched out a grimy palm and quickly folded his fingers around the gold coin Solly placed there.

Before the hand could retreat, Michael grabbed the wrist. "Who exactly are we looking for?" he asked. "What's his name?"

"They call him the Texan. You will know him when you see him."

Michael released the man, and he glided away, melting into the shadows as if he had never existed.

They found José Ramos's two streets over. It was a larger, brighter establishment than those they had visited previously, though the patrons entering and exiting its open door were just as well armed and furtive. They dismounted, and Solly started forward, but Michael put out a hand to stop him.

"I think we'd better check this out first. We don't want to walk into an ambush."

"What do you suggest?" Solly asked.

Michael glanced around them. There were no windows in the saloon and only one door. A narrow passageway, barely wide enough for a man to pass, ran between the saloon and its neighbor. He nodded toward it. "Let's try in there. Maybe it will take us around back."

The passageway was littered with trash and reeked of stale urine and beer. Michael tried not to think of the spiders and other vermin that might be sharing the space with him and Solly just then. He breathed a sigh of relief when they emerged into an alley that ran behind the saloon.

Light shining from the window of a house across the way illuminated the rear of the saloon. Michael could barely make out the crude door cut in the wall of the building. He nudged Solly and pointed toward it, then the two of them crept to it.

A Husband by Law

The knob turned in his hand. Easing the door open enough to peer inside, he looked into inky darkness. "It must be a storeroom," he whispered. "Probably where they keep the liquor. There should be another door leading into the main room." He opened the door wider and slipped inside. Solly followed.

At first Michael could see nothing. He felt his way past crates and kegs, until he came to a wall opposite the door. Pressing his ear to the rough wood, he could hear muffled voices and the clink of glasses.

Solly tugged his elbow and pointed. Twin bars of light outlined a door in the wall just down from where they were standing. With infinite care, Michael grabbed the doorknob and eased the door back a scant inch.

He was looking out onto a table on which sat a large pile of coins, a half-empty whiskey bottle, and two smudged glasses. A pair of large hands thrust into view and poured a drink from the bottle. Michael eased the door open farther. The picture expanded to include burly arms and a barrel chest clad in stained buckskin. The man leaned back in the chair, his head against the wall, but there was something terribly familiar about him.

Heart hammering, Michael opened the door still farther and stared at the battered face of Captain Dunleavy. Behind him, he heard Solly's stifled gasp.

"We'd better get out of here," Solly rasped in his ear.

Michael shook his head. "Not yet."

What was Dunleavy doing in this reputed gathering place for guerillas? Was *he* the Texan their informant had referred to?

Just then, two men approached Dunleavy's table. They had dark skin and black hair, and the smaller of the two wore crossed bandoliers, as if ready to do battle at a moment's notice. They did not sit with Dunleavy, but spoke urgently to him in Spanish. After a moment the man with the bandoliers pulled out a leather pouch and tossed it onto the table. It made a muffled metallic sound, like a quantity of coins rubbing together.

Dunleavy weighed the pouch in his hand, then grinned. He stuffed it into his shirt, then swept up the money on the table and dropped it into his trousers. Then he rose and made a motion for the men to follow him.

Michael and Solly hurried from the storeroom, back through the narrow passageway toward the front of the building. They arrived in time to see Dunleavy and the two men mount up and ride away.

Michael hurried to untie Brimstone.

"What are you doing?" Solly asked as he untied Pepper.

"I'm going after them." He swung up into the saddle and turned the horse in the direction Dunleavy and the others had ridden.

Solly joined him, and they followed, keeping close to buildings and relying on the darkness to hide them. But Dunleavy never even looked back. He rode a few streets over, to a shed under which was parked a wagon. The three dismounted, and Dunleavy lit a lantern. He gave it to the man with the bandoliers to hold, then pulled a tarp from the wagon to reveal a load of wooden crates. Prying open one of the crates, he removed a long rifle.

"Hall's carbines," Michael whispered. "Government issue, I'll wager."

The two men with Dunleavy selected a dozen of the weapons and rolled them into blankets, then lashed the bundles behind their saddles. Dunleavy replaced the top on the crate and pulled the tarp back over it. Then the three of them mounted up and rode off in different directions.

Solly waited until the sounds of their horses' hooves had faded into the night before he spoke. "Did we see what I think we just saw?"

Michael nodded. "Dunleavy is selling arms to the enemy." He wrapped the reins tightly around his hand. "I should go after him."

Solly's hand clamped around his wrist like a vise. "You and what army? You go after him now, alone, and you'll be dead before you've said one word."

"I thought you would go with me."

A Husband by Law

Solly shook his head. "I'm after medicine for Katherine, remember? I couldn't care less if the captain gives away the whole damn farm to the Mexicans." He nodded toward the direction in which the ranger had disappeared. "There's little enough we can do tonight. Better we keep an eye on Dunleavy and hang him with a noose of his own making when we have more proof of his activities."

Michael sat back in the saddle. Solly's words made sense, but it galled him to be so close to getting rid of his enemy for good, yet unable to act. "Seems we're back where we started," he said. "No quinine and no idea where to get it."

Solly was silent for a moment, his brow furrowed in thought. "I have an idea." He looked at Michael. "But first we've got to hide that damn uniform of yours." He began taking off his coat. "Put this on. And take off that hat."

Michael did as his friend asked, shoving the forage cap into his pocket. "What are you getting at?" he asked.

Solly sat back and studied him. "Better, though you've still got that McClelland saddle and that damn West Point posture that fairly screams 'soldier.' But stay back in the darkness and you ought to do all right."

"Just what do you intend to do?"

"You'll see. Just follow me and keep quiet."

Solly rode at a fast clip, Michael spurring Brimstone to keep up. It didn't take him long to realize they were following one of the guerrillas. They'd traveled several miles when they spotted a single rider in the road ahead.

Solly slowed Pepper to a walk. "Remember. Let me do the talking."

They approached the other man carefully. Michael had no doubt that he was already aware of their presence. His body had a certain tension about it, like a man who is holding a loaded gun and quite prepared to use it.

"*Hola!*" When they were still some distance behind the man, Solly hailed him in Spanish. "*Amigo*, may we talk with you a moment?" He held his arms wide, showing he had no weapon.

The guerrilla turned toward them, the pistol he held glinting in the moonlight. "What do you want?" he asked in English.

"I am a doctor," Solly answered. "I am in search of a certain medicine and wonder if you have what I need among your supplies."

Michael could not read the man's face beneath the shadowing brim of his hat, but his voice held an unmistakable note of suspicion. "What makes you think I have what you need?"

"Men preparing for war must set aside many useful things." Solly moved closer. "I am willing to pay in gold for the medicine I seek."

Silence stretched between them like a tightrope. The horses stood motionless, the men on them like statues. In the distance an owl hooted, the only sound in the vast stillness. The guerrilla shifted in his saddle, the leather creaking. "I may know someone who can help you," he said. "But the price will be high."

"I'm willing to pay it." Solly took up his reins and walked his horse toward the Mexican. Michael followed, hunched into Solly's coat, wondering where this long night would lead them, and if he would ever see bed, and Ellen, again.

Ellen dozed in a chair beside Katherine's bed, waking throughout the night to swab her friend's wrists and forehead with cool compresses in an attempt to bring down the fever, which raged. Every sound outside her door brought her to her feet, but time and again it was only a night breeze rustling the tent flap, or a foot soldier tramping home from picket duty. How far would Michael and Solly have to go to find the quinine Katherine needed? When would they return?

By the time the sky lightened with the promise of sunrise, she felt as ragged and worn as an old piece of cloth, every nerve frayed. When soldiers arrived to load her belongings, she sent one of them to fetch Doc Solly's orderly and a wagon for Katherine. She settled her friend as comfortably as she could into this conveyance, wedging blankets and pillows along her sides to cushion the rough ride. Then, with Fly tied on behind, she and Bobby took their places crouched at the end of this pallet, and the company set off to the rousing strains of "Buffalo Gals."

Ellen pulled back the wagon covering as much as she dared to let in air and light. She studied Katherine in the daylight, alarmed by what she saw. The sick woman's skin looked almost golden now, a fearful sign. Solly had warned that yellow skin was a sign of jaundice. Jaundice meant the malaria had reached Katherine's liver, and if left unchecked, death would not be far behind.

She wrapped her arms around her legs and rested her forehead against her knees, trying to ignore the headache that pounded at her temples. Where were Solly and Michael? She glanced out the back of the wagon, at the line of wagons and horses behind her.

Surely the two men would be back soon. They'd been gone since late last night, and now it was almost noon. How far would they have to ride to get the quinine Katherine needed? And what would they do if they weren't able to find any?

She turned to look at her friend again. Katherine lay with her head back, cheekbones sharp in the shadowed light. Sweat beaded her upper lip and glistened on her forehead. At least she was sleeping now. The last bout of fever had made her delirious, muttering about a battle and men dying, and threatening to whip the man who'd insult the Army to her face. Ellen had feared she might have to tie her to the bed to keep her from hurting herself as she thrashed about. But eventually she'd quieted and drifted into a heavy sleep.

Bobby nudged her hand, and she reached down and scratched behind his ears. What was Michael doing now? Was he all right? She picked up the pair of trousers she'd been mending and adjusted the flaps at the back of the wagon to provide more light to work in. The pants belonged to Michael. They were the pair he'd been wearing in prison. She'd traded them for the new uniform she'd fashioned. Was that really only yesterday morning?

She picked up her needle and thread and began to sew. From what she'd seen around camp, Michael wasn't the only man in need of someone to mend his clothes. Maybe when they reached California she'd advertise to take in sewing.

Oh, to live in a real house again, after months in a canvas tent. And the luxury of sleeping on a real bed again, not a mattress stuffed with moss.

The thread snapped in her hands, and she stared down at her white-knuckled fingers, clutching the needle. One bed, she thought, not really seeing the mending. One bed in a house with Michael. She let out a ragged breath, work falling idle in her lap. Every thought and action came down to this: she wanted Michael, wanted him in whatever way, whatever place, for however long she was able to be with him. Her need for him vanquished her shame, gave lie to propriety. The admission frightened her, yet freed her.

She had thought to go to California to live with Uncle David because he was her mother's brother, and because she had fond memories of him playing with her when she was a child. But really, what was he but a stranger to her? How could she be better off with him than she was with Michael?

She loved Michael and she believed he was beginning to love her, but would that be enough? Was she enough?

"Whoa there, whoa." The orderly pulled the wagon to a halt, and she looked out the back of the wagon and saw Michael riding toward her. He was dusty and disheveled, his face lined with weariness, but he was smiling. Smiling at her.

"Everything all right?" He reined Brimstone to a stop behind the wagon and looked down at her.

"Yes." She glanced back at Katherine. "She's sleeping now, but I'm worried about her." She turned once more to

Michael. "What about you? You look as if you've had a hard night."

"It's been . . . interesting." He slapped the dust from his thigh. "But we got what we were after."

"Yes, we did." Solly climbed into the wagon from the front, as dusty and done-in as Michael, but clutching a small brown vial triumphantly. "Nurse Trent, I may need your assistance."

"I'll leave you to it." Michael gathered up the reins and turned Brimstone. "Until we meet again, madam." A mischievous smile banished weariness from his face. To her surprise and delight, he blew her a kiss. Then he whirled and galloped away, a dashing cavalier who had no doubt stolen her heart.

Chapter Seventeen

With a jerk the wagon started forward again. Ellen grabbed hold of the sideboard to keep from pitching forward onto Katherine. Solly handed her the vial and began shedding his coat.

"So this is the quinine," she said, studying the syrupy substance within the brown glass.

The wagon driver stuck his head under the canvas. "What do you want me to do with your horse, sir?"

"You could give him to the first sorry bastard you see afoot." He began rolling up his sleeves. "But once he rides the old bone-shaker, he won't thank you for the favor, so you'd best turn him over to the wrangler and see what he can do about feeding and watering him."

"Yes, sir."

Ellen didn't try to hide her confusion. "Him? Solly, what happened to Pepper?"

"I traded her." He leaned over the pallet and took Katherine's hand, feeling for her pulse.

"Solly, you loved that horse!" Tears sprang to her eyes as she thought of the doctor parted from an animal that had been as much pet to him as transportation.

"It was time I had a new one. The trip down here used her up." He glanced around the rocking wagon. "I don't suppose you have any coffee."

"The orderly brought me some in a jug this morning." She searched among the blankets until she found the crockery vessel. "I'm afraid it's cold now."

"Never mind. Pour some in a cup for me, will you?" He held out his hand. She hesitated, then poured him a cupful.

He knelt beside the pallet and pulled Katherine into his arms. "Katy, dear, time to wake up," he said. "Time to take your medicine." He shook her gently, and she blinked, opening her eyes to look up at him. "How do you feel?" he asked.

Katherine licked her dry lips. "Like I've been rode hard and put up wet."

He poured a measure of quinine into the cold coffee, then carefully capped the bottle. "Drink this, and it'll have you feeling better soon."

Katherine frowned at the mug, but he held it to her lips. "Drink it all."

She coughed at the first sip. "Hell, Solly, that's awful! What are you tryin' to do—poison me?"

"Quinine is bitter, but it's no better than you deserve for letting yourself get run down like this. Now come on, drink up."

He held the cup to her lips, and she drank it all. Katherine smiled as Solly eased her back down to the pillow. "Now, close your eyes and rest," the doctor said.

He slipped the vial into his shirt pocket and sank back against the side of the wagon. His shoulders sagged with weariness.

"Do you want me to stay?" Ellen asked.

He nodded. "Unless you've more pressing business to attend to."

She shook her head. "If I wasn't here with you, I'd be that much more worried about her."

"There's nothing to do now but wait. A few days on the quinine and she should recover."

Katherine stirred and covered her eyes with her hand. "Gosh, Solly, is this what it feels like to die?" she moaned.

"You're a long way from death, Katy dear."

"Don't call me that."

"Call you what?"

"Katy dear."

"Why not?"

She shook her head. "Just don't."

Ellen leaned forward and straightened the blankets around her friend. Was she imagining things, or was her color already improved? "Do you think you could take a bit of broth?" she asked. "To keep your strength up?"

Solly helped Katherine sit, and she allowed Ellen to feed her, opening her mouth like a bird whenever she brought the spoon near. When she had eaten it all, Ellen set aside the bowl and tucked the covers around her. "Try to sleep now," she said.

She glanced at Solly. "You, too. You look all in."

He glanced around the cramped wagon. "And where do you suggest I sleep, madam?"

"There's room for you to stretch out alongside Katherine." She rearranged the blankets to accommodate him. "No one's going to see you, and I'm here as chaperone."

He sighed and shook his head, but reclined beside his patient. Ellen was sure he was asleep almost immediately. She draped another blanket over him and took Bobby into her lap to wait.

"Solly?" Katherine's voice, though weak, rang clear in the stillness.

"Wh . . . what?" His eyes snapped open, and he struggled to sit.

Ellen rushed forward. "Do you need something?"

Katherine shook her head and gave the doctor a fond look. "I just wanted to thank Solly for takin' such good care of me."

"Quite all right. Now go back to sleep." He rolled over onto his side and cradled his head on his arm.

"I'm not sleepy at all. Isn't that odd? I mean, everybody else in this whole camp is probably asleep or tryin' to keep from noddin' off, and me, I'm wide awake."

He groaned. "That's just a side effect of the quinine. Close your eyes and count sheep."

"Why is it always sheep people count? I always thought that was silly. Why should sheep make a person sleepy?"

Solly sat up. Amusement and annoyance battled to gain the upper ground in his expression. "I don't care if you count elephants, Katy dear. Just please be quiet and let me sleep."

Ellen had to cover her mouth with her hand to keep from laughing out loud. Solly eased into his blankets once more.

"Solly, I asked you not to call me that."

He sighed and rolled over onto his back. "Call you what?"

"Katy dear. I asked you not to call me that, and just now you did it again."

He opened his eyes and stared at the canvas overhead. "And why don't you want me to call you that?"

"It makes me feel . . . all funny inside."

"That's probably just the quinine, too. Now, please, I've just ridden half the night and I'm sore and tired and—"

"I thought you swore Pepper never left you sore."

"I wasn't riding Pepper."

"But you never ride any horse but Pepper. You always swore your horse—"

"She's not my horse anymore. Now, dammit, be quiet and go to sleep."

"Not until you tell me what happened to Pepper."

Ellen held her breath, waiting for the answer. He closed his eyes again. "I traded her."

Katherine shoved up on her elbows and stared at him. "What could be worth trading that horse for? You ought to have your head examined."

He closed his eyes. "Yes, I ought to."

"What did you trade her for?" she demanded.

He sat and pulled the vial of quinine from his shirt pocket. "I traded her for this."

She stared at him, gradually sinking down in the blankets again. "You traded your horse for medicine for me?" she whispered.

"Yes." He slipped the bottle back into his pocket, his expression unreadable.

"I can't believe you'd do that," Katherine said softly. She put her hand to one eye, as if wiping away a tear. "I owe you one, Solly."

"Yes, you do."

She swallowed and turned her head to look at him. "You name it. I'll do your laundry for a year. I'll roll miles of bandages—"

He sat and took her hand in his. "No, I don't think that would be nearly enough." He gave Ellen a knowing smile, as if they shared a secret, then looked back at his patient.

Ellen thought perhaps she should leave, but where would she go? Solly had smiled, as if he didn't mind having her here, but she couldn't shake the feeling she was intruding on some private moment. She held Bobby and tried to be as quiet and still as possible.

Katherine grew still also, her eyes wide. "What do you want, then?" she whispered.

"Marry me, Katy dear. Marry me, or I'll never let you out of this bed again."

She swallowed and licked her lips. "I can't think about anything when you call me that," she said.

"Don't think, then. Listen to your heart." He leaned close, eyes searching her face. "Could you care for me at all, Katherine? I know I'm older than you and I've never worn a uniform—"

"Shhhh. Of course I care for you." She slid her arms around his neck. "I love you so much it scares me. What does a respectable gentleman like you see in a wild woman like me?"

He kissed the tip of her nose. "Everything. I see everything I've ever wanted. But you still haven't answered me."

"Yes. Yes, I'll marry you."

He kissed her mouth then, and Ellen looked away, her

heart beating wildly in her chest, tears stinging her eyes. What she wouldn't give to hear Michael say those words, and mean them.

"Wait, save your strength." Solly broke the kiss and gently pushed Katherine away. "We'll have the rest of our lives for that."

"But think of all the time we've already wasted." Ill as she was, Katherine still managed a suggestive smile.

Solly tucked the covers around her once more. "Don't fret over the past. Just concentrate on getting well, so we can enjoy our future together."

He lay down once more and gathered the blankets around him. Ellen settled back in her corner to ponder what had just happened. At least these two had found their happiness. If they could work things out between them, then perhaps there was hope for her and Michael.

"Solly?" Katherine spoke again.

"For God's sake, woman, what is it?"

"You've got it wrong. You shouldn't have said you wouldn't let me up until I agreed to marry you. After the wedding I'm the one who won't let *you* out of bed."

He coughed. "Go to sleep, Katy dear."

"Yes, Solly *dear.*"

The line of troops snaked across the southern desert in a cloud of dust, covering twenty or more miles a day in their haste to reach California. Around the fires at night rumors of war fluttered like moths: the armistice with Mexico was at an end; President Polk himself had said there would be a fight; they were hurrying off to California to protect American interests there; they were preparing to make a flanking movement into Mexico.

Michael listened to the speculation, hearing the thread of truth in every tale. The guerrillas he and Solly had seen had been preparing for war, no doubt. While other men were eager for battle, he wanted nothing of it. After years of soldiering, he was weary of the wandering life. Maybe it was time he settled down, though there was only one woman he had any desire to settle with.

Seeing Solly and Katherine together was only more fuel for his fantasies of married bliss. If those two could be happy together, why not Michael and Ellen?

To the surprise of most, though not perhaps to Michael, Bear Roberts had relinquished his "bride" without a fuss. If anything, Bear appeared relieved to return to life as a bachelor soldier, spreading his bedroll with the other single men and staying up all hours playing cards.

Captain Dunleavy was often at these games, with plenty of cash and mocking banter. "There'll be no war," he declared as he raked in yet another pot of winnings. "No more than a skirmish, if that. We'll defeat them soundly before they have time to raise their bayonets."

Bayonets you supplied them, Michael thought, turning away. The memory of the Ranger selling Army guns to the guerrillas kept him awake nights, wondering what to do. More than once he'd started toward Peabody's tent, determined to divulge all he knew, but the flimsiness of his evidence held him back. He played out the scene in his head: he told the colonel what he had seen and offered up Solly as a witness. Dunleavy was summoned to answer these grave charges. First in anger, then with much wounded dignity, he would deny them and produce half a dozen fellow Texans to swear he had been in their company that night. He would remind the colonel how close he'd come to death at Michael's hands, and declare that the lieutenant, by making these wild accusations, was merely trying to finish what he'd started.

He looked back at the Ranger captain, who sat with his winnings before the fire. As if sensing he was being watched, Dunleavy turned and looked Michael in the eye. His eyes narrowed, and his voice took on a mocking tone. "If it isn't Sir Trent! Where is your shining armor, Lieutenant?"

His fellow cardplayers laughed. Michael straightened

and made a formal bow. "I've no need of armor this evening."

"Oh, no?" Dunleavy raised one eyebrow and gave his friends a knowing look. "Then whatever shall you hide behind?"

Michael clenched his jaw, refusing to give in to the goad. "Ah, you would know all about hiding, wouldn't you, Captain?" he said calmly. "I would go so far as to say you have a natural talent for subterfuge."

He turned before Dunleavy could answer, that in itself an insult, but he did not trust himself to stand before the man much longer and control his anger. Sooner or later he would have to confront Dunleavy, but he could afford to wait until the timing was right.

The desolate country west of Santa Fe was the most dangerous part of their journey. In the past, bands of Indians had attacked the occasional trader who passed this way, and the troops were instructed to be prepared for battle at any time. A more pressing concern was the rumor of border guerrillas, who had begun raiding in the area. Colonel Peabody ordered the picket guard doubled, and the women moved to the center of the column, with troops protecting them front and rear.

This constant state of readiness, coupled with the heat and dryness, put everyone on edge. Solly reported patching up more than his usual ration of brawlers, including two of the laundresses, who stabbed each other in an argument over ownership of a cooking pot.

More than once the strains of "Boot and Saddle," the traditional call to arms, sounded over the encampment, only to have the enemy revealed as another herd of wild horses or a distant dust devil. When the call went out again one evening, just as they had set up camp, Michael raced for his horse with his usual alacrity, but without any feeling of alarm. He had seen nothing threatening in this vast, desolate country.

This time, however, the alarm was not false. Shouts

rang out in the area where the supply wagons were parked, and gunfire echoed around him. Michael spurred Brimstone toward the melee, and arrived in time to see half a dozen armed Mexicans fleeing with one of the supply wagons. They had taken the camp by surprise and were already some distance away. Soldiers continued to fire after them, but their bullets fell short.

"Trent! Evans! Stewart!" Peabody shouted above the din. "Go with Dunleavy and his men after them."

Michael spied Dunleavy and the Rangers heading out after the guerrillas and spurred Brimstone to overtake them. Dunleavy looked back and scowled at him. "What do you think you're doing, Lieutenant?"

"Colonel Peabody's orders, Captain." He met Dunleavy's disdainful look with one of his own.

"As if the Texas Rangers needed help from the regular Army. Particularly the likes of you." He spat on the ground. "Stay to the rear and out of my way."

Michael said nothing but fell back. When time came for action, he'd take his place at the front, with or without Dunleavy's approval.

Though the guerrillas had gotten a head start, the wagon could not travel as quickly over rough ground as men on horseback. The soldiers began to overtake them, and Michael saw one man fall from his horse, hit by a bullet from a Texan's long rifle.

The guerrillas then changed tactics. They made a sharp turn into a gully, tipping the wagon onto its side, crates spilling onto the ground and breaking open to reveal stacks of rifles, pistols, and ammunition. Grabbing up armloads of these weapons, the guerrillas took refuge in the sheltered ravine and prepared to dig in.

Dunleavy ordered his men to a halt, just out of firing range. "They've got enough firepower there to last for days," he said sourly.

"There's twice as many of us," Michael said. "We can create a diversion, then launch a flanking attack."

"When I want your opinion, Lieutenant, I'll ask for it."

Dunleavy glared at him, then glanced back toward the guerrillas. The occasional glint of sunlight off the barrel of a rifle was the only clue to their position. "One point in our favor is that they are shooting unfamiliar weapons," he said. "Their usual *escopetas* are nothing like those new carbines. They will likely be less accurate."

"We don't know that," Michael said. "They could have acquired Hall's carbines before, in other raids—"

"Enough!" Dunleavy shoved his pistol into Michael's chest, the hammer pulled back. His nostrils flared with anger, and his voice was a low growl. "One more word from you, and the Mexicans won't be the only ones shot today."

Michael said nothing, but his expression told Dunleavy just how little regard he had for his threats.

The Scotsman withdrew his gun and gave Michael a considering look. "You think you're so brave, don't you? A regular hero. But I know you. Down inside, you're the worst sort of coward."

Michael had to bite his tongue to keep from replying. Dunleavy holstered his pistol. "All right, Lieutenant, you want to be brave? I want you to lead a direct charge on the guerrillas while Red and O'Neal take a few men and circle around back."

Michael swallowed hard. Depending on the guerrillas' marksmanship, a direct charge was tantamount to suicide, but he'd rather die by fire than disobey a direct order on the battlefield. "Yes, sir," he said, and turned Brimstone toward the guerrillas' redoubt.

Corporals Evans and Stewart lined up with him, as well as three of the Rangers. They loaded and readied their weapons. The smell of gun oil, powder, and sweat hung thick in the hot, heavy air. Michael's mouth felt dry as cotton, and his pulse hammered at his temples. He took a deep breath and raised his rifle over his head. Dropping his arm again, he shouted, "Charge!" and dug his spurs into Brimstone's side.

He saw the flash of the Mexicans' fire before he heard

the report. The shots of his own men crackled around him, and smoke stung his eyes. He saw Evans fall and heard a horse scream as it was shot. His thighs gripped the saddle so hard they ached, and he leaned low across his horse's neck, aiming and firing, loading, aiming and firing.

Though he had lost two men, the others kept coming, and some of their shots met with success. As they raced nearer to the guerrillas, he saw more than one of them slumped in the dirt. Then the Mexicans cried out in alarm and whirled to see a second line of soldiers hurtling toward them. Michael cheered when he saw the Rangers attacking from the rear.

He thought they had won then, and the thrill of victory surged through him. Every sense seemed sharper, every nerve alert with the realization that he had faced down death and lived to tell the tale. He gave the command for his men to surge forward, to join the others in defeating their enemy.

When the bullet slammed into him, the impact threw him forward across the high pommel of his saddle. He lay there, blinking, feeling a fiery pain radiating out from his shoulder. All sound receded, except his own labored breathing, and gray fog filled his vision. He'd been shot. His mind refused to accept the reality, even as he felt the warm stickiness of blood spilling down his back. This wasn't supposed to happen. They had won. How could he have been shot?

Chapter Eighteen

Michael awoke facedown in a wagon, the smell of camphor stinging his nostrils. He groaned, and a hand steadied him. "Hold still there, soldier," Solly's voice was firm and reassuring. "Not the best timing in the world, I tell you. I was about to sew you back together before you woke."

"My shoulder hurts like the devil," Michael managed to say.

"I shouldn't wonder." Solly dabbed some stinging solution on the wound. Michael flinched. "That bullet took quite a chunk out of your shoulder. If it had hit you straight on, you'd likely not have an arm left."

"How bad is it?" He braced himself for the worst.

"Quite painful, I'm sure, but not life threatening. In fact, if you lie still and allow me to do my job, I can almost guarantee you'll regain full use of your arm."

"How could I have been shot in the back?" The question had been forming in his mind ever since he'd felt the bullet's impact.

"Hmmm. That's what Dunleavy's been asking."

"Dunleavy!" Michael tried to rise up on his elbows, but the doctor and a burly orderly held him down.

"Lie still." Solly selected a length of silk from a tray of

instruments. "He's putting it about that you turned tail and ran. That you're a coward."

Again they had to restrain Michael. "A coward! I led that charge! By his orders! How dare he!"

Fury clouded his vision and dulled his other senses to the point that he scarcely felt Solly's needle suturing the wound.

"There, that should do it." Solly punctuated these words by dropping his needle into a basin. "That's all, Orderly. You can leave us now."

When the orderly had left the wagon, Solly came to stand by Michael's head. Michael stared at the doctor's shoes; it looked as if it had been some time since they'd seen polish.

"I've seen wounds like this before," Solly said. "Made with a large-bore revolver. Say a fifty-four caliber. Not one of the Mexican carbines."

"The guerrillas stole a wagon full of guns and ammunition. They were shooting at us with our own supplies." His head felt fuzzy with pain. It was difficult to think, much less hold a conversation.

"Hmmm." Solly knelt until he was eye-level with Michael. "The Rangers use fifty-four-caliber caplocks, don't they?"

The memory of Dunleavy's gun, pressed against his chest, filled Michael's mind, and cold shock washed over him. "Dunleavy could have sent me forward, then shot me in the back," he said.

"You can't prove anything." Solly straightened.

Michael closed his eyes. "Maybe not. But it's one more thing against him."

"As if you needed anything else." Solly pulled a blanket up over Michael's back. "Try to get some rest now."

"May I come in?"

They looked back to see Ellen climbing the steps into the wagon. Michael forced a pleasant expression to his face. Ellen bent over him. Her face was pale, her eyes shadowed, as if she'd spent a sleepless night.

"Oh, Michael, are you all right?"

"I'm fine. Solly's going to have me good as new in no time."

"He'll be on his feet by tomorrow and back to full duty in a week or so." Solly patted Ellen's shoulder. "I told you not to worry."

"Of course I worried." She knelt beside the bed and took his hand. "I saw you when they brought you in. You were white as a ghost, blood all over your uniform . . ." Her voice broke, and she looked away.

Her concern touched him. He cursed Dunleavy for causing her such pain. "I really am all right," he said. Then the sickening realization hit him that she might have heard the rumors Dunleavy was spreading, that he was a coward who had run away from battle. "I understand Dunleavy has said some things about what happened—" he began.

"Horrible lies!" Her face flushed with anger. "You're the bravest man I know. You would never run away." She gripped his hand so hard his knuckles ached. "I'll tell him as much to his face if he dares come near me."

He smiled at the image of her giving the Ranger captain a proper dressing-down. "Don't say anything to him," he said. "He's not worth the effort." He closed his eyes, weariness overtaking him. "I'll deal with him myself. When the time comes."

He slipped off to sleep with Ellen holding his hand, her sweet perfume blotting out the smell of sickness and fear.

It seemed to Ellen that they would never stop traveling. The road to California was a dusty, indistinct scar across the desert, a journey through a purgatory of heat and thirst on the way to a reputed paradise. As the long days of travel wore on, the soldiers and their companions spoke of California's green fields and temperate breezes in terms often reserved for heaven. Even the threat of a coming war couldn't lessen the anticipation of reaching a place where there was plenty of shade, water, and rest.

Ellen knew she was likely the only person among them

who secretly dreaded reaching their destination. In California she and Michael had agreed to part. She knew once they arrived, Michael expected her to search for her uncle. And once her relative was located, Michael would be free of his obligation to her.

But she would never be free of him. He was branded on her heart forever. The thought of parting from him grieved her as much as the death of her mother ever had.

She searched for him now, in the ranks of dragoons up ahead. To her amazement, he had returned to duty only a few days after he'd been shot. He still looked pale to her, and she knew his shoulder pained him, but when she'd suggested he ride in a wagon instead, he'd declared he'd rather take his chances on horseback than be shook to pieces in a wagon.

At last she spotted his familiar figure. He stood out from the other men, with his long gold curls tied at the nape of his neck, and his broad shoulders and ramrod-straight carriage. Her heart swelled with pride as she watched him.

"So, Lieutenant, have you seen any guerrillas lately?" Captain Dunleavy's taunt rang loud in the afternoon stillness as he brought his horse up alongside Michael. Ellen sucked in a deep breath. More than once she'd heard the Scotsman's rude remarks about "the cowardly lieutenant," but this was the first time he'd had the nerve to speak to Michael's face.

Though some of the men around him laughed at Dunleavy's jest, Michael did not so much as turn to acknowledge the ranger. "Too bad that Mexican didn't have better aim," Dunleavy continued. "We'd have had one less coward to contend with."

This time Michael turned to look at his tormentor. He said nothing, just stared at Dunleavy for a long moment, his face like cold, carved stone. Ellen could not see the expression in his eyes, but she imagined Michael was daring Dunleavy to tell the truth, to admit that "the cowardly lieutenant" was braver than the mighty Texas Ranger would ever be.

After a long moment the Scotsman whirled his horse and galloped away. As he flew past Ellen, his face contorted with rage, she shrank from the hatred that shone in his eyes.

"What are you looking so down in the mouth about?" Katherine trotted up alongside her on her mule. "Don't tell me you're worried about all the hot air Dunleavy's been blowing."

"How can he say such . . . such lies!"

"Awww, nobody with any sense believes him. They know he's had it in for the lieutenant practically ever since they met."

"Some people believe it," she said. "I've heard them."

"Well, the lieutenant's a big boy. He seems to be handling it all right."

She nodded, though the thought gave her little comfort. Michael wasn't a man to show his feelings; who knew what this was doing to him on the inside?

"That's not all there is to it, is there?" Katherine asked. "You've been moping around like you lost your best dolly for days now." She leaned over and jabbed Ellen in the side. "Didn't your mother ever tell you frowning like that will give you wrinkles?"

The remark was so absurd that Ellen couldn't help smiling.

"That's better." Katherine grinned. "Tell your troubles to Auntie Katherine, then. I'm full of advice, not all of it good."

Ellen shook her head. "It's nothing, really. Just weary of traveling, I suppose. Aren't you?"

"Tired of the scenery, I'll tell you that." Katherine surveyed the drab plains around them. "It'll be nice to finally get to California."

California again. She was beginning to wish she'd never heard of the place. "I imagine you and Solly will be married there."

Katherine's grin broadened. "Actually, we're thinkin' we might just tie the knot here in the middle of nowhere."

"You mean while we're on the march?"

Katherine shrugged. "Why not? All our friends are here. Solly even knows one of the enlisted men who's a preacher."

Ellen blinked, stunned. "But a wedding . . . out here?" She looked around them at the empty expanse of dried grass and dirt. No flowers bloomed, no brooks flowed. Even the sky was a washed-out blue, unadorned by a single cloud. "But it . . . it's so ugly."

Katherine's look softened. "Aww now, I don't give a fig for the scenery around us. The only thing I'm going to be looking at when I say those vows is Solly. That's scenery enough for me."

Leave it to Katherine to put things in perspective. What did the landscape or the threat of war or the opinions of others matter in the face of true love? Tears stung Ellen's eyes, and she had to swallow hard before she could talk. "Then any place would be a beautiful place for a wedding," she said.

"What do you say? Want to be my bridesmaid?"

Ellen sniffed and nodded. "I'd be honored."

"I kind of like the idea of being a married woman by the time we get to California." Katherine arched her back and stretched. "Can't say it won't be good to sleep in a real bed again, though."

"Yes, a real bed will be nice." Though she preferred a blanket on the ground with Michael to any bed in which she slept alone.

"There you go again, looking like the devil shot your dog." Katherine leaned closer, her face lined with concern. "There's only one thing that could make you so sad. Is something wrong between you and the lieutenant?"

"No, of course not." She didn't dare admit the truth, not even to Katherine.

"Did you ever try any of my suggestions for adding a little spice to things in bed?"

A Husband by Law

Ellen felt her cheeks warm. "I . . . I did."

Katherine laughed. "I can tell by the way you're blushing that they must have worked." She sat back, studying her friend. "So maybe you're fretting about what you're going to do in California."

Ellen looked up, surprised. Did Katherine know something of the truth? "I have an uncle there," she said. "I need to find him."

"Well, don't fret about it. Likely you'll find him." She shrugged. "Solly and I are thinking about mustering out of the Army and settling down. We might go into business."

"Business? Doing what?" She had a difficult time imagining Katherine as a nurse, working at Solly's side.

"Any town can always use another saloon, so we thought we'd do that. And we'd have music and dancing. I always did like to dance."

Ellen remembered the *fandango* where she'd danced with Michael. That night, whirling in his arms, she'd known she was falling in love with him. That seemed so long ago now.

"Why don't you and the lieutenant come in with us?" Katherine's voice rose with enthusiasm. "He could put up a little money and help Solly tend bar."

She looked away, not wanting her friend to see her pain. "I . . . I'm not sure Michael plans to stay in California."

Katherine's shoulders sagged. "Then I guess you'll be an Army wife for true. It's not so bad, really. You get to travel around a lot, see a lot of interesting places, meet interesting people."

"I . . . I don't think he intends for me to go with him."

Katherine was silent for a long while. When she spoke, her voice was solemn. "What do you mean?"

She swallowed a thick clot of tears. What did it matter if Katherine knew the truth? It would be such a relief to confide in someone. "I . . . we . . . we only agreed to be married until we reached California. Until I could get to my uncle."

Katherine looked alarmed. "Well, sure, that was then.

But . . . things have changed now. I mean, you love each other and all."

Did Michael love her? He acted as if he did, but he had never said so. Things were so different for men. Look at Bear Roberts, who had surrendered Katherine without a fight and gone on to live his life as if nothing had ever happened. Maybe Michael would be like that, too. She squeezed her eyes shut but couldn't hold back the tears. They slid down her cheeks in a stream and then a torrent. She felt Katherine's hand on her shoulder, awkwardly patting her.

"Shhh, there. It'll be all right," her friend murmured. "Things will work out, I'm sure of it."

Michael stared straight ahead, trying to blot out the laughter of the men around him. "The cowardly lieutenant," some of them were calling him, egged on, no doubt, by Dunleavy. Certainly he had friends who refused to believe such slander, but he'd made his share of enemies as well. Men he'd beaten too many times at cards, men whose women had turned appreciative eyes his way, or those fellow soldiers who disdained anyone who wore an officer's stripes or could claim a West Point education—those men were too ready to jeer at him behind his back.

Their words hurt worse than the pain in his shoulder, which throbbed with each strike of the horse's hooves against the hard ground. He focused on that pain, grateful for the distraction it provided. Solly had scolded him only this morning, telling him he should be resting in the hospital wagon. The doctor couldn't understand that he needed to be here, proving to his men, and to himself, that he was tough enough to survive this—that he was no coward.

God knows he'd had enough practice hiding his pain—he'd been doing it all his life. Ellen apparently hadn't had that kind of training. He saw how Dunleavy's taunts wounded her on his behalf. Her tenderness moved him, yet made him wary.

She was the one person who might have breeched the

wall around his feelings. He used his wound as an excuse to avoid sleeping with her, to dodge the temptation to give in to the anger and fear that sometimes moved in on him like dark storm clouds. He couldn't afford to let down his guard that way. Dunleavy was like a wolf trailing a herd, waiting to spot any weakness. Michael swore the Scotsman would find none in him.

Dunleavy wasn't the only one on the prowl, however. Michael kept a keen eye on the captain, waiting for his chance to show the world the Scotsman's traitorous ways.

He turned and searched the faces of the soldiers in formation behind him. Most refused to meet his eyes. His gaze came to rest on Corporal Ian Stewart. "Stewart, come here a moment," he called.

"Yes, sir?" Stewart cantered his horse up beside Michael and addressed him with a smart salute.

Stewart had been with him that day they went after the guerrillas. He had been one of those Michael led in the charge. "That afternoon with the guerrillas, when we made our charge, was Captain Dunleavy riding with us?"

Stewart blinked. "Yes, sir. I mean, I believe so, sir. I don't recall him riding off with the others."

"Neither do I. Did you see him, then, when we rode forward? Do you recall his position?"

Stewart's brow furrowed in thought. "I . . . I don't remember. Why do you want to know, sir?"

He ignored the question. "Tell me, Corporal, do you have any idea how I might have come to take a bullet in the back?"

A flush of red stained Stewart's cheeks. "I don't know, sir. Last I saw, you were leading the charge." He straightened, his mouth set stubbornly. "I've said as much to any who suggested different, sir."

"Thank you, Stewart. That will be all."

The corporal's brow remained furrowed. He leaned toward Michael and lowered his voice. "Do *you* know where the captain was when we made our charge, sir?"

Michael answered carefully. "All I can say for certain is that he wasn't in *front* of me."

Stewart's eyes widened, and he nodded. "Yes, sir."

"That will be all, Corporal."

When Stewart had left, Michael felt some of his tension ease. He had planted the first seeds of doubt. Now he only had to bide his time and wait for them to grow.

"Will you stand still!"

"I'm tryin', but I'm just not used to all this fuss and froo-frah."

Ellen removed the last of the pins from her mouth and stuck it in the hem of the dress, then sat back on her heels and smiled up at Katherine. "It isn't every day a woman gets to be a bride. You deserve a little 'fuss and froo-frah.' Now make a quarter turn for me."

Katherine obligingly turned around in the chair on which she was balanced. She had attracted quite a bit of attention from passersby as she stood there, Ellen kneeling in the dirt beside the chair to pin the hem on what would be Katherine's wedding gown. She had accepted both catcalls and congratulations with her usual good humor. "I still can't believe how pretty it is," she said, smiling down at Ellen. "Do you think Solly will like it?"

Ellen grinned. "Don't be silly. He'll love it. He loves you. He wouldn't care if you showed up at the altar in an old tow sack."

Katherine held up the skirt of the blue silk gown. "I never had such a pretty dress," she said, a look of wonder on her face. "It's just perfect."

Ellen studied the full-skirted gown, with its puffed sleeves and wide satin sash. She'd purchased the fabric in El Paso, intending to make a new dress for herself, but now she was glad she'd saved it back. Every bride ought to have a new outfit for her wedding.

The rich blue accented Katherine's pale skin and dark hair, and the styling made the most of her slender figure. Ellen leaned forward to adjust the hem once more. "It will be perfect as soon as I finish this bit in the back. I wish we'd had more time to make you a proper trousseau—another dress at least, and a nightgown—"

Katherine laughed. "I won't be needin' a nightgown. I intend for Solly to keep me warm in bed." She turned around, inadvertently jerking the unfinished hem from Ellen's hands once more. "Oh, Ellen! I always liked sex before, but when you really, truly love a man—why, it's like flyin'!"

Ellen gently turned her back around and took up the hem once more. Katherine's voice sang with happiness, and she felt an uncomfortable stab of jealousy in her breast.

Once she'd pictured herself in a wedding gown like this, in a church filled with flowers and well-wishers. But if she couldn't have Michael as her groom, what else mattered?

She thought of the vows they'd spoken in Michael's tent so long ago. Michael had warned her then he had no interest in a true marriage. Did he still feel that way?

She bit her lip and worked her needle through the slippery silk. She wanted no other man but Michael. If the only pledge they made was the first one they'd exchanged, couldn't that be enough?

Katherine shifted from one foot to the other, the dress swaying with her movement. Ellen sighed. "Will you stand still?"

"What's taking them so long?" Solly paced back and forth in front of the table that had been set up out in the open to serve as altar for the wedding ceremony. "Do you think she's ill? Maybe we should go check."

Michael laughed and put out a hand to pat his friend's shoulder. "Calm down. It hasn't been that long." He glanced toward the tent where the women had retreated to prepare for the service. All morning women had been rushing in and out of the tent, carrying packages and bundles, looking toward the prospective groom and giggling. What the devil were they doing in there? This was only a simple ceremony, after all, not some formal church affair.

"Look at them all, come to gawk like visitors to the circus." Solly frowned at the soldiers and various hangers-on who had gathered to observe the ceremony. From barefoot laundresses to ranking officers in their dress uniforms, it seemed the whole camp had turned out to see the doctor and Katherine the Great wed.

"You couldn't very well keep them away," Michael said. "Not unless you'd waited until you'd reached California and had the wedding in a church."

"No, I've waited long enough." Solly shook his head. "Now that I've talked her into saying yes, I don't intend to give her time to change her mind."

Michael nodded absently, distracted by the arrival of a new group of guests. Gregory Dunleavy and his Rangers strolled through the crowd in their usual rough dress. The man was no particular friend to Solly or Katherine. Couldn't he have had the decency to stay away? Perhaps he'd come to see for himself that Michael was still up and about, little outward sign of his injury remaining. The shoulder still pained him a good deal at times, but he'd returned to full duty after only a week.

"Do you see her? Has she come out yet?" Solly stared beyond Michael toward the tent, which was now hidden by the crowd.

"Soon." Michael forced his gaze away from Dunleavy and straightened his tunic. "If she doesn't come soon, we'll send Macmillan after her."

Private Macmillan paled, perhaps at the thought of confronting Katherine the Great. A slight man in his early twenties, the private, who in civilian life was an ordained minister, had been persuaded to perform the marriage ceremony.

Solly tugged at his stiff collar and attempted to straighten his tie. He was dressed in an old-fashioned morning coat and striped trousers, still carrying the faint odor of cedar about them, from where they'd been packed in the bottom of his trunk. He smoothed his lapels. "How do I look? Old enough to be her father?"

"Not that old." Michael laughed. "She must like something about you, or she wouldn't be going through with this."

A murmur swelled through the crowd, and the company band struck up a credible version of "The Wedding March."

Solly sucked in his breath. "She's coming."

The crowd parted to form a path leading to the altar. Ellen appeared first, and Michael caught his breath as she started down the aisle toward him. Though he had looked at her a hundred times, in a hundred different ways, he felt as if he were seeing her again for the first time, her beauty too glorious to behold.

She walked with the bearing of a princess, head up, shoulders straight, her red-gold hair piled in a crown of elaborate curls atop her head. Her green satin gown shimmered with each movement, flowing over her full breasts and hips. A black, beaded girdle rested about her small waist, and more beads outlined the low, square neckline of the gown.

He directed his gaze up the ivory column of her neck, to the ripe fullness of her lips, across the pink blush of her cheeks, focusing at last on the sapphire depths of her eyes.

His heart began to pound when he met her gaze. For one frozen moment in time, it was as if she were walking up that aisle to be his bride. He longed to say the words that would make her his own, now and forever; to hear her give the answer that would prove she overlooked their different stations in life and loved him only for himself.

Then she looked away and took her place across from him. Jarred back to reality, he turned to watch Katherine make her way up the aisle.

The coarse, common female had been transformed by Ellen's hand into a tall, handsome woman, her slender figure modestly draped in a gown of azure silk. Her normally tousled hair was fixed in curls atop her head, and her eyes glowed like embers against her pale skin.

Michael glanced at Solly. He stared at his bride, mouth slightly parted. Were those tears in the doctor's eyes?

Appreciative murmurs circled the crowd. After weeks of hard travel, the sight of two lovely women was doubly welcomed. Michael stood up straighter, chest swelling with pride that the more beautiful of the two should be associated with him.

His eyes darted to Gregory Dunleavy, and he frowned. The Ranger captain was staring at Ellen the way a hungry coyote would watch a tame rabbit. Michael clenched his hands into fists at his sides. If Dunleavy thought—

"Dearly beloved, we are gathered today in the sight of God . . ."

Reverend Macmillan began to speak, and Michael forced his attention to the ceremony. He only half listened to the words, his gaze continually drifting to Ellen. She was so close he noticed the wisps of hair curling around her ears, and the dusting of powder across her nose. Her chest rose and fell gently with each breath. He stared at the soft swell of the tops of her breasts framed by the neckline of her gown and felt his mouth go dry. They'd had no chance to slip away in private since leaving Santa Fe. Other couples found the cover of darkness privacy enough, but Ellen deserved better than noiseless groping on the hard ground with others attempting to sleep only inches away. Looking at her now, he felt they could not reach California, and the privacy of their own tent, soon enough.

"Is there a ring?"

The words alerted him to his duties as best man. He felt in his pocket and produced the ring Solly had commissioned from the company dentist. He handed it to Macmillan.

"A ring is a sign and a symbol . . ."

As Solly and Katherine recited their vows, Michael thought of his wedding to Ellen. There had been no ring that day, no words of love in any language they could understand. But he had done his best to keep the promises he had made in Colonel Peabody's tent, to protect and provide for her, to fight on her behalf.

He glanced at her and saw tears sparkling in her eyes as she watched Katherine and Solly seal their vows with a kiss. God, she was beautiful. A tropical flower in a jungle of weeds. She deserved a husband as regal as she was—a lord with a fine pedigree and a castle on a hill.

Not a reckless dreamer's son, who spent his life riding from place to place and battle to battle, sleeping in the open or in a canvas tent.

"May I present to you Dr. and Mrs. Marvin Sullivan." The band struck up a fanfare, and Michael turned to offer Ellen his arm. He was conscious of the warmth of her hand on his arm and her tall frame so close to his. He held her more firmly, wanting to prolong the contact, basking in the glow of her smile when she looked at him. If he could not have Ellen forever, he would settle for whatever crumbs of affection she would give him in the brief time they had left.

Chapter Nineteen

Michael and Ellen led the way through an archway of crossed battle swords, serenaded by the cheers of the company. A brush arbor had been thrown up nearby, and beneath it plank tables held a wedding feast. Someone had even procured a few bottles of wine, and everyone raised their glasses in salute to the happy couple.

Solly began the toasts, standing and holding up his goblet. "To my wife, Katherine. For keeping an old man young."

Katherine bounced to her feet. "To my *old* man, Solly, who's got what it takes to keep this not-so-young girl on her toes."

The guests greeted this with whoops and hollering. Waiters began to bring out platters of food, and they settled into an afternoon of feasting and conversation.

"Doesn't Katherine make a beautiful bride?" Ellen leaned close to whisper to Michael.

"Thanks to you." He smiled at her. Did she have any idea how beautiful she herself was?

He opened his mouth to tell her, but she looked away. "I still can't believe she and Solly are married," she said. "Of all the men I would have thought she'd end up with . . ."

"I'm just as surprised Solly married her."

"Why wouldn't he want to marry her?"

He shrugged. "It's just that Solly's a very well-educated man, rather refined. He's supposedly from a very well-thought-of family back East. And Katherine's so, well, coarse and common, ignorant really, with no family at all."

Her smile faded. "If a man and woman truly love each other, their backgrounds shouldn't matter."

He nodded and took a sip of wine to keep from looking at her any longer. Did she really mean what she'd just said? Could there be hope for him yet?

More wine was brought out, and another round of toasting began—to Solly, to Katherine, to Ellen for her talent with needle and curling iron, to Michael for his services as best man, to Reverend Macmillan, to Colonel Peabody, to President Polk.

"I propose a toast!" Solly pushed himself up for the tenth time, swaying slightly as he rose. "To Lieutenant Trent and the lovely Ellen." He grinned at them. "Here's hoping he'll wake up and make an honest woman out of her soon."

Michael heard Ellen's gasp amid the laughter of those around him. He noted Katherine's confused look, and the whispers and shrugs of others. "To Solly!" he announced, standing and raising his goblet of water. "Who's obviously had too much to drink if he can't tell those of us who are already married from those who aren't."

Everyone laughed, and he sat down once more. But he still had the uncomfortable feeling of being watched. When he looked down the table, he met the questioning gaze of Gregory Dunleavy, studying him over the top of his glass.

Ellen let out the breath she'd been holding, grateful to Michael for easing them through the awkward moment. Why had Solly made that toast? Was it possible he knew the truth about their marriage?

She looked across the table at the doctor. He nodded at her and winked. She felt a flush of shame wash over her even as she looked away. Solly did know!

The only way he could know was if Michael had told him. She glanced at him as he leaned across the table, laughing at something Katherine had said. Why would Michael have told Solly their marriage was only temporary . . . unless he was ashamed of her?

Of course, he was gentleman enough never to show it, but hadn't he just said he didn't see how a gentleman could ever marry a woman with a background so different from his own?

She sipped her wine, fighting tears. Over the rim of her glass, she saw Solly lean over and give Katherine a kiss. Her friend's face glowed with happiness as she looked into the eyes of her new husband.

I'll never know what that feels like, she thought. *I'll never be able to truly marry the man I love.*

Dinner over, the party began to break up. Michael excused himself for a moment, while Ellen helped Katherine to freshen up her hair.

"It's just going to come tumbling down in a little while anyway." Katherine giggled as Ellen pinned up a curl that had fallen.

"Are you two lovely ladies hiding your beauty from the rest of us?"

Ellen flinched at the deep voice behind them, and whirled to face Gregory Dunleavy.

"Captain, you startled me," she said, one hand to her throat. She had not spoken to Dunleavy since the day he'd come to her tent looking for Michael, before Michael had been arrested.

He bowed low. "My apologies. I merely came to offer my congratulations." He took Katherine's hand in his own and raised it to his lips. "You make a charming bride, madam."

Katherine snatched her hand away and frowned at him. But before she could speak, Dunleavy turned to Ellen. "And you, my dear, are simply ravishing."

She put her hands behind her back and looked away from him. "Thank you, Captain," she murmured.

"I hope you can answer a question that has been puzzling me."

"Oh?" She looked at him once more. "What was that?"

"What did Dr. Sullivan mean when he told the lieutenant to 'make an honest woman' of you?"

Her face burned, and she laced her fingers tightly together, battling the urge to run away. She forced a smile and tossed her head back. "Oh, Solly was just joking. He likes to tease Michael."

Dunleavy nodded and stroked his thick beard. "I thought for a moment he was implying that you weren't really married after all."

Ellen drew herself up to her full height. "Captain, are you insulting me?"

He bowed again. "Not at all, my dear. I would never do that. I merely—"

"Ellen was just leaving." A firm hand grasped her arm, and Michael led her away. She could feel his anger pulsing through him as he held her to his side. "Are you all right?" he asked, stopping beneath a tree some distance from Dunleavy. "Did he bother you?"

She shook her head. "No. He just wanted to wish Katherine well."

He looked at her closely, as if he saw the lie in the words, then patted her hand and released her. "Would you mind walking back to camp alone? I promised to help with the shivaree."

"Shivaree?" She frowned. "What's that?"

He grinned. "Oh, we'll just serenade the new couple. Make a little noise. I won't be too long."

The memory of Dunleavy's hand on Ellen, and of his leering face close to hers, stayed with Michael as he followed the happy couple toward Solly's wagon. Bad enough that the man was a bully, a liar, a cheat, and a traitor. That he should harass Ellen and disturb her so was beyond bearing.

He was through with biding his time, waiting for the Scotsman to make a mistake and give him the proof he needed to make a formal accusation. He wanted Dunleavy out of his life now, once and for all.

He joined the crowd of men gathered around the doctor's wagon. Some carried torches to illuminate the growing darkness. Others banged pots together or rattled gourds or rang bells.

"Don't forget to give your bride a thorough examination, Doc!" one man shouted.

"Go easy on him, Katherine," called another. "Remember, he's an old man."

Michael joined in the good-natured shouts and taunts, silently congratulating himself on having avoided this particular tradition when he and Ellen were wed. He could not imagine Ellen coming out to greet the hecklers as Katherine did, her hair down around her shoulders and her dress half undone, revealing the lacy undergarments beneath.

"You boys quiet down or I'll knock some heads together," she said.

Grinning, she tossed a fistful of coins into the crowd. As the men scrambled for the money, Solly appeared behind his bride. "Time to say good night, men," he said.

"Good night."

"Congratulations."

"Best of luck to you."

The greetings faded into the night with the men. Michael was among the last to leave, after the newlyweds had retreated inside the wagon. He ought to find Ellen and make sure she was all right, but first he had other business to see to.

Michael found Dunleavy on the outskirts of camp with a group of Rangers and others irregulars, playing cards and passing around a jug of homemade liquor. At Michael's approach, the Scotsman's face darkened, and he started to rise from his place by the fire.

"No, no, don't get up on my account." Michael took a seat on the ground across from him.

Dunleavy glared at him. "If you're looking for trouble, Trent—"

"No, no trouble." Michael held up his hands.

"What do you want, then?"

Michael glanced around the fire, at the Rangers and teamsters and others who formed a circle around him. He'd find no friends among them. But then again, he might yet work their presence to his advantage. "I came to talk to you about something," he said, looking back at Dunleavy. "Alone."

The captain stared at him a long moment, then laid aside his cards and rose to his feet. "All right. Walk with me."

Michael fell into step beside Dunleavy, aware of the stares that followed them as they left the fire and walked to the edge of the clearing. "What do you want?" Dunleavy demanded.

"I notice you seem to have a lot of money to throw around," Michael said casually. "Is your luck at cards that good, or do you have other resources?"

"Where my money comes from is none of your concern."

"Perhaps not." Michael pretended interest in a bit of dirt lodged under his fingernails. "Unless, of course, that money was paid for illegal activities. Activities the Army might find objectionable."

Dunleavy had the gall to laugh. "You must have drunk too many toasts to the doctor and his bride," he said. "You're not making sense."

Time to change tactics. "What do you think of the coming war?" he asked.

Dunleavy eyed him warily. "I think you can hardly call it a war," he said after a moment. "The Mexicans don't have the firepower or the manpower to defeat us."

"Hmmm. I understand some of them are considerably better armed these days."

Did he imagine the look of alarm that flashed through

Dunleavy's eyes? "What makes you say that?" the captain snapped.

"I hear there's quite a trade here on the border between unscrupulous Americans and Mexican guerrillas. It seems there are men who will provide the guerrillas with weapons and other supplies for the right price. You wouldn't know anything about that, would you?" He met Dunleavy's gaze head-on and silently dared him to deny the truth.

Dunleavy stepped back. "I don't have to stand here and listen to your drunken ravings."

"I told you I'm not drunk." Michael glanced over his shoulder, toward the fire where the card players had resumed their game. "Would you prefer to move back to the fire, where I can make my accusations in front of all your friends?"

"You can't prove anything."

"Oh, no? I have a witness who saw you selling rifles to Mexicans in Santa Fe."

"It's your word against mine, Lieutenant." He spat on the ground. "The word of a coward won't count for much."

"A coward, yes." He forced himself to look into Dunleavy's eyes, to let him see that he was not afraid. "Where were you that day, Captain? When we were fighting off the guerrillas."

"I was fighting." Dunleavy's eyes were bright with rage.

"I remember you behind us, ordering the rest of us forward, but I never saw you after that."

"I don't know what you're talking about." He took another step back.

"I can't find a soul who remembers you actually doing any fighting in the battle." Michael looked back at the men around the fire. They were rugged, rough men, known for their courage. "I wonder what your friends would think of a coward who claimed to be one of them—a fearless Texas Ranger?" His voice hardened. "A man who would shoot another man in the back and sell weapons to the very enemy they were all fighting?"

Dunleavy grew pale. His gaze flickered to the fire, then back to Michael. "What do you want?" he asked, his voice barely above a whisper.

Michael tightened his hand into a fist. "Leave. Tonight. Go back to Texas. Go to Scotland. Go to California. Go to hell for all I care. But don't come back here. And stay away from Ellen."

"And if I don't go?" Dunleavy's eyes narrowed.

"I tell Colonel Peabody and General Kearny everything I know and demand an investigation." He nodded toward the fire. "And I start questioning your buddies, asking them to think about where you were and what you were doing while the rest of us were risking our necks in the fighting."

Dunleavy tried for one last show of bravado. He drew himself up straight. "As your superior officer, I order you to stop this nonsense now, Lieutenant."

Michael leaned toward him. "Rank won't protect you in this. When I start talking, people are going to listen."

They stared at each other for a long moment before Dunleavy looked away. "I'll go on one condition."

"You're not in any position to be making demands, Captain."

"All right, then, one *request*."

"What is it?"

"Don't tell Ellen about this."

Michael blinked, surprised. "You really care what she thinks of you, don't you?"

Dunleavy glared at him. "Do you think I would have wasted my time on you if it wasn't for her? I knew if you were out of the picture—you and your long gold curls and West Point education and gentleman's manners—I knew then I could win her."

"I won't tell her. Not because I have any respect for your feelings, but because I see no need to expose her to the whole sordid story." He took a step back. "I think it's time you were going."

He turned and began walking away, but stopped as he reached the group around the fire. "Just one more thing." He looked back at Dunleavy. "I'm not the only one who knows this story, or who knows why I came here tonight. If anything happens to me, you'll be in irons before you can turn around. You'll have lost Ellen and your freedom, and your good name, what's left of it."

Dunleavy scowled. "I'm leaving now. You'd better pray we never have the opportunity to meet again."

Michael thought Ellen would be asleep by the time he reached their campsite, but she raised up on one elbow when he spread his bedroll a little apart from hers. "Did you see the bride and groom safely tucked in?" she asked.

"More or less." He removed his sword and sash and began to unbutton his tunic.

"I've been waiting for you." Something in her voice made him look at her. She was smiling coyly at him, one finger idly tracing the line of her collarbone.

"I went for a walk." He dropped the tunic beside his bedroll and started to unfasten his trousers as well, but thought better of it. The sight of Ellen there among the blankets, her thick hair tumbling about her shoulders, was having a predictable effect on him. He turned his back and began undoing the buttons, wishing the moon would disappear behind the clouds. But a glance overhead showed a sky as clear as glass, stars glowing silver against it.

"What are you looking at?" Ellen asked.

"Only thinking how bright it is tonight." He dropped his trousers and quickly knelt to slip under the covers. After a moment, he heard a sound like something being dragged across the ground and looked over to see Ellen moving her bedroll closer to his. "I want to be close to you," she said by way of explanation, and slid under the covers once more.

He could feel the warmth of her body through the thin

blankets, and with every breath he inhaled the sweet scent of lavender. She brushed her hand down his arm and said softly, "You're not sleepy, are you?"

Sleepy? What man could sleep with a woman like Ellen at his side? "No, I'm not sleepy."

"Good." She snuggled closer, her thigh pressed against his thigh, her breast soft against his side.

Every part of him cried out for her, but some remnant of propriety reminded him of the several hundred other people bedding down in close proximity. There would be no privacy for them until they reached California. California! "We should talk." He eased away from her, though the blanket allowed him to move back a scant inch.

"What do you want to talk about?" She glided her hand across his hip, down his thigh . . .

He captured her wrist and held it. "California. We should talk about what we're going to do when we reach California."

She gave him a puzzled look. "What do you think we should do?"

"I imagine you'll want to look for your uncle. I think we should start with those Englishmen Mr. Leland knew in the San Joaquin Valley."

She nodded. "All right. If you think that's what we should do."

"I do. In the meantime, while we're looking, I'll find a little house for us to rent." A place with four thick walls where they could love each other with abandon.

She smiled, a sleepy, seductive look that raised his temperature another notch. "A house sounds nice. With a big, soft bed."

He should have been gratified that she was thinking along the same lines as he, but under their current circumstances, it only added to his torture. He took her by the shoulders and pushed her away. "If you only knew what that does to me," he said.

Her smile broadened, and she moved her hand across

his hip, toward the front of his trousers. "Oh, but I do know what it does to you, Michael."

"Ellen!" he whispered. "We're not exactly alone here."

A mischievous look came into her eyes. "I know." She giggled. "Don't you think it's, well, rather exciting?"

He sucked in his breath and looked at her intently. Her eyes sparkled with mischief and longing, her cheeks glowed pink, and her moist, full lips begged to be kissed. "Do you know how tempting you are?" he said roughly.

"Am I tempting you?" She snuggled against him. "I certainly hope so."

She slipped one arm around his neck and pulled him close to kiss him. As her lips met his, the warmth between them melted his last remnant of control. "So you want me that badly, do you, Mrs. Trent?"

She opened her eyes wide to stare at him. "Yes," she whispered softly.

"Say it."

"I want you, Michael Trent."

A shiver passed through him that had nothing to do with cold. He brought one hand up to caress her breast. "What do you want me to do?"

"I . . . I want you to make love to me." She gasped as he lowered his head to her breast, to caress the tender tip through the thin fabric of her chemise. While his mouth lavished attention on her breasts, his fingers worked the ties of her undergarments, until it was no longer cloth he tasted, but her own sweet flesh.

He stroked and suckled, teasing her nipples into hard nubs, eliciting low moans. She squirmed against him, eyes dark with passion. "Michael," she said with a gasp.

"Shhh. You'll waken the others." He grinned, enjoying knowing that her desire matched his own.

"Michael, please," she whispered. "You're driving me mad."

"What exactly drives you mad?" He flicked his tongue lightly across one nipple, earning a whimper of pleasure. "Or maybe this." He slid his hand across her belly, to the very center of her passion. He delved into the curls, stoking, teasing, until she was panting with need for him, and his own arousal approached pain.

Footsteps sounded nearby, and they froze, still as statues as the steps approached and then retreated. When all was silent once more, they sagged against each other. "Do . . . do you think he heard anything?" she asked. "Or saw anything?"

"The blankets are covering us," he reminded her. He slipped one finger inside her, smiling at her sharp gasp. "And you were very quiet." He kissed her, smothering her cries of pleasure, feeling her relax at his touch, and then tighten with a different sort of tension.

He moved away, just far enough to strip out of his small clothes. Then he pulled her to him once more. She eagerly welcomed him into her arms, then surprised him by reaching down to stroke him. She moved timidly at first, then with more assurance, her fingernails scraping lightly against his sensitive shaft, until he was gasping with pleasure.

"Shhh," she whispered, her eyes teasing. "Someone might hear you."

He answered by rolling over, pulling her on top of him. She pressed her hands against his chest and smiled down on him. "What if someone sees us?" she asked.

"They'll envy us, for sure." He put his hands on her hips, guiding her onto his shaft. She let out a small cry of pleasure, then began to move in a torturous, wonderful rhythm.

"I . . . I think I like this," she said.

"G . . . good." Then powers of speech deserted him as she increased her pace, driving him deeply into her, sensation shuddering through him, making his heart pound and his breath come in gasps.

He opened his eyes and saw her head was thrown back, her lips curved in a smile of sheer joy. That sight was his undoing, and he felt himself slip over the edge to ecstasy.

She covered his mouth with her own, stifling both their

cries, though in his head the joyous sound echoed, an affirmation of the love he felt but could find no words to express.

She lay atop him a long while, her head resting on his chest, his arms holding her securely. Then she gradually slid to his side. He continued to cradle her, a pleasant weariness overtaking him, edged with melancholy. How much longer would they have to love like this? And how would he ever find the courage to give her up?

Hours on horseback gave a man plenty of time for thinking. Too much time, maybe. As the miles passed beneath Brimstone's hooves, Michael tried to reason out what he would do when they reached California. Should he admit his past and hope his love alone would be enough to convince Ellen to stay with him? Should he plead his case with her relatives first? Should he merely pretend to search for her uncle, knowing she would have to stay with him as long as she had no place else to go?

He discarded the last idea as dishonorable and turned to his remaining choice: to honor the vow he'd made to release Ellen to her relatives and free her from the bonds of this sham marriage. The thought of doing so tore at him, the pain made more unbearable by the fact that it was so unfamiliar.

He had lived a life of few ties. Lovers came and went, and friends drifted in and out of his life. Even leaving his family to go first to West Point and then into the Army had seemed the natural course life should take. He had never known the agony of being separated from one he loved so deeply.

Memory stirred deep within him, and he had a sudden, jolting vision of himself as a boy, weeping uncontrollably in his hiding place in the cellar of the home they lived in at the time. At first he couldn't recall the reason for such sorrow. He must have been about six. His hands tightened on the reins. That would have been the year Dapper Dan bade goodbye to them all, never to return. Dan had set out from breakfast that morning, wearing his best blue suit, only slightly worn at collar and cuffs, and carrying a satchel of clothes and a train ticket. "I have a chance at a good job at last," he'd crowed to his son, eyes bright with excitement. "No more drifting from town to town. It's high time I settled down."

His wife had looked on approvingly, and little Michael and his sisters had watched proudly as their father, handsome and tall, had strolled out the door, whistling. The world had been full of hope and happiness that morning.

Sitting astride Brimstone in the hot desert sun, Michael suddenly found it difficult to breathe. He hadn't thought of that day in some twenty years. Why had it come rushing back to him now? He closed his eyes, trying to force the memories back into the darkness where he'd hidden them so long, but they rushed out, unbidden.

Michael had gone to the train station to greet his father the next day, anxious to be the first to congratulate him. But Dan had not emerged from the cars then, nor was he on the next train. Every day for a week he had waited at the station, first anxious, then despairing. His mother came to take him home on the fifth day. "He's gone," she said firmly. "He's not coming back."

Years later they learned Dan had never gone to the interview. Somewhere between San Antonio and Houston he'd gotten off the train and wandered away, who knows where. "Family life wasn't for him," Michael's mother had said. She'd looked at her son with sad eyes. "I'm afraid you're just like him."

Back then, he'd thought his mother right. Hadn't he spent his whole life trying to be like his father, the handsomest, most dashing, bravest man he knew? He had taken jobs in San Antonio saloons, just so he could hear the stories they told there, about dares Dan had taken and the dashing things he had done. He had entered the Army because Dan had been a soldier once and had claimed those days had been some of the best in his life. He knew from a daguerreotype he'd seen that he looked like his father, with the same blond hair, blue eyes, imposing height. If he was so much like his sire on the outside, it stood to reason he would be like him in matters of the heart as well.

But what if that wasn't true? What if there was more to him than his breeding as the son of a handsome ne'er-do-well? Hadn't he finished schooling and remained in the Army these past seven years? As far as he knew, Dan had never completed school and had never held any job more than a year. Even his stint in the Army had lasted only two years. Michael had lived by a code of honor, defending women in distress and underdogs in a fight. What honor had Dan shown, leaving a wife and three children without so much as goodbye?

He clenched his jaw against the sting of sudden tears. Why should he cry now about that old hurt? Better to turn those memories to good, to remind himself he was more than his father's son. He was his own man, a man in love with Ellen. He could not offer her a fine name or fortune, but he would give her everything else he had, including his heart.

Would that be enough? It wasn't enough for the San Antonio belles and their parents, who had turned their backs on him when he came calling. He straightened in the saddle. He had been a mere boy then. Now he was a man, one who had a reputation for not giving up.

Dunleavy had accused him of being a coward. Maybe the Scotsman had been right in a way. Until now, Michael had been afraid to fight for Ellen, but no more. Now he *would* fight for her, and he would not surrender.

Chapter Twenty

After so many weeks of traveling, California seemed like the landscape of a dream. Michael half feared if he closed his eyes and opened them again, this vista of thickly forested rolling hills and frothing streams would dissolve into the brown desert they'd traversed for weeks.

But day after day, as the dragoons followed in General Kearny's wake, the beauty of the countryside only increased. Flowers grew in profusion by the roadside, and in the settlements they passed, rich gardens flourished.

At last they reached their destination, Monterrey. The sight of the village's neat whitewashed houses and fountain-filled plaza was like a salve for eyes scorched by sun and barren plains. He brought his horse alongside Ellen as the troops halted in the town square. He was startled to see she had tears in her eyes.

"What's wrong?" he asked, reaching for her hand.

She squeezed his fingers and shook her head. "It's so beautiful." A stiff breeze ruffled the hair back from her face. She took a deep breath of the salty air. "It even smells like home."

That afternoon he rented a small house for himself and Ellen. Solly and Katherine found a place nearby. There was an avocado tree in the small courtyard and a market nearby where Ellen shopped. They could have spent the rest of their lives in happiness there, but Michael felt duty-bound to help Ellen find her relatives. She had traveled thousands of miles to see them; he wouldn't keep her from them.

At his urging, she wrote a letter to the group of Englishmen at the farm Mr. Leland had told them about, and placed advertisements in several papers in the area.

"It may be a while before we hear anything," he told her and himself.

She nodded. She was standing at the table in their little house, kneading bread. He did not know when he had seen a prettier picture. Her cheeks were flushed from the heat of the stove, and flour smudged her nose, but to him she looked happy in her work, happy to be with him. He wished he could capture this moment, preserving its warmth and contentment forever.

"What will you do in the meantime?" she asked, bearing down on the dough.

"I've decided to withdraw from the Army," he said. "I'm thinking of going in with Solly on his saloon." The doctor's plans sounded solid. He hoped the venture would provide him with enough income to prove to Ellen's relatives that he was capable of supporting a wife and family.

She smiled. "The two of you will do well together."

"Don't forget Katherine. She wouldn't like being left out."

She shook her head. "No one can forget Katherine."

Solly and Katherine had rented a large house near the main business district. They decided to install their saloon in the lower half of the house while they lived upstairs. Michael and Ellen joined in to clean and paint the interior, and Solly knocked together a bar and some tables and chairs. Ellen made curtains for the windows, and Katherine dragged home a worn hurdy-gurdy, which she announced would provide music for dancing until they could afford a proper piano and someone to play it.

These preparations complete, they set a date to open the

following week and gathered in the empty saloon for a celebratory dinner.

They had scarcely sat down to eat when a knock sounded on the door. Solly laid aside his knife and fork and went to answer it. "We're not open until next week," he told the stranger who waited on the stoop.

"I'm looking for a Miss Ellen Winthrop," said a voice with a broad English accent. "They told me in town I might find her here."

At the mention of her name, Ellen rose from the table and started for the door. Michael followed her. Solly opened the door wider to reveal a broad-shouldered, ruddy-faced man with hair the same red-gold shade as Ellen's. He was dressed in the rough garb of a laborer, a cloth cap in his hand. When he saw her, a wide smile lit his face.

"Little Ellie! My, how you've grown up."

"Uncle David?" Ellen seemed unsure of the identification, and Michael could scarcely blame her. Who would take this rough fellow as a relative of royalty?

"In the flesh. I come as soon as I got your letter."

"Won't you come in and join us for dinner?" Solly indicated the feast spread on the table. "Katherine, bring another chair for Ellen's uncle."

"That'd be just the thing." Uncle David crossed the room in three strides and took the seat Katherine offered, not even waiting for Ellen to resume her place. "My, but you've grown into a bonny lass," he said as he filled his plate.

Ellen continued to stare at him, a stunned look on her face. Michael extended his hand across the table. "I'm Michael Trent," he said. "Ellen's husband."

"Husband?" David stopped in the act of slicing a steak and raised his eyebrows. "Some bloke in town did mention a husband, but I didn't take him serious."

Michael tensed. "Why wouldn't you take the idea of Ellen's marriage seriously?"

The man shrugged and resumed eating. "A bit surprising, is all. Always thought Ellie would take after her mother—"

"Mother was a good, kind woman, and she raised me properly." Ellen's eyes blazed with anger. Michael looked from niece to uncle, confused. This wasn't the joyful reunion he'd imagined.

David shrugged. "Didn't mean nothing by it, lass. Don't go getting your feathers ruffled." He looked up from his plate. "I say, you haven't got a drop of something to wash away the dust, now do you?"

"I'll get it." Michael waved Solly back into his chair and headed for the bar. He poured a drink of whiskey for their visitor, watching him all the while. Now that they were seated side by side, he could see a resemblance between Ellen and this supposed relative, but there all similarity ended. The man shoveled his food into his mouth with both hands, reaching for the butter or pepper without apology, seemingly indifferent to the stares of those around him. Was David some sort of eccentric who delighted in defying convention, casting off all trace of the gentle life to which he'd been raised, or had something happened since his coming to America to change him so?

He returned to the table and set the whiskey before their visitor. "I understand you have a farm in the San Joaquin Valley," he said. "Tell us about it."

"Oh, it's not my farm." He spoke around a mouthful of steak. "Belongs to a chap named Armbrister. I work for him, though."

"What do you do?" Solly asked. He stared at their visitor as if he were a particularly odd specimen of insect.

David shrugged. "Tote barrels, pull weeds, run errands. Whatever needs to be done."

"When Mr. Leland visited, he told us there was a man at the farm named Davey. Was that you?" Ellen's face was pale, and her voice sounded shaky.

He nodded. "Changed my name to Winters when I got here. On account of there being people back home I didn't want to find me." He grinned. "But I'm glad you found me, Ellie dear, you and your fine husband and friends." He looked around at all of them. "In fact, I'm thinking instead of going back to the farm, I'll stay on a while with you."

"You mean you think we all got money to spare, is that it?" Katherine had remained silent until now. Leave it to her to voice what they were all bound to be feeling.

Davey nodded toward Michael. "Well, look at him. Looks like a toff, don't you think? Fancy uniform and all. That takes a bit of ready, don't you know?" He glanced at Ellen and grinned again. "Fancy you ending up with the likes of him. I'd've thought some fool with a title would have set you up proper by now. But then, you and your mama always did think you was a sight better than the rest of us, consorting with earls and dukes and such."

"How can you say such things!" Ellen looked near tears.

Davey looked indignant. "I'll say what I like. And it's nothing but the truth. My sister was no better than she should be. I'm surprised you didn't end up just like her."

Michael didn't understand what they were talking about, but it was clear the conversation upset Ellen greatly. He stood and confronted Davey. "I think you'd better leave now."

"Leave? But I haven't finished me dinner."

"Yes, you have." Katherine took the plate from in front of him. "I think you'd better do what the lieutenant says."

Davey looked around him, at Ellen, her face buried in her hands, Solly and Michael and Katherine glaring at him. "So that's your idea of hospitality, is it?" He shoved up out of his chair. "I'll see you around then, Ellie." He nodded toward her, then stalked to the door. Solly followed and locked it after him.

"I think we'll leave Ellen and Michael alone a while." Solly took Katherine's hand. "Let's go upstairs, dear."

When they were alone, Michael turned to Ellen. She sat, head down, refusing to look at him. "I'm sorry," she whispered.

"What are you sorry for? You certainly aren't to blame for the man's behavior."

"I'm only sorry because . . . now you know."

She looked so dejected, on the verge of tears. He moved his chair closer to her. "Now I know what?" He took her hand. "Tell me so I can help you."

She jerked away from him and jumped from her chair. "You can't help me!"

Her vehemence surprised him. "Ellen, what is going on?"

"I lied!" She grew pale, as if surprised she had said the words. Then she repeated more softly, "I lied to you."

The words made his stomach twist. "Lied to me about what?"

"I'm not the person you think I am, Michael." She twisted her hands together and began to pace. "I'm not a lady."

"You mean your father isn't an earl?" He tried to absorb this knowledge, but it floated on the surface of his consciousness like oil on a mud puddle.

"Yes, he is an earl. That part was true. But my mother . . ." She shook her head. "My mother and father were never married. She was the village seamstress. A very ordinary person." She sniffed and took a deep breath. "Uncle David is her brother."

"But you're still an earl's daughter." He had trouble getting the words out. He felt numb.

"An earl's bastard." The harsh word, spoken in her soft voice, startled him. "It's not the same thing," she added. "I had no place in society, no position. No money."

"But your fine clothes, your elegant way of speaking . . ."

"I was trained as a ladies maid, so I knew how to speak and act. As for the clothes . . ." She fingered the soft material of her gown. "That was all a mistake. When I decided to run away, I mistakenly picked up a bag that belonged to my half-sister Gennette. These are her clothes."

"Oh, Ellen!" He stood, meaning to go to her and take

her into his arms. They were two of a kind, weren't they, each hiding secrets from the past for fear of hurting the other.

"Please, leave me alone." She shrank back from him, putting up her arms to keep him away. "Please," she whispered. "Just go away."

He stared at her, cut to the quick by her words. "Ellen—" he began.

She turned away, hugging her arms to her chest. "Please, Michael. Leave me."

He stared at her, absorbing every detail of the moment—the way the lamplight glowed on her hair, the vulnerable look of her hunched shoulders and bent head. Every muscle urged him to go to her, but her very indifference was a shield to keep him away. He tried to think of something to say to change her mind, but words failed him. In the end he turned and left the saloon, scarcely able to see for the sudden, sharp tears that blurred his vision.

Ellen had never been so humiliated in her life. She never wanted to come out of the room where Solly and Katherine had invited her to stay. How could she face anyone, especially Michael, again? Now he knew what she was really like, the kind of people she came from.

Just when she was happiest, the things she had overlooked had come rushing in to ruin her life. She sat in a chair at the window and stared out at the busy street below. It was her own fault, of course. She should have told Michael the truth long ago. Maybe it would have been easier for him to accept then. Now . . . well, she had seen the horrified way he'd looked at Uncle David.

She had been stunned by her uncle's behavior, too. It had been many years since she'd seen him, but her memories were filled with images of a handsome, good-natured man who had bounced her on his knee and once given her a new ball to play with. Now she saw how much her childish eyes had missed.

A knock on her door disturbed her musings. She sighed,

knowing full well who was knocking. "Come in," she called.

Katherine swept into the room like a hot summer wind. "All right, I've let you stay cooped up in here, crying your eyes out, long enough. Time you dried your eyes and got on with it."

"I'm sorry." She smoothed her skirts and stood. "I know I've inconvenienced you. I'll find somewhere else to stay."

"What's the matter with your own house?" Hands on her hips, Katherine faced her. "Solly's over there right now, no doubt listening to Michael pour out his sorrows. What is the matter with you two?"

Ellen sank down into her chair once more. "Oh, Katherine, Michael and I are too different. He knows that, now that he's seen my uncle. It could never work between us."

"Now if that ain't the biggest bunch of balderdash I ever heard." Katherine plopped down on the end of the bed and fixed Ellen with a stern look. "No one ever died of humiliation, Ellen Trent, and you're not going to be the first. I know your uncle embarrassed you, but nobody's blaming you for the way he acted. All of us have relatives who'd be better off left at home. Hell, my aunt Lucy chews tobacco like a man and insists on spitting in a little tin box she wears on a string around her neck. But I don't go around taking it personally."

"But you saw the look on Michael's face when he met Uncle David. The man even had the nerve to ask Michael for money!"

"You're underestimating your soldier." Katherine stood and put a hand on her shoulder. "The lieutenant is smart enough to know the difference between you and your uncle."

"I lied to him about my background," Ellen said.

Katherine patted her comfortingly. "We all have things in our pasts we don't want others to know about," she said. "Michael is a big enough man to see beyond that."

She nodded. "Maybe. But I don't know if I'm a big enough woman to live with that."

Katherine patted her again. "Yes, you are," she said. "All I have to do is think of some way to prove it to you."

Michael was roused from sleep early the next morning by a furious pounding at his door. He groped for his clothes, reluctant to open his eyes. His head felt as if he'd been hit repeatedly with a hammer, and his tongue was too big for his mouth. What did Solly put in that whiskey to make it so powerful? Maybe he shouldn't have drunk so much of it.

The pounding continued, shaking the door with its force. He struggled into his trousers and shuffled to the door, squinting against the bright daylight streaming through the front window.

"It's about time you answered!" Katherine glared up at him, the brightness of her red and yellow dress making his head ache even more.

"What do you want?" he muttered, hoping he could convince her to leave soon so that he could return to bed.

"You've got to come help Ellen." She grabbed him by the arm.

Ellen's name was like a bucket of cold water over his head. "What's wrong? Is she in some kind of trouble?" He rubbed his eyes, trying to wake up fully. "Is she ill?"

"It's Bobby. He's missing."

"Her dog." He stared at her stupidly, trying to think.

"Dammit, that dog is the only thing she has in this world." Katherine grabbed his arm again. "She's over at my house crying her eyes out. You've got to help her."

The words galvanized him to action. Katherine was right. Bobby meant the world to Ellen. Even if she had sent Michael away, that didn't mean he couldn't help her in her time of need. "All right. Give me a moment to dress."

Two minutes later he was following Katherine back to the saloon. Ellen came running out to meet them. "Michael, is Bobby with you?" she asked, looking eagerly around him.

He shook his head. "I'm sorry. I haven't seen him."

Her shoulders sagged. "I thought maybe he'd gone back to your house. He was always so fond of you."

And weren't you? he wanted to ask her. But now was not the time or place. He took her arm and steered her gently back toward Katherine and Solly's house. "How long has he been missing?"

"He was gone when I got up this morning. Katherine said she let him out just after dawn, and now he's disappeared."

Her voice quavered on the last words, and he longed to gather her close to comfort her. "He can't have gone far," he said, patting her hand. "We'll all spread out and look for him."

"You two look, and I'll join you later," Katherine said as they reached her front door. "I have some, uh, business I have to take care of first."

Ellen turned to Michael, her blue eyes shiny with unshed tears. "Will you help me look for him, please?"

"Of course I'll help you. Which way do you think he'd be most likely to go?"

They started off down the street, searching the alleys between houses and the courtyards behind them for any sign of the little black dog.

"Bobby!" Ellen called. "Bobby, come here."

"Here, boy. Here, Bobby!" Michael shouted. "Breakfast time!"

They asked at all the shops and the houses around the main town square, but no one had seen the wiry-haired terrier. They spied dogs in various shades of white, brown, and black, in all manner of shapes and sizes, but none came close to Ellen's pet.

As their search stretched toward noon, Ellen became more and more dejected. Michael silently cursed the little dog for wandering off and causing his mistress such grief, and wished it were within his power to return the animal to her before another minute passed.

They walked to the trash dump on the edge of town, thinking the fragrant refuse might have attracted the dog.

Buzzards flapped into the sky at their approach, and Ellen raised a handkerchief to her nose as she surveyed the piles of garbage. "I don't see him anywhere."

Michael shook his head. "Neither do I."

They turned away and began walking back toward town. "What could have happened to him?" Ellen asked after a while. "Oh, what will I do without him?"

She stopped and began to weep, and he gathered her into his arms, cradling her head on his shoulder. "Don't give up," he said. "We'll keep looking. We'll get Katherine and Solly and others to help us. He's bound to be here somewhere."

"You must think I'm silly to be carrying on so over a dog." She sniffed. "And I know you have better things to do than spend your day searching for him."

I can't think of a better way to spend a day than with you. He wanted to say the words, but didn't dare, afraid she'd rebuff him as she'd done before. "Ellen, I want to help you," he said instead.

"Why?"

The question surprised him.

"Why do you want to help me?" she repeated.

Because I love you. Again fear held his tongue. He patted her arm. "You're my wife," he said. "Of course I want—"

"Michael, you don't have to keep pretending. You said we'd be married until we reached California and we'd found my uncle. You've met your obligation now." She turned away. "I can understand if a gentleman like you doesn't want to be associated with a woman of my background."

"What are you talking about?" The question came out harsher than he'd meant it, but his head had begun to pound again, and he was having a hard time making sense of her words.

She looked him in the eye, chin up. "You know now I'm not a real lady. What would your family think?"

"My family has nothing to do with it. They're a thousand miles from here."

"Still, with your background, I'm sure you expected to do better with your life."

He grabbed her arm and led her to a discarded wooden cask. "Sit down, please," he said, brushing off the cask.

"I don't want to sit. I want to keep looking for Bobby."

"We'll resume our search in a moment. Right now there are some things I need to say."

At his stern look, she lowered herself to the cask and looked up at him, waiting.

He took a deep breath, wondering how to begin. "You're not the only one who lied," he said. "I'm not a fine gentleman at all. My father was a wanderer and a rogue everyone called Dapper Dan. He was handsome and charming, a fine dresser and a fast talker. But he was a poor husband and a lousy father. He couldn't hold a job or keep money in his pocket if his life depended on it, and he finally abandoned us for good when I was six. I literally grew up on the streets of San Antonio. I am common as dirt, and the people I associated with made your uncle look as proper as a judge."

She stared at him, eyes wide. "But the captain said you were an officer and a gentleman."

He shook his head. "The captain was fooled, like everyone else."

"Your education—"

"Was paid for by a man named Stephen Bowman. He and my mother began keeping company when I was twelve. He took an interest in me and sponsored me at West Point, where I learned to ape my betters and play at being a gentleman. It was the best way to avoid the jeers and punches of my fellow students."

He told her more, words spilling forth like champagne from an uncorked bottle. He told her about the San Antonio belles who had shut their doors in his face, and the stories of his father he had tried so hard to emulate.

As he talked, her expression softened, and fresh tears spilled out from those sapphire eyes.

"I thought you could never love me," he finished. "I thought you'd see what I really was and hate me for it."

She rushed into his arms, pressing her cheek to his own. "I could never hate you," she whispered. "I love you too much."

He crushed her to him, wiping away his tears with her silken hair, filling his lungs with the scent of her. "I love you. God, I love you." He kissed her ear, her eyes, her cheeks, then lost himself in the warm softness of her mouth. She sighed and clung to him, her hands twining in his hair.

After a long while, he raised his head, but still held her close, reluctant to be parted from her for even a little while. "Say you'll never again leave me."

"Yes." She kissed him again, a gentle brush of her lips. "If only we'd known the truth sooner—"

"Shhhh." He put his hand to her lips to silence her. "Listen."

Her eyes grew wide as the sound of a dog barking drifted to them. "That sounds like Bobby!" She shoved away from him and began to run toward the noise.

Michael followed close behind, skidding down a narrow path that ran along the banks of the creek that flowed through town.

"Bobby!" Ellen shouted. "Bobby, is that you?"

The barking increased, and as they rounded a curve in the path, they could see the little dog tied to a tree. He was standing on his hind legs, barking and pawing the air, tail wagging furiously.

"Oh, Bobby, you're safe!" Ellen fell to her knees and gathered the dog to her. She laughed as he licked her face and wriggled in her arms.

Michael looked down on the happy reunion. "Who would have tied him down here?"

"Wait, here's a note." She held the excited dog away

from her and slipped a scrap of paper from beneath his collar.

Michael took the paper and read the message scrawled in bold letters: *"Time to kiss and make up. You know you both love each other, so whut else matters? A soldier, or a coward, is known by how he acts on the battle feeld."*

Ellen looked puzzled. "Katherine did this? But why?"

Michael read the words again, their meaning washing over him like a freshening breeze. "I think Katherine saw what we were both too stubborn and proud to admit." He smiled and knelt beside Ellen. "I knew you were a lady the first day I met you because you acted like one."

She took his hand and squeezed it. "And you'll always be a gentleman in my mind, whether you believe it of yourself or not."

"I think maybe Katherine's smarter than I've given her credit for." He kissed her forehead. "Maybe in the end, we make our own destiny."

"I think our destiny is to be together."

He fended off an enthusiastic Bobby and bent to give her a deep, lingering kiss. "Perhaps you won't mind if I'm not always the perfect gentleman," he said when he released her. "Say, in the bedroom?"

She swallowed, eyes dark with passion. "Is that a promise?"

He smiled. "It's a promise. And you know I always keep my promises."

SEDUCTION ROMANCE

Prepare to be seduced...by the sexy new romance series from Jove!

Brand-new, full-length, one-night-stand-alone novels featuring the most seductive heroes in the history of love....

❏ **A HINT OF HEATHER**
by Rebecca Hagan Lee   0-515-12905-4

❏ **A ROGUE'S PLEASURE**
by Hope Tarr   0-515-12951-8

❏ **MY LORD PIRATE** (1/01)
by Laura Renken   0-515-12984-4

All books $5.99

Prices slightly higher in Canada

Payable by Visa, MC or AMEX only ($10.00 min.), No cash, checks or COD. Shipping & handling: US/Can. $2.75 for one book, $1.00 for each add'l book; Int'l $5.00 for one book, $1.00 for each add'l. Call (800) 788-6262 or (201) 933-9292, fax (201) 896-8569 or mail your orders to:

| Penguin Putnam Inc.
P.O. Box 12289, Dept. B
Newark, NJ 07101-5289
Please allow 4-6 weeks for delivery.
Foreign and Canadian delivery 6-8 weeks. | Bill my: ❏ Visa ❏ MasterCard ❏ Amex _____ (expires)
Card#_____
Signature_____ |

Bill to:
Name _____
Address _____ City _____
State/ZIP _____ Daytime Phone # _____

Ship to:
Name _____ Book Total $ _____
Address _____ Applicable Sales Tax $ _____
City _____ Postage & Handling $ _____
State/ZIP _____ Total Amount Due $ _____

This offer subject to change without notice.   Ad # 911 (8/00)

TIME PASSAGES

- ❏ CRYSTAL MEMORIES   *Ginny Aiken*   0-515-12159-2
- ❏ ECHOES OF TOMORROW   *Jenny Lykins*   0-515-12079-0
- ❏ LOST YESTERDAY   *Jenny Lykins*   0-515-12013-8
- ❏ MY LADY IN TIME   *Angie Ray*   0-515-12227-0
- ❏ NICK OF TIME   *Casey Claybourne*   0-515-12189-4
- ❏ REMEMBER LOVE   *Susan Plunkett*   0-515-11980-6
- ❏ SILVER TOMORROWS   *Susan Plunkett*   0-515-12047-2
- ❏ THIS TIME TOGETHER   *Susan Leslie Liepitz*
  0-515-11981-4
- ❏ WAITING FOR YESTERDAY   *Jenny Lykins*
  0-515-12129-0
- ❏ HEAVEN'S TIME   *Susan Plunkett*   0-515-12287-4
- ❏ THE LAST HIGHLANDER   *Claire Cross*   0-515-12337-4
- ❏ A TIME FOR US   *Christine Holden*   0-515-12375-7

All books $5.99

Prices slightly higher in Canada

Payable by Visa, MC or AMEX only ($10.00 min.), No cash, checks or COD. Shipping & handling: US/Can. $2.75 for one book, $1.00 for each add'l book; Int'l $5.00 for one book, $1.00 for each add'l. Call (800) 788-6262 or (201) 933-9292, fax (201) 896-8569 or mail your orders to:

Penguin Putnam Inc.
P.O. Box 12289, Dept. B
Newark, NJ 07101-5289
Please allow 4-6 weeks for delivery.
Foreign and Canadian delivery 6-8 weeks.

Bill my: ❏ Visa ❏ MasterCard ❏ Amex _____(expires)
Card# _____
Signature _____

Bill to:
Name _____
Address _____ City _____
State/ZIP _____ Daytime Phone # _____

Ship to:
Name _____ Book Total $ _____
Address _____ Applicable Sales Tax $ _____
City _____ Postage & Handling $ _____
State/ZIP _____ Total Amount Due $ _____

This offer subject to change without notice.   Ad # 680 (3/00)

DO YOU BELIEVE IN MAGIC?

MAGICAL LOVE

The enchanting series from Jove will make you a believer!

With a sprinkling of faerie dust and the wave of a wand, magical things can happen—but nothing is more magical than the power of love.

☐ ***SEA SPELL*** by Tess Farraday   0-515-12289-0/$5.99

A mysterious man from the sea haunts a woman's dreams—and desires...

☐ ***ONCE UPON A KISS*** by Claire Cross

0-515-12300-5/$5.99

A businessman learns there's only one way to awaken a slumbering beauty...

☐ ***A FAERIE TALE*** by Ginny Reyes   0-515-12338-2/$5.99

A faerie and a leprechaun play matchmaker—to a mismatched pair of mortals...

☐ ***ONE WISH*** by C.J. Card   0-515-12354-4/$5.99

For years a beautiful bottle lay concealed in a forgotten trunk—holding a powerful spirit, waiting for someone to come along and make one wish...

VISIT PENGUIN PUTNAM ONLINE ON THE INTERNET:
http://www.penguinputnam.com

Prices slightly higher in Canada

Payable by Visa, MC or AMEX only ($10.00 min.), No cash, checks or COD. Shipping & handling: US/Can. $2.75 for one book, $1.00 for each add'l book; Int'l $5.00 for one book, $1.00 for each add'l. Call (800) 788-6262 or (201) 933-9292, fax (201) 896-8569 or mail your orders to:

Penguin Putnam Inc.
P.O. Box 12289, Dept. B
Newark, NJ 07101-5289
Please allow 4-6 weeks for delivery.
Foreign and Canadian delivery 6-8 weeks.

Bill my: ☐ Visa ☐ MasterCard ☐ Amex _____(expires)
Card# _____
Signature _____

Bill to:
Name _____
Address _____ City _____
State/ZIP _____ Daytime Phone # _____

Ship to:
Name _____ Book Total $ _____
Address _____ Applicable Sales Tax $ _____
City _____ Postage & Handling $ _____
State/ZIP _____ Total Amount Due $ _____

This offer subject to change without notice.   Ad # 789 (3/00)

FRIENDS ROMANCE

Can a man come between friends?

❏ **A TASTE OF HONEY**
by DeWanna Pace   0-515-12387-0

❏ **WHERE THE HEART IS**
by Sheridon Smythe   0-515-12412-5

❏ **LONG WAY HOME**
by Wendy Corsi Staub   0-515-12440-0

All books $5.99

Prices slightly higher in Canada

Payable by Visa, MC or AMEX only ($10.00 min.), No cash, checks or COD. Shipping & handling: US/Can. $2.75 for one book, $1.00 for each add'l book; Int'l $5.00 for one book, $1.00 for each add'l. Call (800) 788-6262 or (201) 933-9292, fax (201) 896-8569 or mail your orders to:

Penguin Putnam Inc.
P.O. Box 12289, Dept. B
Newark, NJ 07101-5289
Please allow 4-6 weeks for delivery.
Foreign and Canadian delivery 6-8 weeks.

Bill my: ❏ Visa ❏ MasterCard ❏ Amex _____(expires)
Card# _____
Signature _____

Bill to:
Name _____
Address _____ City _____
State/ZIP _____ Daytime Phone # _____

Ship to:
Name _____ Book Total $ _____
Address _____ Applicable Sales Tax $ _____
City _____ Postage & Handling $ _____
State/ZIP _____ Total Amount Due $ _____

This offer subject to change without notice.   Ad # 815 (3/00)